PENELOPE'S Way

Acknowledgements

I WISH TO ACKNOWLEDGE WITH THANKS THE ASSISTANCE OF
the Canada Council for the Arts and of the British Columbia
Arts Council.

My heartfelt thanks to Carol Shields for her numerous excellent suggestions, which have been incorporated into the manuscript.

And to Fraidie Martz for her enthusiasm and encouragement.

Also to Geoffrey Ursell, my editor and publisher at Coteau Books, for his careful review of the manuscript.

And finally to my agent, Beverly Slopen, for her enthusiastic and unstinting work on my behalf.

Parts or all of the following published short stories and essays have been incorporated into the final manuscript:

"Requiem," *Cross Canada Writers Quarterly*

"Let Me Compute the Ways," *Antigonish Review*

"Death in Calgary," *Green's Magazine*

"The Right Brain of Rev. Scott," *Antigonish Review*

"Chaos," *Queen's Quarterly*

"A Good Day on a Minor Galaxy," *Antigonish Review*

"Doppelgangers," *The Capilano Review*

"The Interstices of Time," *Prairie Fire*

"Evening in Paris," *Fresh Tracks, an Anthology*

BLANCHE HOWARD is co-author, with Carol Shields, of the best-selling novel-in-letters, *A Celibate Season*. She has published three previous novels, *The Immortal Soul of Edwin Carlysle, Pretty Lady*, and *The Manipulator*. Blanche has also published numerous short stories and essays, and has had a theatrical adaptation of *A Celibate Season* produced in North Vancouver.

Born in Daysland, Alberta, Blanche Howard grew up in Lloydminster and Calgary. She has lived in Toronto, Ottawa, and Penticton, and moved to North Vancouver in 1973. She has a Bachelor of Science degree from the University of Alberta, and a Chartered Accountant's degree. She has served on the executive of the North Shore Arts Commission.

To my daughter Allison, who was my first reader

The Bravest — grope a little —
And sometimes hit a Tree
Directly in the Forehead —
But as they learn to see —

Either the darkness alters —
Or something in the sight
Adjusts itself to Midnight —
And Life steps almost straight.

— *Emily Dickinson*

November

NOW THAT SHE HAS TURNED SEVENTY, PENELOPE Stevens is finding it prudent to have a little rest after climbing the first big hill of her daily three-kilometre walk. At the top of the hill, across the street from an uneven row of nondescript houses, a neighbourhood park boasts a circular flower bed set in the middle of the scuffed-looking grass, and a tidy green bench under a spreading maple tree. It is a sunny day, but the seat is damp from yesterday's rain, and Penelope fishes in the pocket of her floppy all-weather garment and spreads out a square of plastic to sit on.

On such a clear November day fog is very likely to form in the Strait of Georgia, and now it begins to grasp the entire city and the valley and the bridge and Stanley Park in its cottony fingers. Penelope leans back on the bench, stretching first one leg and then the other. Soon nothing of the city or harbour is visible except for the two ramparts of Lions Gate Bridge sticking up like buoys in a fluffy sea; then, as she watches, the top floor of Bentall Four is released, and she imagines the office workers staring out over this opaque, intrusive plain and forming a communal bond with her and the other inhabitants on the North Shore mountains.

Municipal gardeners have set out purple and white winter kale in the perfectly round bed, a pleasing visual aid and dutifully admired. It doesn't help; unease, like a miasma of the spirit, is drifting her way as surely as the fog below is reaching for the North Shore.

For some time now Penelope has blamed her unease on the hydro line that bisects her route. Mistrustfully, she eyes the headless giants marching up the mountain, holding batches of death-dealing current in their hands, awaiting the careless moment.

The trees and shrubs under the lines have been cut well back, this year.

Last summer they had been neglected, and the trees had grown tall underneath the lines, and on a very hot day the sagging wires had touched a treetop. There had been a sound like an explosion, and white light that had sparkled in the air, and all the people on the block had run along the street towards the sound, then stopped at the edge of the road, staring along the right-of-way and comparing what they had seen, what they had heard.

By the time the fire truck arrived consensus had been reached: most probably a light plane had crashed. Two firemen, one tall and strong with fearless eyes and a black moustache, the other rotund with white wispy hair that curled under the rim of his hat and eyes that had seen things he couldn't forget, set out at once to climb towards the spot.

VICTOR HUGO ONCE SAID HE NEVER KNEW A MAN WHO wasn't surprised by old age, a statement Brenda would have condemned as the kind of exclusionary dead-white-European-male-chauvinist pronouncement that gave the nineteenth century a bad name. (Brenda is Penelope's daughter.) And Penelope might have agreed — that is, if old Hugo hadn't been right on the money.

Certainly nobody was more surprised than Penelope herself when she actually turned seventy, not even the friends who expressed varying degrees of astonishment at the birthday party Brenda arranged.

Penelope's small house was crowded, but that didn't seem to bother anyone. Forty years ago the house had been a sprawling weathered red cedar summer cottage, in the days when Vancouverites had used the North Shore as their recreational backyard. Over the years it had been winterized and the wraparound veranda had been incorporated into the main body of the house, except for the piece across the back that overlooked a mossy lawn and a ravine. The ground floor had a big kitchen, a small living room, and tiny dining room, just large enough to squeeze the potluck crowd around the table when it was Penelope's turn. Three upstairs bedrooms had been carved out of the attic by dint of gables that at one time rose above the surrounding trees and looked over the inner harbour. Now, however, the cedars and hemlocks and Douglas firs had grown to gigantic proportions, and if Penelope had not been assiduous in pulling out the small seedlings that continually took root the rain forest would long ago have encroached and obliterated the puny efforts of humans.

The kitchen was the only good-sized room in the place. In the centre was a big cedar table that Brenda had made during a stint in shop mechanics, and the birthday party gravitated here, as did most parties. A one-time breakfast nook had been co-opted as a TV space, and here Penelope had squeezed in a worn sofa where she could nap in the daytime if she chose. The kitchen windows were curtainless and looked out on the ravine and caught the morning sun.

But it was the creek that made Penelope fall in love with the little house. A culvert under the road opened at the front edge of Penelope's property and released the little stream from its temporary jail, and it gushed forth happily into the dappled sunlight and rolled placidly alongside the house to the back edge of the property and then swept in a merry little falls over the ravine's edge and on down the mountain. Penelope's bedroom and small balcony overlooked the little waterfall and it wooed her to sleep at night.

The guests reinforced Penelope's astonishment at her being seventy. "No one would ever guess," Penelope's friends repeated over and over, and "You look terrific," although Mildred Summers didn't say this. She trilled her girlish laugh and said, "Oh my goodness!" in an arch and somewhat breathless voice, as if she were greeting Methuselah on his seven-hundredth birthday. (Mildred was ten years younger than Penelope, and if she were to stop to contemplate it — which she was unlikely to do — she would find that she didn't expect seventy to blindside her either.)

Tom from the potluck dinner crowd sidled up to her and quoted, "'Old age came upon me as a surprise, like a frost.' Know who said that?" Tom was eighty and prided himself on his erudition. "Good Queen Bess, the smartest damn monarch ever to rule Britannia."

Penelope liked this hint of hoar frost that coated the hair and cooled the heart. She wondered if the stretch she'd just navigated, the years between sixty-five and seventy, had been a transition, like adolescence or menopause. Not hormonal this time, or probably not, but some hitherto unexplored mechanism by which switches were reset, blood thinned, alarms triggered as brain chemicals found themselves out of equilibrium. Parts of the factory shutting down, resources diverted, output conserved, input reduced, the organism shifting gears to something lower and slower and able to make the last big hill.

Some transition! Botch it and you died.

At sixty-five, she had been comforted by her doctor with, "The ones who survive until seventy seem to coast along until true old age." The doctor had liked to kid her about her age; he had been younger than she was, but was dead now. By his own hand, she suspected, after diagnosing Lou Gehrig's Disease in himself. She still resented his leaving; perhaps if he had hung on, there were knots yet to be untangled? Great secrets to be pondered, as Stephen Hawking was doing? Insights to take with him wherever he was headed?

Tom held out his glass for a second of champagne and joined the others in demolishing the cake, as though the opportunity to drink too much and eat too much didn't present itself often enough – even though they could, all of them, if they wished, overindulge any day of the week. Still, the party was making the men feel frisky in the presence of "the girls," in their "Sunday best" with the occasional string of "real pearls," smelling of the Chanel given last Christmas by desperate grandchildren. For their part, the girls were reviving, under the influence of champagne, their lost skills in the art of flirtation. All of them, men and women alike, were happy to ignore the boring warning voices and bestow on themselves "just this once" the luxury of self-indulgence.

Besides the potluck crowd (reduced now to five originals from eight, with one new addition), there were several Senior Centre habitués from the watercolour class, and even old Doris, who had once worked for Penelope's husband and whom Time had improved, possibly because the only way left for Doris to go was up. And there were younger people, Brenda of course and her five-year-old Jason, along with a rather pleasant but somewhat nondescript man whom Brenda introduced to Penelope as Colin. Colin spent a lot of time talking electronics revolution in a corner with Jim Tran, the husband of Brenda's best friend Connie. Jim had left Hong Kong and its now-threatened free enterprise society which had made him rich.

Connie and Jim's son Tommy was almost Jason's age, and the two boys found the wait for Penelope to open her small gifts (nothing over twelve dollars Brenda had stipulated) almost intolerable. When the time came they were so enthusiastic about ripping off the wrappings that Penelope never did manage to figure out who gave what. (Although she suspects the Styling Gel came from Mildred.)

Midway through the party came the big surprise: Penelope's son Gordon (Brenda's twin), flown in from the east. Brenda shouted, "Ta da!" and Penelope found the excitement all but unbearable, all her loved ones and all her dearest friends here under one roof, every one of them — well, not Grover poor dear, but he was nearby in the Highlands Cemetery, and Grover hated birthday parties anyway.

"Imagine you a minister now!" Connie Tran said, cornering Gordon. Her little laugh of shared familiarity implied that she and Gordon alone knew such a vocation to be ludicrous; that stolen moments of precocious eroticism between them must forever banish any true dedication to the spiritual.

Later Gordon confided to Penelope that he had scarcely recognized in this skinny, smart woman the rather plain overweight Connie Smythe who used to hang around with Brenda in high school. Penelope remembered how she had sorrowed for the shy, hunched-over girl, so obviously infatuated with Gordon, who kept her eyes lowered, hiding their startling blueness.

It was obvious that Connie had internalized her mother's assessments. For Mrs. Smythe had been vocal about her resentment of Brenda and her clear skin, curly hair, even features. "At least you have the eyes," she would say, and Connie would dab unguents on her acne-riddled skin while Brenda actually envied Connie's straight hair, and would badger Connie to help her iron her unruly locks into a semblance of straightness.

Brenda-then had been beautiful, although now only rapt concentration would reveal that Brenda was still beautiful. And only rapt concentration would reveal that Connie wasn't. For Connie had learned a lot about the eye of the beholder. Her eyes were no longer directed at her shoes but were now looking the beholder straight on, their brilliant blueness accentuated with eye liner. Her face was too long and sported a matching nose: a Modigliani face, out of fashion, but her cleverly cut black straight hair, swinging bluntly two inches shorter on one side than the other, had the effect of pulling forehead closer to chin.

She was thin now, and stood very straight. Her black sheath scarcely covered her skinny bottom but was redeemed (barely) in Mildred's eyes by a red lacy over-tunic that ended in a flounce at neck, wrists, and hemline. "Black and red for a party," Mildred sniffed, touching her own suitably pink flowing garment, although the other women were too intimidated to have an opinion. They thought Connie's haircut daring, and fingered their own set-and-permed ash-blonde locks with something like embarrassment. Or shame. "Age is nothing to be ashamed of!" Brenda often declared, stoutly, but the elderly would hide their wrinkles if they could.

"Whatever happened to Betty Grosvenor?" Connie now asked Gordon. Betty had been the one Gordon noticed in high school, but then so did most of the other boys. "I heard she married and moved out to your part of the world. I couldn't believe it when she married what's-his-name, you know, the class nerd." Her eyes drifted past Gordon to Jim who, barely able to sustain this small separation from his asset portfolio, was starting to fidget.

Gordon flushed and stumbled – which didn't escape Connie's notice – and then said seriously, almost censoriously, "Ivan. He wasn't really a nerd you know, we were adolescents, we all figured if you didn't conform you were...well.... Anyway, he's dead."

"Dead!"

"Heart attack."

"But — he wasn't any older than — than the rest of us."

"No," Gordon said, and shook her hand before she could kiss him.

Just for a moment Connie's *sang-froid* crumbled and she was revealed to herself as the ugly duckling Gordon had refused to notice. With a light laugh she gathered up the armour of years and turned away, at the precise moment when Gordon bent and planted a kiss on the back of her head.

I Ie had seen the momentary loss. Gordon's perpetually bewildered air had always made women long to help him, and it was only lately that he had acquired enough self-knowledge to remedy his own complicity in this semi-deliberate plucking of heartstrings. And to follow his own injunction to his parishioners, to "reach out" to one's fellow human beings.

Connie turned and they smiled wryly at one another; a grown-up smile of mutually acknowledged tolerance, even affection. Jim Tran looked rather speculatively at Gordon, and Connie was heartened (things hadn't been going too well between them lately), while Gordon's chest swelled for various competitive caveman reasons that he preferred not to examine.

Penelope, catching the finale, was pleased with Gordon, then began to wonder why the impulse to ordinary human kindness continues to flourish in seeming opposition to the age's ruthless "survival of the fittest" philosophy. She set that one aside for future exploration.

Gordon shook Jim's hand and even Tommy's, and then turned to help old Tom down the steps. (Under normal circumstances old Tom could manage perfectly well, but triple champagne was not a daily occurrence.) When he got to the bottom Tom called back to Penelope, "We're both Scorpios, know that? Only I've got ten years on you, 1913 I was born, just in time for the First World War. Killed my father, never knew him," and he lurched and would have fallen without Gordon's fatherly arm.

"I think you're very brave to let your hair go grey," Mildred said as she and George were leaving, and she touched her own yellow-orange Maggie-Thatcher-look-alike locks. Then she put her hand firmly on her portly, balding husband's arm and turned him away before he could kiss Penelope on the cheek, should he have been so wildly foolhardy as to intend such a thing.

"Don't let that Mildred Summers spook you," Brenda said after the guests were gone. "I like to see people age naturally and I sure wouldn't want your hair turning lacquered orange like Mildred's. Actually I love your colour, like shiny steel, shiny wavy steel. Whose genes gave me this frizz? And you could have passed on your nice skinny figure while you were at it."

AS BRENDA AND JASON GOT OUT OF THE CAR WHEN Penelope dropped them off at the Horseshoe Bay ferry terminal, Brenda's parting words were, "Okay, so you're seventy, it's only a number. Get a life, don't sit around and mope."

Brenda's own stratagem for recovering from failed love and "getting a life" had been to move into a vacant tree house at Plumper Cove on Keats Island, commuting daily via Zodiac and bicycle to her librarian's job in Gibsons on the mainland. Penelope loved the tree house, a sturdy two-storey structure nestled within the aromatic boughs of a ninety-year-old red cedar. She did worry, though, about the day when she would no longer be able to climb the ladder that took you up six feet to a balcony, where both Penelope and Jason loved to lie and watch the wind ruffle the tops of arbutus trees – in winter as well as in summer, since arbutus trees shed their bark and not their leaves.

The door off the balcony led into a kitchen, and because the house was constructed around the tree's trunk a sort of open planning merged kitchen into living room into Jason's bedroom. Having by then come full circle, Jason's bedroom ended with a spiral wooden staircase that led to a loft, which was Brenda's bedroom.

Through the window of Brenda's bedroom, which took up most of the west wall, there was a magnificent view across the narrow strait to Gibsons Landing. The light filtering through needles was lacelike and gentle, and Brenda sometimes sketched there, or read (for a modest fee she had hijacked an electric line from a nearby trailer camp).

The tree house did tend to sway in high winds, or when an occasional venturesome lover discovered the delights to be found in the comforting folds of Brenda's ample body. Brenda and Jason both loved the wind. A promontory protected them from the worst of the winter gales, although occasionally a squamish, as this particular wind was named, would sneak in over the abutment and send them swaying and sailing, the branches creaking and wailing, the whine and guttural groaning of the heavy nails in the bracing joists a grand parody of the old timber sailing ship in which Captain George Vancouver first mapped Keats Island.

Penelope had observed that visitors, including lovers, prone to seasickness rarely visited twice. At the moment she sensed that there were no lovers plural, only a lover, singular, Colin, and furthermore that he was no longer occasional, although Brenda had been unusually coy about whether or not they constituted a relationship.

As she continues her walk, Penelope, pondering what — other than tree houses — might be involved in "getting a life," lists those things she would have liked to do but never has.

1. Live on a boat year-round, sailing from harbour to harbour, south in winter, possibly to California, north again in summer, up and up past Desolation Sound where she and Grover twice sailed, past Toba Inlet and past Bute Inlet, perhaps as far even as the Queen Charlotte Islands.

2. Snowboard. As a child Penelope had a marvellous wooden toboggan that sailed over bumps and thudded to the ground in back-wrenching thumps, and she had skied, too, on ancient wooden slats. Snowboarding, she thinks, would be the thrill of tobogganing *and* skiing all packaged into one.

3. Emulate Madame Curie (a lifelong heroine since Penelope learned in Grade Four that Madame Curie's birthday was the exact same date as her own), except that she fears that all the important elements have now been discovered.

4. Become a Mystic. Ever since she read Kipling's *Kim* in school, Penelope has harboured admiration for the meditative life.

Her attempts to emulate it have, however, come up against a stumbling block: by the time she is successful in clearing her mind of all thoughts she is usually asleep.

5. Work out the Meaning of Life.

The latter seems the most feasible, and timely as well.

The sun is sending out shafts of sunlight that look, through the fog, like the painted rays of a medieval mural, and Penelope is beginning to catch glimpses of the white sails of Canada Place across the harbour. The kale is glowing in the bright sunshine like sprightly scraps of purple neon against the freshly turned earth. Penelope composes herself, but her heart, unlike Wordsworth's (as recited in a forgotten classroom), does not with pleasure fill, nor dance among the daffodils (or, in this case, kale).

A recurring disappointment. According to *Stress or Serenity, It's Up to You*, which, on Brenda's recommendation, she has purchased at Banyen Books, serene masters, yogis, swamis, those sorts of people, find Nirvana in a grain of ordinary sand. Penelope closes her eyes and thinks of sand, vast beaches, single grains, the sandbox of childhood, but her mind can't get around grit. She remembers that the book advises planting the feet solidly on the ground so that earth energy can flow freely up the *kundalini* and into the *chakras.* She does so, and thinks she feels a slight vibration in the ground beneath her. Not a shaking, more of a tingling, a small but distinct shiver, a *frisson* that tickles the soles of her feet.

Electrical, whispers an errant capriciousness, a restive wind that wafts ceaselessly through her thoughts, sabotaging serenity.

The doomed man in Alabama on the front page of this morning's *Sun*, strapped in the loathsome "Chair" with its death-dealing encumbrances. By now, if no last-minute reprieve has come, thousands of volts will have blasted through the delicately evolved neurons and arced across the mortal synapses of his brain. "Fried," Penelope mutters, and starts to get up, then sits down again.

"No," she says loudly and quite sternly. A squirrel stares at her before darting up a tree to saner surroundings. She laughs, then notices that at the spot where the squirrel was squatting a tiny shoot of maple is struggling to right itself. At that precise moment a leaf, dislodged from the tree by the squirrel's trip along its branches, drifts down onto Penelope's hand, and a shaft of sunlight that must have been blocked by the leaf falls squarely on the tiny maple.

Penelope slides off the bench, lowers herself to her knees, and lays her head down beside the shoot. She estimates that, without the interfering leaf, the sun will shine directly on it, unimpeded, for possibly — glancing at the sky — an hour.

As she rests in this unlikely position, on her knees, her rump raised in the air, her arms flattened along the grass on either side of her head, her cheek resting on the ground, she becomes aware that someone, the young woman from the house across the street, is watching.

Risking dizziness, Penelope jumps to her feet and the woman calls, "Are you all right?"

"Fine, thank you," Penelope replies, smiling widely to indicate good health. "Just dropped something."

She waves, and the young woman, whose phone is ringing, hesitates, waves back, then turns and runs into the house, as though missing the call could shatter some unacknowledged fragility.

Reminding herself that age brings enough problems without adding a reputation for eccentricity, Penelope hurries on her way.

She hopes it wasn't The Spoiler on the phone. In the years she has marched along this street on her daily round, Penelope has come to know the woman, whose name she now remembers is Anne Lewis, slightly. At first they merely exchanged half-embarrassed "hellos," for the woman was preoccupied, hanging onto a toddler who bent to examine every leaf and crawling insect, while an excited five-year-old danced impatiently ahead of them, shouting that they would be late for kindergarten.

In time, as the greetings expanded to include the weather and the state of blossoms, the toddler himself grew to kindergarten age, while the older child, a girl, began to lag behind, reluctant to have her friends see that her mother still walked her to school. Lately even the ex-toddler no longer requires the company of Anne, who, Penelope has noticed, is no longer so young. A phase of her life has ended; Penelope knows this from her own experience. Every phase sharply delineated, slipping away like an old skin, nothing left to show for itself except one or two discolouring photos.

Two weeks ago Anne was accompanied by a man, a tall, very handsome, but — to Penelope's eyes — somewhat shifty-eyed stranger who was not the weary-looking man who cut the grass on weekends. Anne flushed as she mumbled her greeting, and didn't meet Penelope's eyes. Penelope knows about boredom and empty days, and she knows a thing or two about temptation as well. The innocuous tingle, the sheathed current, the final convulsion that shatters innocence....

Penelope reminds herself that just because they have vigorous bodies, the young don't necessarily have robust minds. Minds are slippery things, and in her own experience more likely to go off the track when young than old – certainly she herself came perilously close more than once in those far-off days. Everyone has her own private devils, and if there is one thing Penelope has learned it is that devils have to be dealt with on a devil-by-devil basis.

AFTER THE LAST GUEST HAD LEFT THE BIRTHDAY party and Jason had gone to watch cartoons, Penelope and Brenda collapsed on couches and kicked off their shoes, and Gordon made tea. Watching him, Penelope thought how vulnerable he seemed, as though someone should be taking charge of him, looking out for him.

When she was a young mother Penelope used to torture herself by wondering whether she loved Brenda more than Gordon, and on other occasions Gordon more than Brenda, but she learned, in time, that her concern swung between them like a witching wand sensing water. If Brenda were going through a crisis – rejection for the role of Snow White had been a Grade Five catastrophe – then Brenda would be front and centre. And the same held true of Gordon, except that his crises were more subtle, requiring skill in the art of divination.

Penelope had seen something on Gordon's face, some pain or failure, when he was talking to Connie, and she wasn't surprised later, after Brenda had gone out with Colin, that Gordon confessed, hesitantly, that he was seeing a psychiatrist.

What did surprise her was that Gordon was seeing the psychiatrist because he had come into possession of a sensibility that she herself had always longed to have, but whose existence he didn't believe in.

GORDON, WHO WAS THE REV. GORDON STEVENS OF THE Unitarian Church of Etobicoke, was most emphatic about the fact that he did not believe in auras when he met with Dr. Weinburg, to whom he had been referred.

"Then why are you seeing them, do you suppose?" Dr. Weinberg asked, with a smile of complicity, as though they shared a secret. He had an untidy moustache and smelled of cigars.

Gordon shrugged. "I'm still inclined to the migraine theory," he said.

"Certainly that is possible, very possible. Why would Dr. Holmes reject it, do you suppose?"

Gordon hesitated. It was Dr. Holmes, a neurologist, who had first suggested migraine aura, after the hospital's new MRI scanner — which had given Gordon a panicky claustrophobia when his head was shoved into the shiny new headgear — had revealed neither lesion nor tumour. Dr. Holmes had asked if there was some trick of lighting in the church. "Strobe lighting, for instance?"

Gordon, wondering just what misimpression Dr. Holmes might be under regarding Unitarianism, denied strobe lighting, and in the face of such denial Dr. Holmes admitted that very little was known about the mystery of biochemical brain function. He leafed through a text with the single word "MIGRAINE" across the binding and read out a small excerpt that agreed with everything he'd just said. An aura or even a full-blown migraine can, in some instances, be traced to a specific place or event which operates as the triggering action.

"But why now?" Gordon asked. "And in any case, that wouldn't explain the diversity — well, almost suitability."

"Suitability?" Dr. Holmes was scarcely able to conceal his disappointment.

Recklessly, Gordon plunged ahead. "Harbit-Jones has to analyze everything in the cold light of Cartesian logic, and his aura is green."

He was babbling, inappropriately, he knew this — but he seemed to have lost the ability to stop himself. "A clear, brilliant green, almost no other colour, while his — ah — friend's, is blue — she's a warm and giving kind of person, you see, otherwise she'd have some difficulty in her relationship with Harbit-Jones, although it's interesting, there was an occasional flare of red, it's my guess there is some anger...."

Dr. Holmes was looking at him with the bland expression of one concentrating on blandness. Picking up a prescription pad he scribbled a referral. "I think," he said, as gently as he could, "you should see Dr. Weinberg."

Gordon sighed. "Jungian or Freudian?" he asked.

"I don't know. It's not my field."

Dr. Weinberg, as it turned out, was neither. He was, he said, of the bloodhound persuasion; he sniffed out trails and byways that might lead to the light, "Or, in your case, out of the light." Gordon laughed, rather immoderately.

"Now," Dr. Weinberg said, "was there anything else you perhaps confided in Dr. Holmes that you haven't told me?"

Gordon fiddled with his wristwatch. He didn't meet Dr. Weinberg's eyes. "I did mention that the colours matched the personalities of their owners," he mumbled, noting the unlikely polish on Dr. Weinberg's shoes, which he could just glimpse under the desk.

"Tell me about that," Dr. Weinberg said. "Start at the beginning."

BUT GORDON'S STORY WAS INTERRUPTED BY BRENDA'S return and Gordon clammed up at once. Those two, Penelope thought. Engaged in rivalry so deep from Day One that to this day neither of them would give an inch. Once upon a time Brenda had claimed that she was seeing auras and Gordon had ridiculed her; the last thing he would be likely to do now was to hand her his capitulation on a platter.

WHAT SUBTERRANEAN DISTURBANCE IS STRUGGLING TO illuminate Gordon's psyche? Penelope wonders now, as she hurries on her way home. She longs to know more, but Gordon has gone back to Etobicoke, and anyway such revelations cannot be forced. They will surface in their own good time. Is Gordon seeing the auras from the pulpit? Which would be disconcerting, although revealing, given that they match the personalities of their owners. Then she wonders what colour hers would be. She would like it to be blue, a colour she finds restful, but she suspects restless violet streaks that ripple and pulse like northern lights.

The Spoiler's would be black and red, of that she is reasonably sure. Anne Lewis was so anxious to answer the phone....

Penelope reminds herself that the call may have been merely a friend for a game of bridge. Or Anne's husband, fearful at some subliminal level that it would not be she who answered. Still it could very well have been The Spoiler himself, bold and careless, too powerful now to be dismissed.

Penelope begins to walk more quickly, then forces herself to stop and admire the fluorescent orange-red of a Japanese maple.

Would Anne's life be changed if she missed the call? The Spoiler defeated? The husband tormented? Or would a noncommittal answering machine have informed someone — friend, lover, husband — that she wasn't available at that moment, (the moment she waved to Penelope), and that if the caller would just record a message...? Leaving the moment forever lost in a welter of insignificance, even the memory disappearing after a week or two.

Sharp, familiar, palpitations remind Penelope and she slows down, her thoughts whirling in some unidentifiable distress. A song she once sang, in ancient times in Sunday school, wanders through her mind.

"God sees the little sparrow fall," Penelope warbles, her voice, in her ears, sounding unused, sliding off the notes as she tries to retrieve the next line. "He marks...no, meets, its...." what? Shining? Tender? No matter, the point is that the sparrow's fall did not go unnoted. It was marked.

If she hadn't shouted "no" and frightened the squirrel he would not have jumped off the bent shoot, allowing it to straighten before being irretrievably damaged. Nor would he have dislodged the light-blocking leaf as he ran along the branch, just at the moment when the sun was positioned to shine through. Penelope herself, kneeling beside the shoot, may have destroyed other shoots that were competing with the small maple. She and the squirrel and the falling leaf may have given it the Darwinian edge it needs to survive.

If the tiny maple now has enough light it might grow into a large tree, and cast a great shadow, so that other shoots will be discouraged from flourishing. Eventually, in a year of drought, it might challenge the parent tree for water, and the older tree might die, falling with a crash that takes out hydro wires. And possibly – it could happen, it has happened – someone will be killed.

PENELOPE CROSSES UNDER THE HYDRO LINE AGAIN. She thinks she can hear the wires humming their twin songs of love and death.

When the two firemen started up the mountain the eyes of the onlookers strained after them, until the men were swallowed up by trees and shrubs. The crowd, Penelope among them, waited, and then there was another flash and a frightening noise. The firemen didn't reappear. Still the people waited, uneasiness rippling through them like an unnatural stirring of ectoplasm, or like sound so high it may have been imagined.

A long time later, after the police had come and then an ambulance, the sound of its siren sliding into minor keys as though it too were in mourning, they learned what had happened. Just as the two men reached the charred clearing another arc slammed them into the ground and squashed the breath from their lungs. The younger of the two managed, gasping and weeping, to crawl out a little way, where he was eventually rescued. But by the time the main power switch in the distant hydro station had been turned off and it was safe to go back in for the other man, the older man was dead. Later, Penelope saw in the paper that it was his last shift before retirement.

WHEN PENELOPE GETS HOME SHE SITS DOWN WITH THE newspaper and a cup of tea. Scientists with computers, she reads, have been amazed that the omission of even the twentieth figure following the decimal point of pi will change a given result dramatically after a couple of hundred generations. They call their new theory "Chaos."

"Aha!" Penelope shouts. "They've caught on, have they?" Muttering, she castigates them for the choice of name. "It isn't chaos, you poor saps," she rails. Can't they see that "chaos" implies that there are no rules, that nothing matters? If it made no difference whether or not the young woman answered the phone, that would be chaos. If the squirrel's dislodging the leaf affected nothing, that would be chaos. If God did not see the little sparrow fall, if it made no difference whatsoever that Penelope Stevens had wandered briefly over this earth, if her passage left no mark and was not marked, then that would be chaos. Chaos is randomness, and chaos and randomness seem to Penelope to be the twin enemies of serenity. It is precisely because the twentieth decimal after pi makes a difference that she feels a stirring of hope.

As she drinks the soothing lemon-flavoured tea she thinks about Anne Lewis, snatching so eagerly at life that she can mistake The Spoiler for her need. And then she thinks of the dead fireman. She imagines him getting up on that morning of his final day, seeing the sun and dreaming of the morrow, his first day of freedom, when he would amble out to the golf course and never again have to run into burning buildings, nor rescue cats from trees, nor resuscitate aging men whose hearts had failed.

When the accident happened Penelope thought it was the randomness that made the thing so unbearable, but now she sees that it isn't like that at all. If nothing in the world will ever be the same again after a squirrel runs up a tree and a leaf comes fluttering down, what enormous waves must crash around the planet when a man dies? However meaningless the death might seem.

A shaft of sunlight clears the surrounding trees and reaches the kitchen window, and as it touches and warms her she marvels to think that, in merely one day of her life, she has been able to change the destiny of a woman and a tree and even a forest, and cause reverberations that will be felt for generations to come.

But what really tickles her, makes her smile, then laugh loudly, derisively, in the silence of her sun-drenched kitchen, is that scientists have taken so long to discover it.

She decides to enrol in the "Science for Seniors" course being offered at Capilano College and find out what else they might have missed.

DECEMBER

THE NIGHT GEORGE SUMMERS DIES THEY ARE having the monthly potluck dinner in Penelope Stevens' small house, and Penelope can't prevent the uncharitable thought from snaking across her brain that it is just like George to choose *her* house in which to make his final exit instead of waiting a month until the dinner will be at his own house.

For something like thirty years, on the first Thursday of the month a group of four couples has rotated potluck dinner venues, although they are no longer four couples. Penelope's husband, Grover, is dead; Nancy has re-married, (Dick, silently grateful to have found Nancy); Tom is a widower; and Mildred and George are the only couple remaining of the originals. Or were.

On the night in question there is one other, a friend of George's, a sturdy man with greying hair who, like George, had gone through UBC's school of engineering on his veteran's credits, and whose name Penelope missed but which turns out to be

Edwin. Edwin doesn't have much of anything to say until he sparks the final conversation, the one that may or may not have caused an exasperated George to collapse over coffee.

During pre-dinner drinks they begin the litany of the symptoms of aging – "the organ recital," as somebody has dubbed it – and George, as usual, is grumping over the definitive grievance. "Sleep," he says, flatly. "That's the bastard. If a person could just get a proper night's sleep most of the other crud would clear up."

"Think gravity," Penelope says.

All eyes turn on her.

"Now think no gravity. Think anti-gravity. Think anti-gravity paint."

"What the blazes are you on about?" George demands.

"If you want to put yourself to sleep, think anti-gravity paint."

SLEEP, FOR PENELOPE TOO, HAS BECOME CAPRICIOUS, descending uninvited when television Weather discharges its roiling clouds across green-and-brown North America, or, alternatively, deserting her as she pulls up the covers and switches off the lamp.

Penelope is not one to accept arbitrariness. She does not get up and drink cocoa, as her mother might have done, or swallow a sleeping pill (if, indeed, she possessed such a thing) as her late husband would surely have done. Instead her mind gropes for the anti-gravity paint and, once it has been slathered onto the bottom of her single mattress, she raises the mattress with one finger, holds it lightly while she slides open the balcony door, tilts it gently (this is harder, gravity is grabbing the edges) to get it through, piles on the necessary equipment — which she has stored in a box on the floor — carefully positions the mattress at hip height and rolls gently onto it. She wriggles her ankles into loops, then, using a pole, she pushes off while at the same time giving the mattress a firm shove upwards. Since the pole is affected by gravity and the shove must be strong enough to counteract it, this is a bit tricky, but after a couple of undignified tumbles Penelope has mastered it.

GEORGE HATES STUFF LIKE THIS. HE GLARES AT HER from under bushy brows. "Penny," he says, slowly, articulating as though hers is a deficit of comprehension, "I swear you're getting nuttier by the minute."

"George!" Mildred says, in the exact tone of remonstrance she has used for thirty-nine years.

"Penelope. My name is Penelope."

"Oh Christ!" George clutches at his bald head as though he's forgotten there is no longer hair to tear out. "If there is one thing I can't stand it's people who get cute in their old age and change their names."

"Penelope has always been my name," she answers, reasonably. She leaves it at that. She's learned, quite recently, that it is not necessary to justify oneself for personal decisions — she wishes she'd known that when Grover was still alive.

George's colour shifts from pasty to florid and Mildred says, quickly, "Come on everyone, dinner."

By this time, Edwin, the newcomer, unused to their free-wheeling familiarity, is looking more than a little uncomfortable. Penelope hands him a plate and motions for him to help himself to food, then smiles encouragingly. Emboldened, he blurts out the fateful words that will lead, eventually, to Penelope throwing out the remainder of the anti-gravity paint. (Not an easy task.) He blinks, half-smiles, and says, "I could have used some of that stuff when we were flying over Gimli."

There is a small silence until everyone is seated around the table, and then Penelope urges him to tell his story.

"Do you remember, quite a few years back, when that new Boeing 767 ran out of gas...."

"Sure. 1983. Over Gimli," George says.

"What is Gimli?" Nancy asks.

"A place, sweetheart, a place." Dick squeezes her hand. He doesn't need brilliance, he needs (and is grateful for) a nurse.

"Oh cute, Nancy. You missed Generation x by five or six decades, so don't try to pretend you weren't around during the war."

Dick raises one hand, but Nancy pats his knee and Dick sets the hand back on the tablecloth. George is likely to become cantankerous during his second glass of wine — not to mention the third and fourth — and they have all come to accept it.

"Why, was the war in this Gimli?" Nancy is deliberately baiting George, of this Penelope is reasonably sure. She is also reasonably sure that everyone else — with the possible exception of George (and Edwin, of course) — knows this.

"Gimli is in Manitoba!" George shouts, and in despair pours himself more wine. "The Commonwealth Air Training scheme, you nit!"

"Steady on," Dick says, in defence of Nancy's honour.

"George," Mildred remonstrates.

"Commonwealth? A business sponsored air training?"

"The *British* Commonwealth!" George thunders.

"I'd forgotten all about that," Mildred says, and suddenly her eyes sparkle. "They were from all over, the men I mean, and the Aussies were stationed near us, right there on the North Hill in Calgary...."

Penelope, from years of experience, knows that the explosive content of the conversation is approaching a critical mass. Turning quickly to the abashed-looking newcomer she says, "Now Edwin, tell us about it."

"Well, like I say, I was on it. The new Boeing 767. When it ran out of gas."

"Fuel," George says, but in deference to Edwin's status as a guest, friend, and fellow engineer, he lowers his voice and merely adds, "not gas."

"My goodness!" Nancy gasps. "I certainly hope the captain got rapped over the knuckles. They're getting awfully careless, aren't they? I always say, it's almost safer to drive south these days."

"Nancy, if a plane runs out of fuel, what makes you think the captain or anyone else survived?"

"Well, because Edwin is alive to tell the tale," Nancy answers, rather triumphantly, and during the general laughter George covers his retreat by pouring more wine.

"Yes," Edwin goes on, "the 767 was a brand new aeroplane that year, and they had a brand new way of measuring fuel, that's how the mix-up happened."

"Litres instead of gallons, it was only a matter of time before the bloody metric system killed someone."

"Actually," Penelope interposes, "it was being weighed. Not measured. Weighed in kilograms, I believe."

Edwin beams at Penelope. He wonders if she is a widow. "We were up there at thirty-five thousand feet when suddenly both engines stopped, one after the other, and we started to go down."

THEY WERE CRUISING COMFORTABLY AT THIRTY-FIVE thousand feet and Edwin, who had never before flown over the prairies, was looking down at the flat fields blocked precisely in green and sometimes yellow squares, creased where rivers and creeks had clawed out their massive circulatory systems. He was admiring the shiny new aircraft, on its very first flight across Canada, and listening to the great engines purring along. He thought he might doze awhile.

When the noise lessened he wondered if they were coming down to a lower cruising altitude. Then the noise lessened again and several passengers looked up curiously. Some glanced out the windows before returning to their magazines. It seemed to him that the sound stopped altogether, but seasoned travellers know that a jet is often very silent during any kind of descent, even a minor altitude change, and this jet was an unfamiliar breed.

Many of the passengers had earphones on and heard nothing.

But Edwin, who had been a pilot during the war, was now aware of the great silence, no throbbing of giant turbines, no swish of air conditioning, nothing except a slight whistling. He made no fuss. Then others began to notice the wheat fields coming closer, and suddenly an alien presence stalked the aisles. Fear, Edwin thought it was, or gravity, or God.

"MY GOODNESS!" MILDRED'S ROSY FACE IS A PICTURE of consternation, as though they, crowded there in Penelope's little dining room, are in mortal danger. "Then what happened?"

"Well, nothing really. We glided in. You see, the captain looked down and recognized the old airstrip at Gimli, seems he'd trained there during the war, and so he just set her down as gentle as you please." Edwin is not a raconteur.

"No, it was the co-pilot — can't remember his name — he was the one who'd been stationed there," George says. "The captain was Bob Pearson, did a hell of a job. Had to calculate air speed and angle of glide dead-on to get enough lift for such a heavy aircraft ...."

Mildred interrupts. "Was anyone around, to see you come in?"

"Oh yes, that was the really funny thing. There were a lot of people out at that airstrip for a car rally they were having. Boy, you should have seen the look on their faces when we all slid down that chute as cool as you please, right there in the middle of their drag racing!"

"Imagine!" Penelope says. "Just think what it must have been like, looking up and seeing that giant silver plane about to land and not hearing one single sound. They must have wondered if it was a UFO."

"Yes. Well," Edwin says, as though to finish off the story, but then, remembering why he has recounted it in the first place, "So you see why I'm so interested in your anti-gravity paint. Mind telling some more about it?"

THE FIRST NIGHT PENELOPE IMAGINED LAUNCHING HER gravity-treated mattress she soon realized she needed equipment on board, not just her covers. She rested the mattress on the balcony railings, steadied it enough so she could climb on, then sat up and gave a push with her foot, quickly pulling the foot back into the safety of the gravity-free zone.

The balcony was fifteen feet above the ground. Suddenly Penelope noticed that she was not sitting on the mattress but had risen above it by six inches, and that the covers, too, were beginning to grow restive. Of course! Anything on top of the treated mattress would be weight-free as well. She grabbed at the covers and at the mattress, and wished she knew whether gravity travelled in straight lines or went around corners – if only she'd looked all that stuff up *before* she got into this situation. But since there was nothing to do now but play it by ear she tried to tuck the covers tightly around her legs and hung onto a pinch of mattress fabric.

While she was wrestling with the covers her hand accidentally slid outside the protected area, and in pulling it back she banged the mattress harder than she intended and caused it to reverse direction and begin to fall. Newton's First Law (she had learned it that very day) said that an object would remain in a state of rest or in a straight line at constant speed until it was compelled to change that state by an impressed force. Since this meant that gravity-free objects would continue to travel at the rate of initial propulsion, she hit the grass with a fairly hard bump, which caused enough of an equal and opposite reaction for the mattress, with Penelope still on it, to move upwards, and it wasn't until she was eight feet above the ground that she thought to hang out her hand.

Unfortunately, by this time she was rattled and hung only one hand over the side, so that the mattress started to tilt to that side and before she had time to pull her hand back gravity caught the angled, untreated covers and mattress top and woman, and she plunged onto the grass in a heap of mattress and blankets and bruised pride. She packed it in for that night.

"JUST THINK," SHE RECOUNTS TO HER SOMEWHAT confused audience, "if nosy Mrs. Moore next door had been watching the way the Gimli drag racers did, what a shock she would have had if she happened to glance out the window and spotted me in my nightclothes on the lawn, balancing my mattress on one finger!"

"My, Penny — I mean Penelope — you do think of the oddest things," Nancy says, and then, as if to validate her observation and give it status, she turns to her new husband. "Doesn't she, Dick?"

All eyes turn speculatively to Dick, since no one to date has ever heard him express an opinion. He thinks for a moment, then says, "You know, I was stationed at Gimli myself, before I was sent overseas."

Nancy beams. "Dick! How interesting! Isn't that fascinating, everyone? Dick was stationed at Gimli."

"Big deal," George growls. "Not exactly the Burma hump, was it?" During the war George ferried bombers over the Burma hump, a fact he usually manages to slip into whatever conversation is taking place.

Over the years Penelope has formed a mental picture of George and the Burma hump, which she sees as a great cone of land rising out of the ground like a camel's hump. She imagines George's World War II bomber climbing and climbing, its engines groaning and grinding, barely clearing jungle forests that crawl with rainbow-hued snakes of astonishing iridescence, and man-eating plants that snatch indiscriminately at passing protein. She remembers George as he was when she first knew him, young and rather handsome with curling black hair, and she imagines him sitting in the open cockpit with his aviator's goggles on and his white scarf blowing behind him, risking his life as he clears the great obstruction with only inches to spare, gallant, elated, wildly and luxuriantly alive in his sleek, muscular body, full of vitality, full of joy, and she often thinks it may have been the last true happiness George ever knew.

She is so lost in thought that she almost misses Tom's unusual intervention (since Peggy's death he seldom speaks). He has, as he often does, left the table to leaf through some book or other —

in this case, *The Canadian Encyclopaedia* — and now he returns, holding the tome open and peering over his rimless glasses. "Listen to this," he says. "Gimli means 'the great hall of heaven' in Norse mythology."

This seems telling, or auspicious, and they all stare silently into their wine glasses as they try to puzzle out wherein the significance lies.

EVENTUALLY PENELOPE MASTERED FLIGHT. AFTER GETTING caught in a windstorm that almost tumbled her upside down, she realized that the mattress top and sides, as well as the covers, all required paint. She herself could remain paint-free, since she could pull the treated covers over her head if necessary.

Then there was the vexing matter of direction. Treated oars would move her back and forth, although rowing was tiring. "Down" was simple enough — she hung both wrists over the edge of the mattress for "down" — but for some time "up" could only be achieved by getting close to a roof or a tree, or even the ground, and giving a mighty push up with an oar. But then Newton's law kicked in and she was stuck with whatever speed and direction her propulsion had given her.

The problem actually kept her awake for a couple of nights, until she remembered the years that she and Grover had sailed. In no time she rigged up a mast and sail and coated them with the paint. Now she could hoist the sail, which was levered so that it could serve as either spinnaker or parachute, and take advantage of up and down drafts, as well as horizontal breezes.

This three-dimensional sailing was the most luxurious thing Penelope had ever known.

"IT MAKES ME THINK OF THE FREEDOM THAT FISH ENJOY," Penelope says, "although I suppose it should remind me of birds, except that birds have to flap their wings most of the time in order not to sink, while fish can, like me, float."

The potluck crowd are silent for a moment, and then George says, as though it were some kind of personal insult, "Where the hell did you come up with something that weird? It's a total impossibility, in case you didn't know."

"What makes you think so?"

"Ever hear of Newton?"

Penelope doesn't deign to answer.

"Newton's Law of Gravity, bodies attract one another in proportion to their combined masses and inversely in proportion to the square of the distance between them — of course, old Newton's been upstaged by relativity, but the basic principle still holds." George often brags that he's never forgotten anything he learned in engineering school; and, by way of proof, when in his cups (which often occurs after prolonged potluck dining and wining), he will recount stories of outrageous conduct "before the invention of bloody political correctness," ribald jokes, panty raids, and the most inventive of all the pranks — which George implies was his brain wave — the hoisting of a small British car called a Flying Standard atop Lions Gate bridge. (The way Penelope remembers it, the students in veterans' classes were older than other students and disapproved of such antics.)

"*Sir* Isaac Newton," Penelope says, carefully, as though she too may have difficulty in getting her point across, "also said that gravity can only be observed, it can't be explained, and that he personally had no idea what it is, for all he knew it could be God."

"When? He never said any such thing. You're making it up."

"We studied it in the Eldercollege course I'm taking at Capilano College." She can't contain an almost imperceptible note of "in your face," since George was particularly disparaging when she enrolled in "Science for Seniors." "Slop for the Aging-challenged," he dubbed it, in spite of (or because of) Penelope's outrage.

Mildred remarks that if the Almighty is gravity, He, She or It has a lot to answer for, and they all begin to try to top one another with cries of "unholy bloody bags under squinty slitty eyes," "falling arches, rising ankles," "plugging prostates preventing peeing," "hanging guts make me nuts," until Tom removes his pipe (which he is no longer allowed to light) and makes his second intervention of the evening.

"Look at it this way," he says. "Maybe gravity is merely the messenger, calling us home."

ONCE UPON A TIME GEORGE WAS IN LOVE WITH PENELOPE. Penelope knew this, but what she wasn't sure of at the time was whether or not she was in love with George. Certainly, as Brenda would have put it, she was "in lust," but she suspects factors other than either love or lust flagged her attention: boredom, frustration with the strictures of the fifties, the feeling that her own lack of identification with society's mores was some sort of personal madness: all of these, stirred in the melting pot of human emotions, may have disguised themselves as love.

But perhaps George himself was not exactly in love with "her" (whoever "she" was). Perhaps George was in love with the Burma hump, with danger, with the freedom that comes with riding the third dimension of air, with youth and joy and all the things he had left behind in the jungles of Burma. Perhaps, she thinks, she had come to seem a substitute.

There wasn't time for much of an affair (for which Penelope, over the years, has become grateful). Stolen moments before and after school meetings, at the hockey rink, during ballet lessons, while a child practised her scales, an occasional kiss, some heavy breathing.

"Come on! No fancy sidestepping!" Penelope chides herself sharply. (She is committed to total honesty – "Now that it's safe," a derisive voice mocks, but she stops that one in its tracks with "better late than never.") A few motels whose shabbiness was a given, since money was too scarce to cover champagne or even flowers, much less a good hotel.

Penelope's husband and Mildred caught on, although neither of them let the knowledge rise to their conscious minds. Instead the potlucks were frequently suspended for headaches, flu, crushing schedules, and then, after several months, tentatively at first, and finally definitively, they were reinstated.

Penelope has come to believe that every life has a central

event, or a defining epoch, and that George had lived the only part of his life he would ever give two damns about above Burma. She also knows she couldn't have saved him; it was all she could do to save herself.

ON HER NOCTURNAL VENTURES SHE USUALLY FLOATS down the back lane, keeping as much as possible in the shelter of trees so she won't be mistaken for a UFO. Sometimes she stares down at the tops of the houses she passes on her daily walk and thinks about the people she has come to recognize, Anne Lewis, the children, even The Spoiler, and laughs at their surprise if they should look out and see her floating above them. Occasionally, when she begins to feel sleepy, she fastens her mattress from a hook under her balcony roof, the upright mast preventing her from drifting into the ceiling, and falls asleep, waving gently in the breeze. (Once she tried doing this in a tree but was awakened by a squirrel.)

One night, feeling particularly venturesome – and longing to hover over the tree house and send silver streams of danger-retardant love down on Brenda and Jason – she flew high over the sparkling lights of Lions Gate Bridge, hoping that no motorist spotted her and caused a pileup, then cleared Stanley Park before losing altitude out in the middle of English Bay.

She hadn't counted on the solitude of a vast ocean at night, even with the lights of Point Grey winking near her. Nervously, she ventured out into the Strait of Georgia, but then, panicking, she thought she had better not go further, that if she encountered fog she would be lost, and so she turned and headed for the shallows off Spanish Banks.

She was four feet above the water when a so-called "rogue wave" roared in and crashed over her, wetting her and the mattress, and by its downward thrust forcing her beneath the waves. Fortunately the tide was out, and the sand, on which she and Grover had once stranded their sailboat, was a mere three feet beneath the surface.

Wet through and through, she launched her soaking mattress and flew above the treetops almost recklessly, and the next day thought she'd better grow gills if she ever wanted to fly the ocean again.

THE SECOND LAST WORDS GEORGE SPEAKS, JUST BEFORE he falls face down across the table between Mildred's Fruit Cocktail Pie (made with Borden's sweetened condensed milk and decorated with Christmasy red and green candy sparkles) and Nancy's Rum Baba (a new recipe), are, "You and your stupid anti-gravity paint! Sometimes you make me so goddamn mad...." But after he falls he manages to stretch his hand through the whipping cream and grasp Penelope's hand, and whisper "Penny...." Then he sighs, and then he dies.

BY THE TIME THE AMBULANCE HAS COME AND GONE AND Mildred's daughter has taken Mildred home and the others have left, light is beginning to filter through the Douglas firs that surround Penelope's house. She falls on the bed, exhausted, wanting and needing no part of her nightly ritual.

To her astonishment, no sooner does she lie down than the mattress takes matters into its own hands, points itself east, and climbs up and up and over the white peaks of the Rockies, which lean against one another in the moonlight like weary giants. Then she is whisked high over the dinosaur-littered badlands of Alberta and the flat farmlands of Saskatchewan, before the mattress finally pauses and hovers above the flatter plains of Manitoba.

By the time they get to Gimli the mattress is at thirty-five thousand feet, even though Penelope has been hanging her arms over the side until she has pins and needles in both hands. She sees a silver dot in the distance, and before she knows it she is face to face with the giant 767 that came down in Gimli. Somehow she finds herself inside. She slides off the mattress, which drifts disconsolately up and down the aisle.

The cabin is so large that she can scarcely see the far side, for it is obscured in a whitish mist, as though a cloud has seeped through the aeroplane's silver skin. There is strangeness in the air, as though magic, or unseen forces, are whirling in a great wind inside the numinous cloud at the edge of her vision. She notices a lone man at the back. She goes up to him – it is George. She slides into the seat beside him.

He is trembling and sweating. "We've taken a direct hit, Penny." He grasps her hand and holds it so tightly that Penelope is afraid he will break the fragile bones. "Listen! – The engines have gone."

Now she, too, becomes aware of the great silence. George

loosens his long, white aviator's scarf and it billows out behind them. "We can't afford to lose any speed," he gasps, and his voice breaks. "Speed is all we have to counteract the force of God."

Penelope puts her arms around him and cradles his head of thick, curly, black hair against her breast, like a child's. A surge of some unidentifiable emotion — she isn't sure what it is, although it reminds her of love — hits her like a tsunami, almost toppling her. Perhaps it is pity, but a wrenching, terrible pity, more searing than the pity she felt when Grover died, a sorrow of such inestimable weight that it feels like a black hole around her heart, sucking in and collapsing onto itself in a leaden mass.

The loudspeaker clicks on. "Gimli!" Tom's voice, enhanced many times by a synthesizer, announces, as though Gimli were a stop on a tour bus. "Gimli everyone! The Great Hall of Heaven!"

"There, you see? Gimli is down there. The pilot will take us in."

"There is no pilot," George says, and now he is shaking so that she can scarcely hold onto him.

Penelope can see into the cockpit and she sees that this is true, that there is no pilot. The semicircular panel of black instruments is dark and the dials are limp and powerless, except for one that is whirling around and around counter-clockwise, and which Penelope thinks must be the altimeter.

"Penny," George whispers, and begins to cry. "Save me."

But just then a giant hole is blown out of the top of the airliner. Penelope manages to grab the mattress and as she jumps onto it George is torn from her arms and she and the mattress are sucked out of the hole into a starlit night. The airliner and George fall out from under her, and she watches as the plane begins to spiral in tighter and tighter circles, until it explodes in a fireball that lights the sky, and she cries out.

PENELOPE SITS STRAIGHT UP IN BED. SHE IS TREMBLING, and she can still see, etched on her eyelids, the light of the exploding fireball, and hear, echoing in her ears, George's final despairing plea. She feels a sense of overpowering loss, which puzzles her, since she knows she isn't grieving that much for George, at least not for the George he turned into after they flattened the Burma hump.

She read once that despair is the perilous and pitiless knowledge that God is not there, or if there has deserted you. That you are on your own amidst the frozen slush and gravity-ridden black holes, that the universe has nothing to offer but a giant celestial shrug.

She gets out of bed and opens the curtains. A thousand, a million perhaps, tiny dew-globes on the birch's bare branches are shimmering in the early sunlight, and a cone from the fir tree above plops heavily onto the grass below.

There is a strong force, the instructor at Capilano College said, and a weak force and an electromagnetic force, and then there is gravity. Quantum theorists, seeking a unifying principle that will explain the universe, tiptoe through a carnival where pions and kaons and virtual mesons disappear and energy incarnates itself into matter. They say that gravity is the holdout, the obstinate force that resists integration. Even now, in the post-Newtonian world, they say, gravity, still, can only be observed.

JANUARY

B RENDA STEVENS THINKS COMPUTERS ARE GREAT; no tree house should be without one, she says, and although Colin Forman doesn't think this is particularly funny he joins in the general laughter.

Colin is a computer expert who has taken a leave of absence from Vancouver Public Library to install a computer system in the Gibsons Public Library. He bought Kids Pic for Jason and is helping Brenda install Windows, and urges Internet as well, but the phone company balks at putting a line into its natural enemy, a tree.

Colin thinks no tree should harbour a house, but he isn't sufficiently dedicated to getting Brenda out of hers to make a commitment. They have been dating ever since Colin's first exploratory trip to Gibsons a year ago, and now that he is a "full-time temporary," they see a good deal of one another.

Brenda herself has not been particularly anxious to commit, but lately Time, capital-T Time, is getting to her. Inexorable, she thinks, and searches the Windows thesaurus for synonyms. Unbending, unyielding, harsh, unrelenting, cruel, relentless, merciless, implacable, immovable, firm. Right on. She is beginning to think marriage might be a good thing. Jason could use a father.

Of course he has one somewhere, but Brenda wouldn't recognize him if she stumbled over him in the dark, which is more or less how she *did* meet him. On the beach in the moonlight, gathering the white oyster shells that wink back in the silver light. Blearily, though. Through tears.

THAT WAS BEFORE BRENDA OWNED THE TREE HOUSE. A friend named Rolf from her California days had fled to Canada to avoid the Vietnam war and had built the tree house as the perfect hideout from FBI agents who, he was sure, were scouring the continent for him. Day after day Rolf would take his binoculars and scan the ocean and the hills, expecting to see a bevy of belted raincoats and fedoras landing at the dock or creeping through the ferns in his direction. To access his hideaway he used only a rope ladder, pulling it up behind him, convinced that the agents would never think to look up in the air in their search.

One day a member of the Royal Canadian Mounted Police did stroll by, glanced up briefly with a puzzled expression and tipped his hat to Rolf, who had been sitting on the balcony in the Lotus position and chanting a mantra. Rolf lived in terror for weeks, sure that police everywhere were buddies and that they would put out an all-points bulletin. But the store owner, who liked Rolf and occasionally hired him to help in his garden and build fences to keep the deer out, said the Mountie was merely

on his annual check of gun registrations and didn't think anything of Rolf's tree house since he was used to the eccentricities
of the Gulf Islanders, and anyway, wasn't there an amnesty on
Vietnam draft dodgers?

After that it wasn't the same anymore. Twenty-five years of
tree-bound paranoia left Rolf longing suddenly for cities and
exhaust fumes and even a three-piece suit, anything but the
monotonous sound of wind and waves, and so he loaned the tree
house to Brenda for a one-week getaway, took the ferry to
Vancouver, and gave himself up. (It turned out that nobody
wanted him, and so he stayed in Vancouver, shaved, got a reasonable suit from the Salvation Army, and was able to start training to be a stockbroker.) Which was how Brenda eventually
acquired the house for herself and Jason.

BEFORE COLIN THERE HAD BEEN GIL, WHOM BRENDA
still thinks of as the true love of her life, and what she wanted
the house for that week was to give both her and Gil a breather
from passion. They worked at the same library then, and the
rest of the staff couldn't help but notice the way their two bodies drifted together in the shelter of the stacks, defying the disapproving book spines of those who had learned the harsh
lessons of illicit love: Anna Karenina, Emma Bovary. Brenda
had urged coming out of the closet and Gil said, "Stacks, you
mean," and they had giggled together and risked holding each
other's hands tightly against their fiery bodies. That was all
they'd been able to manage for the six weeks since Gil's wife had

found one of Brenda's headbands in the car.

Brenda was in the third day of her retreat on Keats Island when Gil phoned the grocery store and asked them if they could fetch Brenda, it was an emergency. The owner and his wife and their two bored teenagers, as well as a couple of fishermen, were hushed as Brenda, trembling in case it should be Penelope, or Gordon, or Connie, picked up the receiver.

She hadn't thought it would be Gil. He couldn't phone at this hour, his wife might hear. The words dropped into a silence so total that the sound seemed, to Brenda, to reverberate like a boom box from the granite face of the nearby mountain. "There'll never be anyone else," he began, and she thought the ocean itself momentarily stilled. He said he couldn't leave his children. And the wife that went with them.

She ran from the store and, in the falling darkness, began to pick up the white oyster shells, as though the act of gathering might provide a bulwark against emptiness. She stumbled, and straightening, saw propped against a peeled log that shone whitely in the moonlight, a man's partly-clothed body, and when the stranger held out his arms she sank into them and wept.

They made love often that night, and afterwards Brenda would not have been sure whether or not she'd dreamed this chance lover if it hadn't been for the unmistakable onslaught of morning sickness.

THE CHRISTMAS BREAK THIS YEAR GOES ON UNTIL THE fifth of January, and so there are a few days left before Brenda and Jason have to get back to Keats Island. During the Christmas excitement Penelope passed over Brenda's remark that she was thinking that marriage to Colin might be a good thing. Penelope isn't so sure. "You truly loved what's-his-name didn't you?" she asks now. "Are you sure that's over?"

Brenda's face has begun to settle into a kind of resignation; laugh lines that used to explode from her dimple, and still do, amble back slowly now, as if they hope there won't be a next joke to take them out of their new, soberer grooves.

"Gil," she murmurs, as though the name itself were fragile. Her face goes soft and vulnerable, and Penelope would like to pick up this Gil – whom she never met – and shake him until his teeth rattle.

"Short for Gilbert, but he'd punch you out if you ever called him that." Brenda bows her head so that her unruly black hair screens her, then, after a moment, gets up and watches Jason hang upside down from Penelope's birch tree.

Penelope lets it go. She's dropped the penny; Brenda is smart enough to pick it up.

OVER THE HOLIDAYS MILDRED HAS TAKEN TO DROPPING BY, ostensibly to discuss the January potluck dinner which is supposed to be held at her house. "Switch with Nancy," Penelope advises, but Mildred invokes the spirit of dead George "who loved to entertain, you know that, Penny, especially the old crowd, we all go back such a long way." She says this openly and without rancour, and Penelope dismisses a momentary unease

49

that, cometlike, streaks through her brain.

When Mildred drops by for the third time, this time with her special blackberry jam ("Why?" Brenda wants to know, bemused that Mildred is suddenly so chummy, but all Penelope can come up with is that Mildred is lost without George, that she will adjust in time), she (Mildred) thinks rather crossly that it's too much for Penelope, a child tearing around the place, what is Brenda thinking of? Mildred doesn't say this, however; she regales them instead with a description of George picking the blackberries from which the jam was made, cursing each individual thorn so loudly that other pickers hurried their children out of earshot. Then she sighs and says, "Oh poor George, you'll have to excuse me, Brenda, I still can hardly believe it!" and Brenda wonders why it was that she didn't like Mildred much when she was growing up. "She was such a cranky mom. I never knew she could be so much fun," she says later.

"She has another side to her," Penelope cautions. There are things about the relationship that Brenda doesn't know and will never find out — at least, Penelope hopes not — although she is at as much of a loss over Mildred's inexplicable hovering as Brenda is.

While Brenda is on the mainland she has been invited to meet Colin's mother, who lives in Kerrisdale. Kerrisdale's aging, comfortable, well-appointed homes and spacious apartments are now worth the moon because of their proximity to the centre of the city, and also because Kerrisdale itself carries a certain panache as a place to live. Not quite Shaughnessy, but sort of a second cousin once removed.

"How do I look?" Brenda asks, and Penelope tries to see her

without the love-distorted blur that rises and shimmers in front of her like heat waves from the pavement; tries, in fact, to see her through the unblinkered gaze of a prospective mother-in-law. Brenda is a big, sturdy woman with long, rather frizzy hair which she is attempting to contain in a ponytail. She is wearing, over jeans, a loose top of some silky material that boasts a crimson poinsettia splashed across her right breast.

Penelope suggests that she might want to wear one of the flowery skirts she dons for festive occasions. Brenda rejects the skirt, but does add several strings of handcrafted beads and a pair of matching earrings bought on Keats Island.

Mentally, Penelope commits Colin's mother to the scrap heap.

AFTER BRENDA GOES OUT, PENELOPE TRIES TO PERSUADE Jason that it can be fun to watch programs that are neither cartoons nor *Sesame Street*. On *Nova* a stone is flying through the air with unstonelike leisureliness and diving like a controlled kingfisher into a pond.

"That's an instant replay," Jason informs Penelope rather patronizingly. Brenda has explained that Penelope is getting old, and that he, Jason, must try not to do things that will be too hard for her to cope with. Brenda meant physical things, but Jason, in common with much of the rest of humanity, equates physical slowness with some lack of mental acuity, and so he tries, when he remembers (which he rarely does) to be patient.

"Who wants to see a replay of a stupid stone? I want to see Wayne Gretzky," Jason says, jumping up and down on the couch.

"I'm going to be just like Wayne Gretsky when I grow up," he announces. Not in looks you aren't, Penelope thinks but doesn't say. Jason is a dark, almost swarthy child with flashing black eyes and olive skin and a shock of black, frizzy hair (Brenda's legacy). Penelope often wonders about the father, although Brenda has assured her that it couldn't be Gil, she knows that.

Jason swings an imaginary stick and sends a cushion flying across the room. Jason has not yet learned to skate (ice on Keats Island is as rare as the proverbial snowball in hell) but Penelope tries to look impressed.

She attempts to explain why the instant replay of the stone is in a different league than Gretzky's goal. "You didn't know the water would look like that, did you? But by the time you see the Gretzky replay you already know he's scored, but maybe you blinked and missed it, or some skater got in the way, or it was just too fast...."

"Not for me," Jason brags, falling off the couch in slow motion and onto his head. "I didn't miss it, I can follow the puck even when it goes – goes – like this!" and he scoots across the room and crashes into the opposite wall.

But in spite of his sophistication Jason does allow himself to watch when the pebble plop is repeated. Once again the displaced water rises majestically like a celebration and forms a king's crown, perfect even to the spherical weightless jewels suspended above its glistening points.

"See!" Penelope exclaims. "Who would guess it would look like that?" Jason may not be excited but Penelope is; here they are able to see something they didn't even suspect was there, something their own senses are incapable of delivering, a hidden thing, a spectacle that lurks unseen just beneath the surface of the seeable. Like a magician, a conjuror of awesome power who lets us capture the unknown and unseeable in the tiny caves of Time.

"I don't know what you're talking about, Grandma. I want to watch Barney."

Penelope gives up, switches channels, and returns Jason's cushion to its proper place, muttering as she does so to the television, "Oh you are a mountebank, aren't you?" A nice juicy word, mountebank, she thinks, one you don't get a lot of opportunity to use. She looks it up. From an old Italian phrase for "mount-on-bench," it was originally "an itinerant quack who appealed to his audience by means of stories, tricks, juggling, and the like." The word now characterizes anyone who, with cynicism and manipulation, practises charlatanry from a public platform.

Exactly what the TV is doing, passing off illusion as reality, pretending its little sleight of hand is nothing more than a memory aid, a small jolt to help us recall something we have actually seen.

She catches purple Barney the Dinosaur out of the corner of her eye, and suddenly, over Jason's protests ("It's just getting to the good part, Grandma") she switches back to PBS long enough to remind herself of who started all this. Professor Edgerton of M.I.T.

It must be fifty years ago, but she can still recall the first strobe-lit stills of the interstices of time and the graceful ballet that was being danced in a realm beyond the scope of our senses.

The disbelief she felt, that everybody felt.

When the revelations of Dr. Edgerton's wildly-clicking camera made the cover of *Life* with the image of bumpy water pouring from a tap, she was, she remembers, almost giddy with excitement. She was a young woman then, but no different, no different, she reminds herself. Awed, intrigued, filled with wonder. Now the astonishment is gone; romantically-suspended lovers who run through moonlike gravity scouring beaches in search of the perfect shampoo have turned wonder into banality.

Penelope finds her own jadedness disturbing. She used to think — and she remembers this clearly, it was when Grover would pour water from the little pitcher he kept on the drinks tray into her scotch, something Penelope still misses, it's no fun drinking alone — anyway, she used to marvel that no one would have guessed at the tortured stream filling her glass. Now she takes it for granted that flowing water is bumpy rather than graceful, just as she takes for granted that the camera will slow Time and show a diver bending to almost touch her toes, then gliding down, splashing crystalline water upwards in glistening lumps.

In those days wonderment was to be found in simpler things, in photographs of moons and microbes and bumpy tap water. Penelope checks herself before this thought can take hold; she doesn't intend to fall into the aging-trap of discounting today's glories for those of the old days. Wonderment still abounds, is all about us for the looking, and she thinks of storms on the surface of Mars and explosions on Jupiter, and of men and women floating upside down where gravity has never been.

PENELOPE BURSTS OUT THE MINUTE BRENDA COMES IN
the door. "Let me tell you what I've been thinking, about Time,"
she says.

This doesn't surprise Brenda in the least; in fact, she is glad
that Penelope's theories and discoveries still agitate and excite her
as they have always done. She and Gordon used to mock them,
refuse to listen, bury their heads under cushions, complain to
Grover (who stayed neutral), but no technique sufficed to deflect
an enthusiasm once begun.

All Brenda says, as she pulls an ornament off the Christmas
tree, is, "I came back early so we could undecorate the tree. Oh
God, this silly angel with all the crappy golden hair. Remember
how Gordon carried on until you bought it? I was traumatized,
we were only, oh six or seven at the time, and nothing would do
but he'd have it. It made me so goddamn mad, I already had a
complex about frizzy black hair even back then. My first experience of unadulterated, green-eyed, soul-eating jealousy, one of
the lousier emotions of the western world. — Speaking of Time,
doesn't it seem as if we just put these damn decorations away
from last year? Am I crazy or is time speeding up?"

"That's it, Brenda, just what I was telling you. Now take that
expression you used to use, never trust anyone over thirty...."

"That sixties crap I bought into, you mean. Don't remind me.
I guess I never thought thirty would happen to me."

"That's because you were measuring Time by the standards of
the years between ten to twenty, when Time creeps in its petty
pace, et cetera."

"Or hey, how about ten back to nothing? I guess by those

standards thirty did look a long way off. And now I've dinged old forty and I'm on the slippery slope. How can a person be expected to know the rules will change?"

"Exactly what I mean. About Time. It's dwindling exponentially. The spaces getting progressively shorter like the old slide rules we used in school."

Brenda is silent for a moment, intent on unhooking a fragile blue globe. "Whatever happened to E equals M C squared? I thought the speed of light was supposed to be constant and limiting, and speed, if I remember the little I managed to absorb in high school physics, is distance times time. So Time should be constant too, shouldn't it?" Brenda begins to unclip the tree lights. So far all Penelope has done is accept each decoration from Brenda and set it on the floor.

"That's the question," Penelope says. "You've hit the nail right on the head. And I should warn you, it'll get worse, in case you think improvement lies ahead. So why do you suppose it seems to be speeding up? "

"Our perception?" Brenda hazards. "I don't know. Colin tried to guide me through Stephen Hawking on the subject, but all I understood were about two words, 'and' and 'but'. *He's* on to better things now, something called Banach-Mazur Distances which are beyond the fourth dimension. N-dimensional. Multi-dimensional spaces are called Banach spaces, and the distances between the spaces are these Banach-Mazur distances. Colin's mother just beams at him like he's Einstein when he spouts this stuff."

"Oh yes, I forgot, Colin's mother. How was she?"

"Oh — nondescript and doting but relatively harmless I think.

I should have listened to you and worn something else, I don't think she realizes that everyone wears jeans and runners nowadays. Maybe they don't in Kerrisdale. But I don't expect to live there myself." Brenda yanks off the last of the Christmas lights and says to her mother that she would love to stay up and untangle the mystery of Time, but right now she has to hit the sack before she falls over in a coma.

THAT NIGHT WHEN THE HOUSE FALLS SILENT EXCEPT FOR its bodily functions, the muffled heart thump and warm breath when the furnace kicks in, the creaks as its aging joints warm, the high-pitched complaint as the refrigerator hums its protest, the clicks of mini-icebergs forming in the freezer, and the occasional bump in the night of – Penelope likes to tell herself – something unimaginable, Penelope watches the repeat of the program.

What she'd missed when Barney interrupted earlier today was Professor Edgerton using strobe lights in the opposite way to what he'd been doing. The magical pictures of the stone were taken at speeds measured in microseconds; now he was slowing down the shutter speed and running the results on an ordinary projector. Spying on the slow-movers.

Outside the boundaries of Time starfish run amok. The reckless rose, careless of its quick beauty, bursts in seconds, and the hands of the clock (as Penelope is beginning to suspect) spin round and round its face.

Penelope looks up "Time" in *Bartlett's Familiar Quotations* and finds Proust, someone, she thinks, who spent enough years in contemplation of time past. "In theory one is aware that the earth revolves," Proust wrote, "but in practice one does not perceive it, the ground upon which one treads seems not to move, and one can live undisturbed. So it is with Time in one's life."

Maybe so in the nineteenth century, before we'd *seen* the earth revolve. Back then all that was known about the movement of starfish or clock hands is that they weren't where they were when we left them, and so they must have moved.

Penelope scrabbles through the junk drawer for a pen and her Meaning of Life notebook. What it boils down to is this:

We can't see slow things move any more than we can see what the fast things are up to.

Whatever Time is, we are only able to see its passage if it progresses within the boundaries of some inner organ of time perception.

If it moves either faster or slower, we'll miss it.

As she falls asleep she marvels that Dr. Edgerton was able to show us Time in the camera's eye. The eye of the beholder. Time that comes through as fickle, inconstant, subjective. Time as illusion. Time that lags and speeds up. Time that ambles along for years and then begins to jog, and run, and race — just when we most need it to slow down.

TOWARDS THE END OF THE HOLIDAY BRENDA TAKES Jason to visit Connie Tran and Tommy.

Theirs, Brenda and Connie's, has been an enduring friendship, in spite of their separation after high school for a year while

Brenda headed for California and Connie took a job in a bank. Mrs. Smythe had said that if the universities in Vancouver, which Connie would be able to attend while living at home, weren't good enough for her she could darn well earn the money for the room and board she would need to attend the University of Victoria on Vancouver Island. By the time Connie had enough money Brenda had returned from California and decided to go with her to Victoria.

That was after Gordon had given up his attempt to rescue Brenda in California, although, as it turned out, he had succeeded. Something on Gordon's face when he left – disgust? pain? rejection? – had hurt Brenda, so that, like a landscape that shifts suddenly from right to left and leaves the viewer disoriented, where before she had seen love, sweetness, openness, flower children, she now saw garbage, lurking rats, abandoned compost, and a shoddiness that befouled like smeared ink the kindly Christian concepts they all chanted.

So Brenda came back and went with Connie to the small university in a town that shared little with San Francisco except a common language. In their last year both Brenda and Connie managed to get scholarships. After graduation they took their saved money and treated themselves to ten reckless days on Waikiki Beach.

One day, tiring of sun and sand and Mai Tais and musclebound surfers, they strolled up a narrow road of shanty houses on the outskirts of Honolulu. A woman wearing a tent-sized muumuu of brilliant tropical prints sat outside a tiny house on a wooden armchair. Waves of rich brown flesh rolled downwards from her jawline and disappeared beneath a purple hibiscus above her breasts, and arms like small trees surged out of the armholes. Above her a weathered wooden sign swung from a slat above a window. "Madame Pele, Fortunes," it proclaimed.

As they approached, the woman, who had appeared to be dozing, opened her eyes and stared at them. Both girls stopped, as though on command.

"Your fortunes, five dollars," she said, in a voice that carried not a hint of obsequiousness — a voice, in fact, that would brook no refusal.

Brenda looked at Connie and they nodded in unison and dug into their bags for five dollars.

The woman took her time. She looked hard at them both and then said, "You do not belong to the United States."

Connie admitted that they were Canadians, and the woman accepted this news as of little consequence. She started with Connie. "You have chosen the path of least resistance," she said. Her voice was melodious, a singsong cadence that was reminiscent of the soft Hawaiian language, but both young women were startled by the elegance of her pronunciation and by her choice of words.

She strolled through Connie's life like a Sunday walk. Bossy mother, ugly duckling, brains, worldly ambition, all of these came tumbling out, but in language veiled enough to make the commonplace sound faintly congratulatory.

"It's my *future* I want to know about," Connie said finally. By now both girls were entranced, mesmerized almost, willing to suspend disbelief forever.

But suddenly Madame Pele appeared to lose interest. "You'll settle for a *very* dark man who will shower you with worldly goods," and although, later, Connie and Brenda laughed at this variation of tall, dark and handsome, from that day on Connie began her search.

"And," Madame said, finally, "you will have two children, a boy and a girl. The girl will carry the foreign features of your husband, and the boy will be very fair."

She turned to Brenda and suddenly her moonlike face creased into a broad smile that revealed teeth of almost fluorescent whiteness. "Aha! You are one of those!" she said, but refused to explain.

She spoke of "the other face you keep hidden, carved from you in the womb, a watcher and keeper, a rival, a lover, except that the love will be forbidden and never consummated." She said that Brenda would spend her life searching for a substitute and, when she failed, a stranger would father her child — but suddenly Madame, in great agitation, heaved her bulk out of the chair and turned away.

"What?" Brenda cried. "You haven't finished with me. I want to know what will happen. You owe me!"

The woman half-turned and reached between her sweaty, gleaming, brown breasts and extracted one of the five-dollar bills and handed it to Brenda. "Take it and go," she whispered.

"No!" Brenda shouted. "Tell me. I can take it. I want to know the worst."

"How can I tell you," the woman mumbled, so that they had to strain to hear, "when you have not decided?" and before they could stop her she moved, with surprising agility, into the little house and shut the door in their faces.

Brenda was about to bang on the door when a large brown arm reached out the open window and pulled off the sign, then retreated. The window slammed shut, and Connie tugged at Brenda's arm. "We leave tomorrow, we can't afford a dust-up," she said.

They went back to their hotel and celebrated their last night by getting blasted out of their skulls, with hangovers so fierce that they came within an inch of missing their plane the following day.

BRENDA NAVIGATES THE WINDING ROADS OF WEST Vancouver and up a steep drive to the Tran's front door and Jason insists on ringing the bell, not once but twice. The door is thrown open by Tommy, who crashes against Brenda and almost topples her as he tears down the front steps.

In her jeans and pink velour T-shirt Connie looks waiflike, Chaplinesque, a child who has stumbled inadvertently into opulence. She sells upscale real estate now, in West Vancouver, and Connie's and Jim's combined incomes would support a far grander house. But in this Connie has proved curiously stubborn. "This is our home," she tells Jim. "It's plenty big enough for the three of us. If you need to show off, get a Jag."

Connie and Brenda take their coffee into a marble-floored sunroom that looks out on the magnificent panorama of Georgia Strait and Burrard Inlet — four white sails against the blue, the beaches of English Bay, the distant towers of the University of British Columbia on Point Grey — and have just begun catching up when the boys, who refused to come in a few minutes before, burst into the house demanding cookies. Connie sighs. "I used to think I'd like two," she says. "Kids. But now I think if I raise one and keep my marbles I'll be doing damn well."

She settles the children with cookies and milk in a small den and turns on a dinosaur video. "Brontosaurus," Jason yells, but Tommy disagrees. "It's a tyrannosaurus, you nut," and he punches Jason's arm and they scuffle a bit before becoming absorbed in a world that existed long before boys.

Connie returns with two glasses and a bottle of white wine, a California Chablis Jim "has an interest in," although nowadays Jim usually sticks to local wines, quite acceptable, he says. (He also has an interest in a winery in the Okanagan.) Connie doesn't bring cigarettes because she is trying to quit. Brenda recognizes the signs, the restlessness, the compulsive twitch of the reformed smoker mechanically reaching for distraction.

Connie pours the wine and hands a glass to Brenda, then raises hers. "Cheers," she says, and then, settling herself comfortably, "Okay, down to the Brassy Tackies." Connie has always loved puns. She and Brenda, and sometimes even Gordon, used to spend hours making them up, and she and Brenda — although never Gordon — would shout them at startled passersby. Jim hates puns. Perhaps, Connie rationalizes, puns only work if they are in your native tongue.

"Does Colin compute in bed?" she asks with a sly grin.

"Hey, now that you mention it, that's exactly what he does.

No graphics, goes without saying. He'd never let himself glance at anything that might be construed as porn."

"Plain black and white then. Okay. How's this for catchy software, Let Me Compute the Ways." They giggle and Connie tops up her glass.

"Main Menu: U – undressing. F – foreplay...."

"And C, don't forget C. Contraceptive check. That's a biggy with Jim."

"I, I suppose. For Intercourse."

Connie fetches cigarettes. "The hell with it," she says. As she bends to light her cigarette she murmurs, "Could be O first."

"O?"

"Oral."

"Oh." Brenda grins. "Colin has never even hinted at O, I'm not sure he knows about it. Just as well, I don't think I'm a Portnoy."

"You don't approve." Connie bends her head, ostensibly to inhale the luxurious, tranquilizing, deadly smoke as smokers do, with half-closed lids over eyes turned inward for the rush, sucking with the passion of an Ondine rising from beneath the waves to bestow a deadly kiss even though it will kill her lover and she will be cured of love.

"You know me better than that, Con. I'm strictly for whatever turns you on."

"Or *him*, as the case may be."

Out of the corner of her eye Brenda sees Connie's face contort, one side of her mouth jerking up as though an invisible wire were attached to the corner and an invisible hand yanking it. Her right eye shuts in a grotesque wink and then repeats the process twice more.

Brenda changes the subject. "Mother has a theory...."

"What else is new?" As an adolescent, Connie joined Brenda and Gordon in mocking Penelope's theories, her belief, for instance, that potatoes were healthier baked than mashed and that the skins should be eaten because of the Vitamin C. ("Too lazy to peel them would be my guess," Connie's mother had sniffed. Mrs. Smythe – the Y pronounced like I – mashed hers on Monday, fricasseed the leftovers into cakes Tuesday, made scalloped with latherings of cheese Wednesday, and fried them with onions in butter – a favourite of the late Mr. Smythe – on Thursday, fish and chips on Friday, White Spot Saturday, and pot roast with potatoes Sunday.)

"Mother gets smarter as I get older," Brenda says. "Anyway, she thinks we can't and shouldn't blame men for objectifying women, that the male brain has evolved a visual receptor that helps get him upright and scattering his seeds about, and that this interior eye is constructed so that whatever female he meets can be fitted more or less into the mould that's most ideal for procreation."

"Sort of a Procrustean bed."

"Right. Hence youth, breasts, et cetera. Also she says it explains the Muse that inspires artists to greater heights, like that naked woman on the lawn in that Picnic painting, early Impressionist, Manet or Monet, I can never remember which."

"Where all the men are sitting around fully clothed in nineteenth-century suits and starched collars."

"Right. She says male conjecture is a type of invasion."

"Wow. She *is* getting smarter. I don't even understand that."

"Think Updike, Rabbit, Couples. Guy meets girl, guy takes in bra size, checks leg length, and before he can stop himself — Mother doesn't say this but I think this is what she means — before he can stop himself, assuming he tries, he's conjecturing about what it's like where pelvis and legs meet."

"The Split Infinitive," Connie murmurs. "Sure. Doesn't matter that he knows perfectly well, in general terms, he has to contemplate the individual instance every time, because that's the way his brain works."

They are silent for a moment, pondering the inequities of male and female sexual behaviour, and then Connie says, "So the object of scrutiny — us — feels invaded. I mean, it *is* a kind of putdown when you think of it. No wonder girls get low self-esteem."

"I remember being so embarrassed about my largish top that I would slouch around and squash them with my books."

"So I wonder why we — women — don't stare at a guy's trousers and wonder how his dick hangs." Connie says this so indignantly that Brenda laughs, and Connie pours more wine into her own glass. Brenda covers hers. "Have to drive the perilous West Van ravines," she says, and then, after a moment's hesitation, "I don't know how she explains the so-called deviations, they don't seem to do a lot for procreation when you think of it. Anyway, Colin keeps his fantasies, if he has any, on a tight leash — it's funny, that should make him appealing but doesn't. Women are always attracted to the creeps. In Mother's day there were more safe-

guards, she probably went through life with just one notch on —
her knickers, I suppose."

"I wouldn't knock that," Connie says. She looks wistful, or
sad, and Brenda wonders if all is well in the Tran household.

JUST AS BRENDA AND JASON ARE LEAVING CONNIE'S HOUSE,
Brenda says, "I'd like another. Kid, that is."

"Who were you thinking of having it with? Colin?"

"I guess. I don't have a big list to choose from. He'd be your
perfect parent, coaches hockey and he doesn't even have to,
already loves Jason nearly as much as he loves his mother."

"Remember that fortune teller in Hawaii?"

"Fortune teller? Nope — that was twenty years ago, for Pete's
sake. All I remember about Hawaii is having the granddaddy of
all hangovers on the trip home."

"She said I'd have two, a boy and a girl."

"Well, better make up your mind soon, kiddo. We're both
pushing forty-one, menopause can start any time."

"Jim doesn't know that."

"About menopause? Come on...."

"No. That I'm forty-one. He thinks I'm thirty-five."

"Christ — !" But before Brenda can say any more a series of
tics distort Connie's face, wave after wave, like a northwester roiling the still waters of English Bay, sending up breakers with clus-
ters of pinched skin like bubbling froth riding the surf, rolling
over her right eye, closing it in a leering, seemingly interminable
series of bizarre winks, ten times, twenty times....

"What the hell is that, Con?"

"Nerves," Connie says miserably. "That's why I'm taking the whole two weeks off."

"A month might be more like it."

As Brenda and Jason wind down the curving streets with their sprawling, ostentatious homes and perfectly clipped gardens, and owners who fought every tree and fail to look at the view they sued for, Brenda muses that wealth might not be all it is cracked up to be. Although she wouldn't mind giving it a try.

BRENDA DOESN'T KNOW IF IT MEANS SHE HAS PASSED whatever test was posed by Colin's mother, but Mrs. Forman has asked her over for lunch. Penelope is minding Jason. Mr. Moore from next door drifts over to the fence with his budgie and offers to let Jason hold it. (Mrs. Moore is out or he'd never dare.) Jason, his face a study, excitement, awe, gratitude, and something – well, holy's a pretty strong word – but something indefinable, a sort of luminosity that seems to come over children when they touch their fellow animals, holds the trembling bird carefully in the palms of his little hands, and whispers, "His heart beats so fast." Then Mr. Moore catches a glimpse of his wife's car a block away and quickly gathers up his bird and disappears into the house.

Mrs. Moore doesn't like Penelope, although she doesn't say this even to herself. What she says is that Penelope is "common," a judgement her own mother had made on the entire North American continent when Mrs. Moore did the unforgivable and emigrated from England. Furthermore, she doesn't *approve* of

Penelope living alone — after a certain age people shouldn't live alone, they pose a threat to everyone including themselves. She has been watching Penelope.

Mrs. Moore's disapprobation isn't entirely Mrs. Moore's fault. Penelope has been wary of getting too close to a neighbour ever since the one who rushed over to banish Penelope's loneliness whenever she spotted her sitting outside in the sun with nothing better to do than read a book, and so she is polite but cool. Mrs. Moore (Penelope has always refused Betty, or even Elizabeth) interprets this as being "uppity" which has come about because of Penelope's obstinacy in refusing to "know her place." Her place is many notches below Mrs. Moore's. Imagine, she declaims to Mr. Moore, her having the nerve to think *she* is too good for *us!*

And perhaps Penelope does. Mrs. Moore is a lightweight whose unused brain capacity has been invaded by anger. Now she watches Penelope through anger's distorting lens and has convinced herself that Penelope's behaviour is sufficiently bizarre that she may soon pose a threat to them all. She has even gone so far as to plan a pre-emptive strike, but Mr. Moore refuses to help, and Mrs. Moore is not one to ride into battle without someone by her side.

AT THREE A.M., IN THE MIDDLE OF A DREAM ABOUT starfish and clock hands, the solution to the enigma about the subjective feeling of Time speeding up comes to Penelope. A voice offstage, so to speak, is shouting like a circus barker, "Fast shutters for slow, slow shutters for fast!" and immediately

Penelope awakens and knows the answer. *We* must be something akin to giant cameras.

She claps her hands and is about to shout out "fast for slow, slow for fast," so she won't forget, when she remembers that others are sleeping in her house. She writes the words down instead, and then she thinks about how Dr. Edgerton did it all with shutters, or rather with shutter speeds. (She is rather relieved, if the truth be known, that electricity doesn't enter into it.)

When our personal shutters open slowly the world speeds by, just as the galloping starfish do. Penelope thinks her personal shutters must have begun to open very slowly indeed, even though she has no idea where these shutters are located. But everything else in her has slowed down, why wouldn't shutters?

Jason's shutters probably blink in microseconds, and that slows his perception of time passing. Penelope plans, excitedly, to explain this to Jason — after all, he saw the program, he might understand it, if he'll just pause long enough to hear her out.

"Christmases are sure a long way apart, aren't they Grandma?" he'd said that very day, and "Last time, Santa slid down the tree," but then he wasn't sure if that was true, it had been so long ago. And when he and Brenda first came to visit he said, "Grandma, we'll be here a long, long time so you won't need to feel one bit lonesome."

Penelope plans what she'll say. She'll say, imagine you are a giant camera that has fast, lightning fast, shutter speeds. Christmases would seem to be an eon apart, wouldn't they? That's why it seems so long since Santa slid down the tree.

She won't tell him the downside — Jason will figure that out soon enough when the decorations no longer surprise and delight with their all-but-forgotten variety. And holidays begin to speed by. She won't tell him she was surprised when Brenda and Gordon actually survived adolescence — well, not Gordon, that was easy, and then she laughs, quietly, so as not to waken Brenda and Jason, thinking that she was damned surprised when *she* survived Brenda's teen years. Raising kids in the sixties and seventies was no picnic. Maybe it never is. At the rate time is whizzing by Jason's adolescence won't bother her; it'll be over before she knows it, he shouldn't even be out of baby clothes yet, the way she feels.

The camera effect. Looking out at the world through shutters whose openings are gradually spaced further and further apart. Perception that isn't a continuous act but a series of blips, or pulses, slowing as we talk more slowly, slowing as we hear more slowly, slowing as we move more slowly. Slowing as our hearts beat more slowly.

She rehearses the exact words she'll use to Brenda and Jason when she lets them in on her discovery.

"HOW LONG DO BUDGIES LIVE, GRANDMA?" JASON ASKS at breakfast as he and Brenda are getting ready to catch their ferry back to Gibsons and then the water taxi to Keats Island, and Penelope looks up "budgie" and finds that its life span is pitiably small by our standards. But then, she explains quickly, that may only be the way it seems to us, especially with its heart beating so fast.

Because what Penelope is thinking, after weighing the evidence presented by Dr. Edgerton and the camera shutters with slow speeds and fast speeds, is that there may be a connection with heartbeat. That consciousness could be something like radar, sending out blips in time with our own pulses. That budgies may be using up all the little spaces of time that aren't accessible to us, and, as far as they are concerned, live as long as we do.

When geese in winter flee this country in their precise V-formations, she explains to Jason, perhaps they see themselves as plodding along like starfish, with all the time in the world to line themselves up with the left wing of the goose ahead. No, she doesn't know how fast the hearts of starfish beat, but if the camera effect relies on heartbeats it must be very slowly indeed.

AFTER BRENDA AND JASON LEAVE, PENELOPE HAS TO accustom herself once more, not so much to solitude, but to the loss of energy that has been sparkling through her little house. A child makes the surroundings tingle and vibrate, and Brenda does too, in her way, because she lives in the present and is focussed on future possibility in a way that Penelope no longer can be. Penelope thinks she misses this the most, not having a future to plan for, and then she pulls herself up with a sharp reminder that Mildred has agreed to relinquish the first monthly potluck dinner since George's death to Nancy and Dick, and that's just two weeks away. And she'll be starting another Science for Seniors course next week.

As she gets into bed she thinks that there isn't much comfort to be found in knowing that Time seems to be flying by for no better reason than that her perception of it is slowing. Nor solace in the thought that, when death comes, she has already experienced it millions of times in that tiny interval between one pulse of consciousness and the next. Nor in wondering whether she's generated the pulses in her brain in time to her heart's beats, or whether she's just picked them up from Somewhere or Something that has consciousness to burn.

Then she wonders if Dr. Edgerton ever asked himself that question, about where the consciousness was coming from, and, if he did, whether he found such speculation at all comforting. She wishes she could have talked to him about it, but he is dead now, perhaps photographing multi dimensions in the lonely reaches of Banach-Mazur spaces. In this world he photographed the interstices in Time, and no doubt he wondered what else was hidden in there, what other marvels were lurking that neither he nor his camera could discover.

In the dark of a restless night she wonders if he knows, now.

FEBRUARY

IT IS TWO MONTHS SINCE GEORGE SUMMERS DIED, an event that is concentrating Penelope's mind rather wonderfully. She didn't feel this kind of imperative after Grover's death — all she can recall of that time is a shocked interior silence she assumes was grief, and later, a hesitant and solitary voice that precluded the possibility of interior dialogue.

But George's death has reminded her that her own future no longer stretches deliciously into a haze of possible fame, glory, and even riches, although that's not exactly news. It's the tendency of the road ahead to peter out with neither bang nor whimper that is sharpening her focus; the way it smudges into an indeterminate greyish-brown distance, a possible oblivion.

Penelope is determined to settle the question once and for all. (Before you die, whispers the fearmonger who plies his nasty trade below stairs — but she knows better than to give that one an inch.) What she intends to settle, she points out frostily, is not so much the plausibility of immortality — she is prepared to keep an open mind on that — as the quixotic conundrum it trails in its wake: who, exactly, survives? Among the selves that have heaved

75

into consciousness in their day, that now slide and slip below the surface like tectonic plates, which will prove to be the essence?

For George's death is a potent reminder that there was once a woman who is no longer contained in Penelope, with whom she registers not a scrap of recognition, whom she would pass in the street without so much as a friendly nod. The faithless wife who longed to leap at and under George Summers. The strumpet who fantasized by day and especially by night of their falling together in a tangle of sweaty limbs; of their glorying in, exulting in, the rock-hard thrusting that, when she did experience it, failed to live up to its advance billing.

That woman is not to be found anywhere in the emotional detritus of Penelope's past. All she is now is a memory, a curiosity, a being to whom Penelope attaches a slight aura of shame, an outgrown primitive who once bore Penelope's name.

She wonders how many other women she has mislaid. They must be scattered through her like errant *doppelgängers*, temporarily petrified, the way DNA fragments are sometimes encased in amber. Awaiting resurrection. Or, at the very least, a proper burial.

In European folklore there is a superstition that if you meet your *doppelgänger* you will be dead before the sun sets.

Penelope remembers, suddenly, when she first heard the word. It was an evening very many years ago in France. Her parents kept the children while she and Grover went on a month's holiday, everyone agreeing that a break would be "good for Penny's nerves."

SHE HAD BEEN GOING THROUGH A TIME OF DISLOCATION. She would be stricken with sudden and extreme fears, as though whatever had once existed at her core had been swallowed up. It was as though, in giving birth to Brenda and Gordon, a road had appeared that she was not prepared to take, yet more familiar paths had become dangerous and subject to invasion.

She and Grover rented a house from M. and Mme. Truffault in the village of Roujan, in the Languedoc area of southern France, and in the warm Mediterranean evening they would laze in the tiny garden, sipping a potent local *muscat*, absorbing the evening sounds. The mourning dove, its three repetitive notes seemingly underscoring the uselessness of it all. Two sets of bells from the church and the *hôtel de ville* echoing the hour, first one and then the other, as though Time itself were willing to wait for the other's harmonious expression.

An impassioned conversation started up and drifted over the garden wall, the voices musical in their lilting foreignness, and Penelope remembers now the feeling she had of waiting, although for what she couldn't have said. A presence perhaps, or another person — it was as if there were a danger zone inside her into which something, or somebody, was about to drop.

Then she heard the word *doppelgänger.* "What's a *doppelgänger?*" she asked, and Grover explained that it is supposed to be your double, a ghostly double exactly like you, even dressed the same. Some people, he said, swear they've met this double face to face, and then he held up his hand and listened again. (Grover liked to display the bilingualism he'd acquired during his prisoner-of-war stint.)

"They are saying that — some man, Claude something, in the next village, bumped right into his *doppelgänger* in his own vineyard and died before sunset."

Penelope remembers the shock as the words struck and resonated with something in her that was tuned to the same harmonic frequency. Agitated, trembling, she jumped up and mumbled an excuse and ran outside for a walk through the narrow, crumbling streets. She caught a reflection of herself in her yellow sundress in a store window, and then saw a flash of matching yellow behind her. She began to shake, in case the following shade should grasp her shoulder and spin her around and accuse her of stealing her life. And demand that it be returned.

Dread settled over her like a shroud, enveloping her from head to foot and blocking all the light, and she fell just as the clock in the *hôtel de ville*, which was half a minute early, finished striking five. As she fell she caught an impression of flames, or crimson streamers, swirling above the landlord's house.

She was out for about five minutes, a fact that was established only after a heated discussion between the fat *patron* of the *boucherie* and the woman who baked for the *boulangerie*, centreing around the exact time lag between the *hôtel de ville* chimes and those of the church. When she came to she was lying on the sidewalk and she saw faces bending over her and heard a babble of foreign words. She felt a rising panic, and then one of the women, the one in a blouse of the same yellow as Penelope's dress, shouted, "Monsieur Stevens!" in the direction of their nearby residence.

"Anxious attack," said a doctor who prided himself on his mastery of English, declaiming the words as though naming would cure her.

When they were back in Canada she let a subliminal awareness surface: George Summers was regarding her with surreptitious interest. George was opportune, Penelope sees this now. He slipped under her skin like a jigsaw piece whose border more or less matched the empty place where Penelope's shadow began. The space the *doppelgänger* might have co-opted.

But even then, while saving herself, Penelope was nagged by the possibility that their passion, hers and George's, was subtracting some possibility that should have been Mildred's. Did she, does she, owe Mildred?

THAT WOMAN, LONG QUIESCENT, WHO LUSTED FOR George Summers — perhaps she wanders still, a dispossessed shade, in some subterranean chamber of Penelope's brain. The more Penelope thinks about this the more likely it begins to seem, for there was at least one temporary resurrection — an episode Penelope forgot, or dismissed as an aberration.

A month after Grover had his stroke — ten years ago last fall — Penelope was asked if she'd be willing to fill in for awhile at his accounting business. She knew the ropes, had always worked during tax season and occasionally at other times when the workload was too much for Grover.

Such work, she recalls, seemed to grant her legitimacy. It was the one time when she felt that she attained the status of a real person in Grover's eyes, and perhaps in the world's eyes, her own even. Why? The balancing of the myriad workloads of home, children, cooking, gardening, cleaning, the invisible woman's world where debits never equal credits and assets tend to be unquantifiable is infinitely more complex than double-entry bookkeeping. Penelope decides that status conferred by the world has no logic, or perhaps it operates under a logical system that uses a different subset, like arithmetic done on a base other than ten. Perhaps status-granting is embedded in the primitive animal pecking order, part of the spiral helix.

Before that though, when she and Grover were young and newly married, each of them had loomed so large in the other's view that the external masquerade was, for a time, blotted out.

THEY WERE LIVING IN THEIR FIRST LITTLE HOME, ON A small orchard in the interior of British Columbia. A city boy's untutored fancy.

Counting off the laggard days in a prisoner-of-war camp in France after Dieppe, the image of the Okanagan Valley – where Grover had once, as a boy, gone to camp – was what sustained him. In the dismal barracks he was warmed by that distant sun; on the hard-packed earth of the exercise yard he persuaded his captors to let him plant saplings. A kindly guard supplied him with books on fruit-growing, although those he read were in French and written for French farmers and were thirty years out of date.

As the months turned into years he tended the small trees. At the end of five years, when he was about to be released, he was relishing the first sweet black cherries and imagining the sun-ripened peaches, the plump pungent apricots and crisp apples yet to come.

And so Grover used his veteran's credits to buy the orchard. His French books had told him nothing of the complex irrigation systems the arid Okanagan Valley demands, nor of how strenuous the work would be. That the dream didn't fit the reality — and what dream does? — was neither here nor there; it had nourished and sustained him when he needed it, and he was prepared to give a great deal to make it come true.

The sun in that desert valley could be fierce, but in the sweet early morning there would be a softness as the wind carried the news of daybreak down from the mountains. In spring, rows of sweet white and pink apple blossoms, fields of delicate pink peach blossoms, cherry blossoms that turned branches into soft white tubes, fell and patterned the earth like durable snow. Earth, trees, birds, blossoms, everything was young, bursting with promise; and now Penelope wonders what was being promised, and whether she and Grover ever found it.

The trees had to be sprayed with fierce chemicals, lime sulphur that bonded with clothes and whose acrid, sulphury smell could be detected even years and hundreds of washings later, malathion that seeped through cloth and penetrated skin and might eventually destroy the body beneath (although no one knew that at the time), DDT that killed the mosquitoes and made the birds' eggs too fragile to hatch (no one knew that either), and weed killer whose deadliness Penelope trembles to recall. Even the detergents which, to great acclaim, were just then coming on the market sent phosphates into the lake and, in time, clouded the water with algae.

The safe, beautiful landscape turned, then, subtly treacherous. Ecosystems that took millennia to learn to live among the cactus and greasewood could be wiped out in a season; human biochemical systems of uncounted fragility could be destroyed with one or two insidious reactions.

They had been happy, though, at the beginning of destruction. Their brains, when she thinks back, lazed with easy acceptance, as though they were wrapped in cotton wool. Their strong tanned bodies supplied all that was needed of joy and challenge, and desire.

The orchard sloped up from a deep and flawless lake, and in summer a hot dry wind swept up the valley and into the trees, turning the leaves inside out. In the early morning she would walk to the boundary of the orchard with Grover when he went to prune or spray or change the sprinklers, then go back into the house and feel lonely – although she wasn't sure if what she felt was truly loneliness, for it was blended. She crept into the cool house and shut out the wind, and it seems to her now that she felt lonely and glad at the same time, and thought she could imprison forever the sweet contrasting air of the house.

On hot summer days she would pick cherries or apricots or peaches alongside Grover all morning, and then they would run down to the lake and dive into water as clear as window glass, and lie on the sand and let the hot wind caress their tanned skins. It flashes into her mind now that the wind that cooled and dried their wet bodies had cooled the heat between them as well, had sucked out all the moisture, and that youth and joy and all the things that once had rioted under the blazing blueness had gone with it and were irretrievably lost.

There were times, though, of rebirth, little separations that were followed by forgotten warmth, shared crises that once again concentrated friendship. The good moments in bed, the happy times camping with the twins, their joint pride in the children.

After five years they cut their losses. The air in Vancouver, where they moved, was kinder, less searching. In the armed forces Grover had, for a time, been assigned to accounting; now he set up a small bookkeeping business. Penelope worked along with him when she was needed, until the day he failed to write up a journal. The pale dependable lines between which he inscribed his careful numbers had stretched evenly before him until suddenly one of them lifted from the page and stabbed him through his right eye.

In the brief time that remained to him, Grover added this to his list of treacheries.

IN THE DAYS FOLLOWING GROVER'S STROKE SHE DID AGREE to do some work at the office, the ambivalence she felt about leaving Grover lessened by his enthusiasm. "Keep an eye on the bastards," he mumbled, and Penelope knew too well the depth of his mistrust. "Skim off the receivables, kite them, won't find me so easy to fool."

On the first morning Penelope donned her "costume," her old tweed suit, black pumps, white blouse, silver chain, and made a hurried departure.

She crossed Lions Gate Bridge behind a dawdling driver. Normally she wouldn't have minded taking her time on a clear, crisp, fall morning, through the green expanses of Stanley Park that exploded here and there with flashes of red tucked among the giant trees, but she was in a hurry. She hadn't yet met the manager assigned by the firm that had agreed to temporarily manage and assess the business, that would probably buy Grover out.

Penelope wonders now if she felt any sort of foreshadowing. She doesn't remember any. Perhaps she should have, if her Chaos theory has merit. If even a falling leaf — and there is no shortage of that commodity in Stanley Park — can change the future, then coming events cannot fail to cast their shadows before. Can they? But then, she reminds herself, those were bleak times, scarcely conducive to the serenity that fosters insight — or second sight, as the case may be.

The young woman in the car in front of her seemed unsure, one minute darting forward, then slowing unpredictably in the morning rush hour traffic. She was driving a shiny red sports car, and her long, waving chestnut hair gleamed in the slanting morning light. Now, instead of moving briskly through the first light after leaving the bridge, she slowed, and the signal turned from green to amber. She braked abruptly. The driver behind Penelope blasted his horn.

Startled, the young woman glanced over her shoulder. Suddenly, as the light turned from amber to red, she lurched forward. There was a shriek of brakes, a hurtling blue truck, and Penelope heard herself shout "No!" into the closed interior of the car, as though she had the power to stop what had already finished. Then there was confusion and screaming, and men running around the union of twisted blue and red metal, now fused forever in helpless ardour.

An angry policeman motioned Penelope off onto a side street. As she swung around the flashing lights and running people she saw blood on the pavement, and something else, something unidentifiable that might have been human.

Later, Grover told her he'd seen it on the news and it had given him quite a turn. He said they'd shown the jaws of death prying open the car door. He said it was obvious from the start that the driver would be dead, crushed in the collapsed interior of her shiny car. "Never knew what hit her," Grover said, a tiny triumph hiding in the words.

Penelope was glad she hadn't known that at the time. As it was, she was barely able to control the shaking that spread from her stomach to all her limbs as she greeted the new manager. Nothing much registered on her except that he was very young, which, for some reason, seemed to increase the overweening dread the accident had fostered in her. His head of waving chestnut hair was the exact shade of the young woman's in the car, and then the thought popped into her mind that Grover would have taken his long, luxuriant hair as a personal affront. There had been a time, back in the sixties, when Grover had refused to hire "long-hairs," as he called the young men who scorned the brush cuts favoured by their fathers.

"How do you do, Mr. Delaney," she said.

The firm had supplied its own receptionist (except for Doris during tax time Grover had managed without one), a young woman, dressed in a skirt shorter than Penelope had ever worn even during the war, and who now lifted her pencilled eyebrows to new heights. Penelope wondered if her old tweed suit looked shabby.

But Mr. Delaney's polite smile disparaged no one; if pressed, he might have identified in himself an agreeable egalitarianism that — at least around the office — expressed itself through the use of Christian names and other laxities. She was to call him

David, "And this is Heather," he said, gesturing at the reception-ist, "our girl Friday, not to mention Monday to Thursday, and occasionally Saturday."

Penelope said her name and then, as if to excuse herself, told of the accident. It was David, not Heather, who brought coffee. Penelope gulped it gratefully, feeling a slight enhancement of courage. She was struck by the extraordinary evenness of David's teeth when he smiled.

Later, when she showed him her rows of neat figures and bank reconciliations and her precise notations of discrepancies he startled her with a quite undignified whoop. "Penelope, you're a gem!" He laughed and looked up, and Penelope was shocked when the word "beautiful" popped into her head.

Penelope smiled, and as she returned to her desk she looked out the window, seeking refuge in the street below. A whisper from the advancing wind was stirring dead leaves and dust in a miniature whirlwind. The Nisga'a feared the whirlwind, which was said to house a demon in its still centre. They believed that if the demon were to escape it could take possession of the soul of an innocent bystander.

THE OFFICE THEN WAS IN GASTOWN WITH ITS VIEW OF the ocean and the North Shore mountains, but when they first settled in Vancouver the office had been small, barely big enough to accommodate two desks.

She had been alone in it the day George came bounding in with his tax return, a different George then, tall, slim, curly-haired, funny, smart. She remembers the two of them joking lightly, and that she became intensely aware of the maleness of his presence, and then of the warm, delicious wetness between her legs. Suddenly George leaned across the table and kissed her.

Penelope remembers her jaw dropping as she stared. In the fifties a married mother was supposed to be inaccessible, although Penelope suspects now that she may have been overly naive in buying so fully into society's outward appearances. Nevertheless she hadn't expected temptation to present itself ever, much less in such an accessible and desirable form, and in the seconds that she sat gaping, multiple possibilities whirled and tumbled through her scrambled brain.

Finally George laughed. "Was it that traumatic?" he asked.

She came around the desk, and then their hands were seeking, grasping, searching, as though they might find and capture a wholeness that had so far escaped them. George was fumbling with the buttons on her blouse before common sense marshalled itself sufficiently to dike the floods of adrenalin. Penelope pushed away just as they heard Grover's step on the stairs.

No wonder Grover became suspicious. Penelope remembers rushing to the washroom and seeing in the mirror a face that was bright red and hair that stuck out at absurd angles.

When she came back George was gone and Grover was puzzled. Especially when Penelope didn't meet his eyes.

WHEN SHE GOT HOME AFTER THAT FIRST WORKING DAY following Grover's stroke, his eyes were filled with questions whose answers she didn't know. She served his dinner, but when she tried to help him with his fork he shoved her hand, and the fork flew across the room, stabbing the double purple African violet on the windowsill.

She schooled herself to pretend it was an accident.

Later he tried to make amends, hunting for those syllables that he could work his disobedient tongue around. "Wha — whash — thish guy like?"

She shrugged, dismissing David. "Practically a boy." She was surprised to notice how she dissembled. But Grover was skilled in duplicity; he wondered what she was hiding.

"Won' get it for no-nothing," Grover grunted. He meant the business; he had already rejected the first offer.

Grover told her then that the girl with the chestnut hair was dead. Penelope forgave him his tiny satisfaction.

The next day Penelope couldn't bring herself to drive and took the bus instead. In the office, David's words of praise fostered a countervailing harmony that sprang to life inside her head. "You're too fast for me, Penelope," he said, and caught her eyes before she could protect herself.

She thought suddenly of the clear blueness of the deep lake where she and Grover had lived, and an unexpected and foreign delight welled up in her. She remembered standing on a dusty cliff where sagebrush rustled in the hot breeze and fine black dust wriggled into the crevices between her toes. She remembered diving from the cliff and separating the dark water and feeling the promise of ancient mysteries; she imagined she'd seen shapes pressed against the rock ledge. She arched her back and let herself rise through the green and then through shimmering incandescence until she left the monsters behind, for they could be deadly if they were allowed to wander.

She reversed a three and a nine and spent half an hour looking for her mistake.

Later, on her way home, she saw David in the lobby of the building, standing under the sign that said NEW, the "s" having succumbed. She stepped behind a pillar. David stuffed a newspaper into his pocket and went out into the warm wind, and she thought of the mistral that had hurled itself against the *patrons* of the *boulangerie* and the *boucherie* in Roujan, so that they whispered of the madness the wind could cause, along with a certain lack of accountability, especially in women.

Without a moment's hesitation she started after him. As she pushed through the revolving door it flashed into her mind that Grover would be waiting, but the memory had no power. Her body had separated itself from her will and was operating on its own; she felt detached, even curious, wondering where it would lead.

In the parking garage across the street Penelope shrank against the walls of the concrete ramp as the drivers spiralled downwards. An impatient Lincoln driven by a fat man with a mean face and a cowboy hat barely missed her.

As David passed her he honked and waved. His car was long and slim and white, scarcely seeming to have enough height for the tallness of him. She risked a great deal to turn and watch. Then she hurried down the oil-spattered wasteland she'd just come up and out to the sidewalk. Her bus had gone without her.

She lied openly this time, said she'd looked in on Grover's ancient Uncle Gustav who was in Evergreen Extended Care Facility. Grover had, over the years, visited Uncle Gustav whenever his conscience wouldn't let him wriggle out of it, and now the burden had fallen on Penelope.

She stroked Grover's poor head and kissed him, ashamed to see the relief in his eyes. She sat over dinner with him far longer than she usually did, chatting about the days in the orchard and their modest success since. Then they watched M.A.S.H., an old rerun they'd seen twice before, and afterwards she helped him into bed and felt the familiar lurch of pity, and wondered why she couldn't get used to it, the way Hawkeye and B.J. and Radar and the rest of the M.A.S.H. unit did.

THAT NIGHT, AS GROVER PREPARED TO DIE, HE AND Penelope both dreamt their tangled dreams. Grover dreamt that he had become Uncle Gustav, that he shook with what once was called palsy but had been upgraded to parkinsonian tremors. He was grumbling about Diefenbaker, as Uncle Gustav did, the decline of decency, the appalling, tasteless food in the nursing home. As Grover struggled to waken, the bizarre thing happened that had plagued him since the stroke: weak and unable to move, lust flooded through his failing body and he groaned and waited for it to recede.

Uncle Gustav. Did lascivious thoughts sometimes slip along the gnarled neurons and across their ancient gates? Not likely; Uncle Gustav seemed to find the minutiae of failing functions more enthralling than the thrashings about of concupiscence. Yet sometimes he did refer obliquely to the looseness of morality among the "young," as though some racial difference, some anthropological chasm, deeper and more penetrating than mere language or pigmentation, set the young apart from the old.

Which was, or should be, absurd. After all, what was aging? Nothing more, Grover mused, than a continuing metamorphosis, worm to butterfly, tadpole to frog. He wondered whether the frog, in some incontrovertible central kernel of its frog brain, imagined itself as still tadpole, still sleek and fluid, smooth-skinned and silent. Catching sight of its wrinkled hide, was the frog amazed, the way she – that woman, the one who cheats – was? "I don't feel any different inside," she would say, wonder lifting her voice as her fingers traced the tiny gullies in her cheeks. "Inside, I'm the same as I was when I was a girl. Sometimes it takes me by surprise. Sometimes I forget."

Grover forgot too. He had forgotten now, waking with an erection. He didn't know *who* he was – or no, he knew that he was "he," but he didn't recall what "he" had been named, nor where this room, with its wallpaper of old-fashioned roses bordered in Wedgwood blue, could be, nor who was the black bulk in the other bed, nor even what the name was of this world into which the unchanging nature of his manhood had ushered him.

IN THE OTHER BED, FIGURES UNROLLED BEFORE PENELOPE on a seemingly endless tape as she fell asleep, and suddenly she felt the hot summer sun of the Okanagan Valley. She was wearing her old pink shorts with the white halter, the kitchen a steaming sauna. Fruit jars stood gaping open on the long white table, and David was filling them with syrup. The syrup was flooding over the mouths of the jars and down her front, trickling down and down between her legs. David came toward her, but the hot syrup was making it hard for her to breathe and she reached out to him to ask him to wipe it away, and as he bent to his task she saw the golden liquid exploding upwards in a fountain into the heavenly sky, and she wakened with a shout...

And woke Grover.

"Sorry, sweetheart, nightmare," she murmured, and he grunted and said he had to go to the bathroom. She eased him onto the wheelchair and left him to perform this one act in the privacy he still clung to.

Afterwards she lay awake, wondering if dreams were the province of demons.

GROVER WASN'T WELL BUT HE WOULDN'T LET HER CALL the doctor. She was to go to work, he was quite capable of phoning if he needed her. "I could get the homemaker...." she began. He turned his chair around and grasped the remote control – the final thing he would ever have power over – and zapped the TV on at full volume. She thought she'd better take the car.

During the day she stole little glances at David, strobelike glimpses that confirmed what she already knew. A document may be picked up gracefully. Understanding can manifest itself in a delicate flush. The shape and hue of blue eyes may be a work of art. She felt dizzy with pleasure.

David left early, at four o'clock, and at once she too straightened her desk and left the office. She cruised around and around the block, waiting for the exodus of cars from the parking garage. She passed a seedy hotel and beer parlour with its faded "Ladies and Escorts" sign six times, then whirled around again past a few drunken escorts staggering along the sidewalk without ladies. The departing cars continued to fail her.

She turned into the traffic and, suddenly frightened, drove as fast as she could across the clogged bridge.

Grover was grey and helpless and she called the doctor, who told her to get him into the hospital. Poor, poor man, crying a little as she held his spotted hand, but still able to turn away when she kissed him in front of the ambulance attendant.

She stayed with him the next day, but at four o'clock, although Grover's condition was stable, a change came over her. She left the hospital and drove to Gastown and circled around the familiar block for nearly an hour. Then she glimpsed the white car a block away at a red light, and she manoeuvred with manic intensity through the maddening traffic and the narrow clogged streets and then back across the Second Narrows Bridge where she'd come from. Once she almost lost her quarry. She rounded a corner dangerously, and then had to brake suddenly as David parked his car. She watched while he ran up the steps of a white wood-trimmed split-level house.

When she got back to the hospital Grover too had changed. He was in a plastic tent, gulping oxygen, and when he opened his eyes she saw relief cross his grey face, as though he'd thought —

what? It flashed through her mind that maybe, with the end so close, he had the power to see.

She sat with him all the next day, but again at four she was invaded, and she told the nurse she'd rush out for a bite while Grover was sleeping. She parked where she could watch David's house, pulled down the sun visor and huddled into the space between the steering wheel and the door.

David ran with an awkward loping gait up to the house, while Penelope waited for revelation. She saw someone open the door and glimpsed a pale skirt and hopeful hands that drew him in. Then the door was shut, and someone drew the drapes, and she started the car and skidded slightly on snow at the corner.

SHE FLEW UP THE COLD STEPS OF THE HOSPITAL AND practically into the arms of the doctor. "Oh Mrs. Stevens, we've been trying – he asked for you...."

He was dead. He had asked for her, and she had been – where? Staring into a strange woman's house. A young unknown woman who waited for a golden man with almond-shaped eyes and chestnut hair.

Had Grover known? Had his spirit left his poor, damaged body and watched her huddling in the old Chev on a strange street, staring into the lighted kitchen of a strange house? If so, what had he thought?

When she phoned David he told her to take her time. "I'm off to Hawaii in a few days anyway, leave it till I get back." His voice was respectful.

She thought how strange it was that the house should seem antagonistic merely because Grover was dead. Always before it had welcomed her in an easy companionable sort of way, but now it retreated, closing its doors and drawers and making it quite plain that they wanted to be left that way. Even the African violet on the windowsill had not survived the stabbing, or the neglect.

She phoned Brenda and Gordon, and when they cried she felt as though she had betrayed them.

AFTER GROVER'S FUNERAL, AFTER BRENDA AND GORDON LEFT (where were they living then? Penelope can't remember) she dreamed she was following the hearse, and when it stopped David sprang out and ran up to the white door. It opened, but before he went in he turned and looked at her with the beautiful, almond-shaped eyes, and she felt ashamed of her old tweed suit. The young woman in pink shorts and white halter ran to him, her legs long and glistening brown, her fruit boiling on the stove, and Penelope saw her reach up to the golden young man and kiss him. She wondered how that could be, for she was the same woman who had driven the red sports car and was now dead, and in her dream Penelope wept in the vast blankness of her coffin-shaped truck.

At four o'clock the following day she was in the middle of dismantling Grover's bed when she felt the wind change. She went into the bathroom and put on her lipstick and combed her hair, then pulled on boots and a heavy coat and left on her quest.

She parked close to David's house. A young Jamaican woman stepped out, skirt flattening against her thighs in the rising wind. The young woman inhaled deeply, risking the madness that came with the mistral. Penelope understood, then, that David had gone to Hawaii where the hot wind blew across great beaches.

She and Grover had lain on beaches where the hot wind blew. They had waited until the sun failed and the moon rose and they had made love openly and dangerously on the still-warm sand, and then they had held hands and walked up to the high house on the clay hill above the lake.

IN THE EARLY DARKNESS PENELOPE WENT TO THE CEMETERY. Little drifts of snow between the graves were softening, although the wreath was still frozen. When she picked it up the stiff leaves cracked beneath her gloves. She cried then, finally, for Grover.

Later the house relented and welcomed her back. She made cocoa the way Grover had liked it, and watered the African violet, thinking that perhaps it would come up again from the roots.

She pulled back the curtain and saw that most of the snow in the yard had melted. A small puddle held the light from a street lamp. But the wind had died and it was getting colder; soon the mountain lakes would be frozen.

She dropped the curtain but continued to stare at the place where the light had been. She would not need to work much longer; she'd take what was offered, close the deal as quickly as possible. She wondered how she would manage to fill the long evenings. Now that the wind had died she probably wouldn't dream again.

GEORGE SUMMERS AND GROVER HAD TRAINED TOGETHER
in the airforce, and when George and his new bride moved to
North Vancouver they became fixtures in Penelope and Grover's
circle of friends. The potluck dinners had been Mildred's idea,
and although Penelope had never cared that much for Mildred
she went along with it.

A couple of months after Grover died, Mildred and George
invited Penelope over for drinks. "We have something we want
to discuss," Mildred said, her voice plump and musical.

George poured drinks, sherry on the rocks for Penelope, a finger of vodka and orange juice for Mildred, two fingers, hold the
oj, for himself. Then the three of them arranged themselves in a
neat, stiff triangle on the tangle of cretonne daisies and dahlias
that covered the sofa and matching chairs. Mildred raised her
glass.

"To poor Grover," she said, and sighed, her rosy face settling
into appropriate sadness as they tipped their glasses to whatever
wisp of Grover still attached itself to them.

George knocked back his drink in one go and lumbered out
to the kitchen "to top it up." Mildred glared after his retreating
back. The silence deepened. Penelope resisted a wild impulse to
toss her sherry at the tendrils of the spider plant, open the sliding glass door and gallop down the street into the safety of her
own car. She didn't. Instead she pressed her knees tightly together
and sipped her sherry until George, unable to stall any longer,
ambled back and eased himself into his chair.

Mildred cleared her throat. "As you know," she began, with a
solemnity befitting an announcement of men landing on Mars,

"we drive to Arizona every winter."

Through the apprehension that chilled her, Penelope nodded and smiled. Mildred looked pointedly at George. George rattled his ice around in his glass, then drained the watery contents and heaved himself up to a semi-crouch before being checkmated. "George?" Mildred said, ending the word on an upswing of unmistakable portent.

George sank back. The ice cubes, as a source of inspiration, failed him, and finally he mumbled, "Come on along if you want."

"Yes!" Mildred cried, her voice lilting with melodic overtones. "Yes, Penelope! Get your mind off — well, off your loneliness!"

"Hotter than hell, should warn you," George muttered.

"I'm not...." Penelope began.

"It takes a year," Mildred said. "Everyone says it. A year until you're yourself again."

Penelope didn't ask who she was in the interim. She downed her sherry and held out the glass to George who sprinted with it to the kitchen.

Such hope in Mildred's eyes, such fervour. Why, Penelope wondered? Perhaps being sequestered on the desert with George was boring. He hated shopping and seemed unable to make small talk, he was bellicose and frequently despondent, he swore and in the evenings drank too much, and all too often he relived the glory days of World War II, ferrying bombers over the Burma hump.

Penelope downed the sherry, thanked them, said she'd think it over, and got the hell out of there.

MILDRED PHONED EVERY DAY, HER VOICE NO LONGER RICH
and melodic, increasingly at the edge of exasperation.

Still Penelope stalled. The drive to Phoenix would not be
much fun, of that Penelope was reasonably sure. She could
scarcely remember that there had been a time when she would
have thought it a heaven-sent opportunity.

After a suitable interval she phoned to decline. To her relief
George answered. "Thank Christ you've still got your head
screwed on straight!" he muttered.

She heard the click of the extension. "Hi Penny," Mildred
trilled, and George mumbled "Leave you girls to it," and hung up.

Penelope repeated her invented reason. She would have to
mind her bank balances from now on, she still had to finalize the
deal but it looked as though the business might not be as lucra-
tive as Grover had thought. (After she had been cured of George
she had sworn never again to lie. Still, to save face for Mildred?)

There was a short silence and then Mildred said, in a voice as
harsh as the rasp of an old saw, "You owe me, Penny."

PENELOPE IS GLAD, NOW, THAT SHE GRIEVED SO FOR
Grover, that forty years of marriage didn't end merely with a
shrug and a whimper.

The marriage wasn't perfect (if it had been, would the *doppelgänger* have kept up its restless clamour?). Grover's failure – she
sees this now – was that he was too slow for her. She interpreted
his stolidity as purposeful, as "passive aggression," to use the
buzz word of the seventies. Mistaking plodding determination

for stubbornness, silence for hostility.

He was a slow kind of person, quiet, wary, a man who took his own good time. While she was, still is, quick, impulsive, dancing feverishly through days too still to contain her, sharp with repartee, eager to engage life. Sometimes he had to hide from her. She mistook retreat for rejection.

Marriage should be a no-fault contract like no-fault insurance, Penelope thinks. If you careen wildly into the other in an attempt to break off some of the rigidity, nobody is to blame. If you park yourself like solid concrete so that the other is bound to crash, it's because concrete is what you were cast in. Pick up the pieces, make allowances, plaster over the cracks, blame God or Darwin or your parents but don't blame the other. That's about the best you can do.

She wasn't perfect herself, Penelope would be the first to admit that, but she knows now that expecting to be perfect is a kind of conceit in itself. She came to terms; she was human and grieved humanly. The thing that comforted her — David — may have been bizarre, but that too was human.

Guilt, Penelope has learned, is something that women do exceedingly well. She felt a shame that was like the annihilation of the Self over not having been there for Grover's final need. It took a long time, but now she can accept that this doesn't exactly qualify her for entry into the criminal class.

She was much more one-dimensional back then, when Grover died. Now she thinks of herself as n-dimensional, like those Banach-Mazur spaces Brenda was talking about.

In the ten years since Grover's death she has been fierce in expunging guilt's more exaggerated manifestations, and she is proud of her growth. It took her the first five years to allow herself occasional treats, but now, when she feels the need to tip her hat in her own direction she sheds her customary sweatpants and runners and dons the good outfit she bought at last year's Chapman's sale, a violet two-piece silk suit, soft and flowing over her calves, with a long ribbed top that fits around her skinny hips. She parks her car at the Seabus terminal and rides over across Burrard Inlet, past the pyramid of yellow sulphur that occasionally sparks outrage from environmentalists, past rusty freighters with incomprehensible Chinese lettering on the bows, towards the sails of Canada Place, where, in summer, the Royal Princess and the Rotterdam may both be tied up, and you can get a first-class view of them as you walk across the overpass above the rail lines. Then she takes the Skytrain to a good hotel, The Four Seasons, The Hyatt, the Hotel Vanouver, and goes into the dining room to be waited on by a deferential waiter: a glass of the best French wine, and possibly filet mignon, or at least something she would never allow herself at home. Sometimes there is a pianist, and once even, magically, a harpist.

That old tweed suit — nowadays even if she'd spent too much, expecting to amortize the cost over twenty years, she'd get rid of it as soon as it made her feel shabby. Yet it took another two years after Grover's death for her to pass it on to the Salvation Army, and even then she scrutinized bag ladies on the street for months to see if by chance the suit still had some life left in it.

She still scrutinizes bag ladies. But differently. In the past she didn't truly see them, if you define "seeing" as fitting things into a pattern where they can be classified. Bag ladies were outside an invisible boundary and therefore inadmissable for viewing. (Perhaps they threaten by their randomness?)

Well, she's shucked off that pile of garbage, as Brenda would say. Nowadays she not only notices bag ladies, she listens to them, and — be honest — occasionally envies them. There is something basic, Robinson Crusoe-like, in wheeling one's possessions about in a Safeway cart and living off the land, and sometimes Penelope thinks with a sort of longing about Hindus who shuck off worldly possessions when they get old and head for the hills with nothing but begging bowls. Or the modern version, abandoning the finally-mortgage-free home with three bathrooms to trek off in a tiny trailer to a pad in Arizona and a porta-potty.

But she isn't too hard on the self she was then, after Grover's death. Hindsight is great but you have to factor grief into the equation. At that time her brain seemed to be swaddled in cotton batting, and when even her own children thought the trip to Arizona might do her good, get her mind off things, she finally caved in.

"WE CAN TRADE AROUND, TAKE TURNS DRIVING," George growled as they piled into the car on a rain-drenched morning when clouds shade sea into mountains and the operators of Vancouver's Grouse Mountain ski hill mingle their tears with the streams of rapidly melting snow.

"I don't think Penny would be comfortable driving someone else's car," Mildred interposed, then without a pause for breath she sat in front with George. She'd navigate, she announced, at least through Washington and Oregon. "We avoid the I-five, back roads are more fun, and I'm a great navigator," she said.

Something in Mildred's voice gave Penelope pause. A warning, like a muffled foghorn, seemed to be struggling through the numbness, and in that moment, that irreversible second when it has only just become too late, she knew that the price of distraction might be too high.

The first motels featured a bedroom for Mildred and George and a make-down couch in the living area for Penelope. King, queen, neutered hag, she thought as she fell asleep. On the second night she dashed for the bathroom and collided with George. (His prostate was giving him trouble.) She would have toppled if he hadn't grabbed her, and just then, as though they were in a bad sitcom, Mildred woke and switched on the light and sat up. The thin strap of her blue satin nightgown fell over her plump shoulder, partially revealing the whiteness of her breast.

"What are you two up to?" she demanded querulously, and Penelope skittered into the bathroom and locked the door, and when she heard George shout, "Oh for Christ's sake!" she flushed the toilet so she wouldn't hear the rest.

"Get two units," she told George the next day.

"But, Penny," Mildred began, "that'll cost extra...."

"I'll pay," Penelope said.

Mildred protested; Penelope had given her to understood that she hadn't been left all that well off, but if she wanted to throw her money around she guessed it was up to her.

They rode in silence for the rest of the day.

EVER SINCE SHE'D KNOWN HER, PENELOPE HAD RECOGNIZED that the kind of seductive behaviour that was Mildred's was probably a learned manipulation dragged along from a charmed girlhood. But that was easily overlooked because Mildred's nature was open, sunny, uncomplicated. Through the years Penelope had come to realize that nothing existed for Mildred until she herself had experienced or discovered it; that the doings of others, unless they impinged on her directly, were outside her purview, but it hadn't mattered.

Mildred's world — at least it seemed so to Penelope — divided itself into two classes, those who were good-looking and those who weren't trying. Mildred knew that the good-looking — among whom she counted herself, and George — were a superior species to whom the latter, the not-good-looking, owed duties of service and respect.

Mildred had always been favoured. Miss Stampede Queen — plumper now, but still unbowed. Penelope, Mildred saw, didn't try, even though she had the basics, enviable thinness, nice skin; nevertheless Penelope was accorded a grudging wariness not usually bestowed on lesser mortals, because of George. A wariness that could, and often did, slide into fury. But if Penelope wanted to let on that her great thing was integrity, then Mildred wasn't about to call her bluff. Until the time was right.

And so they had chatted at the monthly potluck suppers and occasionally exchanged news of children on the phone, and that, Penelope reminded herself, is where she should have left it.

BUT HAVING MADE HER BED — AN OVERLY APT ANALOGY — Penelope kept up appearances. "How did you sleep?" she would ask, when Mildred and George finally straggled into the dining room, half an hour past the agreed-on time.

Mildred would bow her head and massage her brow (carefully, so as not to disarrange her sprayed locks) and wave at Penelope to sit. "Sorry, I didn't sleep a wink. You don't know how lucky you are to be able to sleep, but of course all by yourself, no one to disturb you...."

"Shall I drive, give you a break?" Penelope asked, as they were putting the bags into the car. George's arm had been bothering him so Mildred had been doing all the driving for the last two days. But Mildred was already in the driver's seat handing the map to George. "I've marked the route," she said to him. "I can't face the freeway today. All you have to do is try to stay awake."

She drove over slippery mountain passes at a speed that would have left the drivers on the freeway pulling over into the parking lane and gaping in wonderment — or so it seemed from the lurching discomfort of the back seat — and sometimes would turn off without explanation. "Not yet — Christ!" George would shout, and Mildred would wave airily and glance (dangerously) at the map and explain brusquely that this was a shortcut, didn't George remember from last time? Twice they got lost.

By the end of the day Penelope would be exhausted, as though something, an invisible vacuum cleaner, or an eccentric vampire, were sucking off her energy. She began to have a spooky feeling that there was a fourth person in the car who wasn't Mildred but wore her clothes. Alone at night her mind would circle like a police dog, sniffing for traces of Mildred, and when she would finally fall asleep she would waken and suffer a brief lapse, forgetting who Mildred was and having to search for the name of this woman she had known for over thirty years.

Penelope thought there were modules in the brain, little cogs like the ones that made her sewing machine perform different stitch patterns. The cog by which she recognized Mildred, built up over all those years, had gone awry. It no longer contained Mildred as she was now revealed; other modules, Elspeth's at the Senior Centre for instance, or Doris's who had worked for Grover sometimes (and once, briefly, caught his eye) would be better fits. Occasionally Penelope would even call Mildred by Elspeth's or Doris's name, Mildred's first hint of what she would come to believe – or pretend to – as Penelope's deterioration.

Elspeth at the Senior Centre was still alive. Over the years she had come to carry her meanness with a sort of pride. "My Aunt Annie," she once bragged to Penelope, "was said to be the meanest woman in Ontario." As for Doris, Penelope came to realize when they were working for Grover that her extreme propriety hid a devious nature. Whenever she made a mistake she presented it to Grover in such a way that it could be construed as Penelope's fault. Grover himself had similar leanings, something to do with keeping Penelope in her place, and so Penelope lost confidence.

No-name Mildred, as Penelope took to calling her (to herself) could just about as easily, with a little trimming here and stretching there, fit into Elspeth's mould or Doris's mould as into the one formerly reserved for her in Penelope's brain.

THEN, IN SEDONA, ARIZONA, A PLACE OF LIGHT AND DAZZLING red rock, and a weightlessness that was perhaps the altitude, perhaps something else, Mildred as remembered and believed in, returned. Mildred, really Mildred, agreeable, dismissable, laughing and splashing in the pool, exclaiming over the density and proximity of stars in the furry blackness of the night sky, marvelling at the brilliance of red rock and sunsets.

Their motel was near the airport, and George was thrilled when a local "Red Baron," white scarf, leather gloves, flew an ancient World War I Tiger Moth biplane each morning from his ranch near Flagstaff to the airport for breakfast. George joined the retinue that trailed after him (George himself had actually flown a Tiger Moth when he took his Basic Training at Camp Borden). Mildred was amused and tolerant. "He should have kept up his flying," she told Penelope.

Penelope was disarmed, at least temporarily. Perhaps she'd overreacted? Perhaps Mildred had truly been ill?

Really-Mildred lasted for three days, until they met a group of thirtyish young people, women in homespun cotton gowns, men sporting ponytails and ragged jeans and T-shirts that said, "Children of a Minor Galaxy," who urged them to pause and feel the energy, and told them that Sedona was at a conjunction of something they called ley lines. Penelope breathed in rapidly, and felt light again, as though energy were indeed surging through the brilliant earth and up through the soles of her feet.

George grunted and called them "that bunch of hippies," and said maybe the thin air at this altitude, or more likely some not-so-thin grass, was what was affecting their alleged minds.

"Hippies are extinct," Penelope pointed out. "These are New Agers."

"Penny believes in that stuff," Mildred said flatly, although this was news to Penelope.

"WHEN CAN WE?" GEORGE HAD ASKED IN THOSE HALF-forgotten days, and the flushed, dark-haired young woman who was no longer Penelope had said, "How do people go about having an affair?"

"I think they rent a hotel room and register as Mr. and Mrs."

"But when? I have to be in the office until two, and I leave just in time to pick up the twins at school."

"Do you go to any evening meetings?

"Parent-teacher."

"Pretend you're going."

"I always go with the next-door neighbour."

"Christ, I thought people *drifted* into affairs."

"In novels everyone has them, especially in England where they're always civilized and witty."

"I can forego witty and even civilized if we can just get started."

"Do you have the feeling that it's somehow un-Canadian?"

Love would find a way of course, and Penelope believed then that this was, indeed, love. And George — but even then she knew that he was much more dedicated than she was. Both of them had, of course, been in love before — but not like this, they assured one another. George had been captivated by Mildred's undoubted beauty and her cheery, easygoing ways. As for Penelope, the time had been ripe for marriage, and she had grasped at Grover's settled, dogged affection.

"It's like magic," Penelope said, touching George with fingers that seemed to have acquired a brand new sensibility. But then she was stricken with a sudden and terrible shyness. She had never slept with anyone but Grover – in pre-pill, pre-sexual-revolution days, this was the norm. (For women, Penelope reminded herself.)

"What's the matter?"

"Nothing. I – ah – feel sort of shy. I've never...."

"Neither have I."

"I mean, I've never – uh – with anyone but Grover."

"Oh. Well I've never done it with a tie on before."

George had been so different then, rather sweet and tentative. Poor George who had loved her with such fervour – more, she suspected, than she'd loved him. When the affair ended she was no longer afraid of what might slip in. She suspected her passion had been nothing more than a catalyst for the exclusion of raiding *doppelgängers*. George had been a necessary but temporary skin placed over the lesion to give it time to heal.

YET IN AN ARIZONA MOTEL PENELOPE DREAMED OF THE young George for whom she had once longed and who had longed for her. In the dream he was even more handsome than he had been then, as handsome as David from the office, who Penelope could now see he resembled. But at every attempted assignation either Mildred or Grover would pounce, and Penelope woke with an ancient longing that spoke of youth and joy and had no business lighting up her aging body. Such yearnings had been expunged long ago, or so she thought; buried deeply in the acceptance that creeps year by year over passion like a roving glacier, smothering desire under tonnes of translucent ice.

(It occured to her now that if the woman who had wanted George Summers and who had resurfaced so singularly for David could evoke such a splendour of feeling later, she might not be lost after all.)

In the hard light of an Arizona morning George metamorphosed instantly into his stolid self, a man she no longer felt anything for except a basic goodwill and a sort of pity. By the time breakfast was finished, the resurrected Mildred too had disappeared, and they rode to Phoenix with the stranger.

On the flight home, which Penelope took suddenly and without dissembling ("No, I'm sorry, I just want to go home") she pondered the mystery of selves. Two personalities, one Mildred. Were they, the personalities, real and roaming about, awaiting the unguarded moment — a loss of attention, a momentary distraction — to slip into a living body? She shivered, and thought of the casting out of devils.

PENELOPE SQUATS ON HER STEP IN THE LOTUS POSITION (which Brenda taught her at Christmas) but is unable to sustain it for longer than a few moments. Long enough, however, to clear the disturbance that is agitating the air in the wake of her memories. (Brenda taught her to cope with negative energy by enclosing herself in a glass cage, but this always reminds Penelope of the Cone of Silence in the old *Get Smart* TV series and makes her giggle.)

Penelope decides to go on her daily walk and think it through.

The day will be sunny once the sun burns off the mist, and Penelope takes this as a benevolent omen. As she walks she organizes the evidence, imagining it in neatly-printed rows, on the lined paper of her Meaning of Life notebook.

FACT ONE: she and George once had a mutual infatuation about thirty-five years ago

FACT TWO: the affair was brief, not through nobility, entirely, but — let's be honest — also because of fear for the children, as well as lack of opportunity

FACT THREE: somehow Mildred figured it out

FACT FOUR: the last thing George said, the person he called for, was "Penny."

No-name Mildred will be unlikely to dismiss that final plea. Yet George's death should have freed them both, from guilt, from lingering resentment, from obligation. Shouldn't it?

So does she owe Mildred? George is, after all, gone. Where? Well, as Hamlet pointed out, that *is* the question, and Penelope begins to intone, "Whether 'tis nobler in the mind...." memorized in Grade Twelve and destined, apparently, to stay with her forever, or until the end of her days, whichever comes first. Sternly, she stops the recitations. (Although it is one of her firmly held beliefs that the current educational trend away from memorization is a serious deprivation. She has, over the years, pulled out, examined, and often understood what had previously been beyond her. Furthermore, she has derived enormous pleasure from sonnets and soliloquies whose commitment to memory she had originally regarded as a refined torture.)

But she has work to do. Who survives, who should feel guilt, who owes whom, where has that person gone. Weighty matters.

It may take her longer than she expected to work it all out.

MARCH

"**D**EAR MOTHER,
   This will come as a surprise to you, no doubt — considering I have no other visible means of support — but I've quit my job."

Penelope can read no further for the moment because of a filled-up bursting feeling she remembers from childhood, joy, or something resembling joy, a sort of dizzying enchantment that came with sun-up and lungsful of sweet air and quotidian rebirth. She savours what had been forgotten, and only after the ordinary sweeps away this bubbling effervescence does she pause for sober second thought.

Penelope knows, as every enlightened twentieth-century mother knows, that it is not acceptable to try to keep grown children at home. But knowledge, as Penelope constantly relearns, does not always, or even often, translate into feeling. How much simpler the world would be if right thinking would invigorate, good deeds inflame, and charity deliver something headier than a brief, self-satisfied glow!

But oh, the swirling energy of a younger loved one! How can

you not yearn for it? And there are so few people in the world one truly loves, at least not in the way she loves Brenda and Gordon. And Jason, of course.

She dismisses the errant expectancy, reminds herself that at forty-one Brenda is not likely to come home to live, and goes back to the letter.

"I ran up against an intolerable situation at work and if there's one thing I've learned it's that without self-respect you have bugger-all.

"I mean, letting a senior citizen off without paying a two-buck fine is hardly a capital offence, common humanity if you ask me, and scarcely rates a lecture from the new head librarian about library finances and taking the law into one's own hands (civil disobedience is what she implied). All articulated in a voice well above library guidelines, and right in front of the chairman of the Board! Showing off at my expense, the old bat.

"Yes, a woman! Can you believe it? It's kind of wrecking my belief in female solidarity.

"Oh sure, it'll be tough and jobs aren't a dime a dozen, but there is no way I'm going to sit still for the kind of crap she's dishing out.

"Kind of makes me sorry I voted against unionization. The old head librarian was so great, none of us wanted to muck the place up with rigid rules, but this old hag (okay, she's younger than me — young hag), anyway, this blinkered female bureaucrat is the kind that needs a union breathing down her neck.

"The hell with it. Anyway, I've got UI coming, it doesn't cost that much to live in a tree house, that's an advantage I hadn't counted on.

"I sure as hell am *not* counting on Colin. To my surprise he was lounging in my leafy bower when I got back to Keats Island after giving notice – I told you, didn't I, that he finished the contract at our library some time ago? He's no longer working exclusively with the Vancouver library either, now he's doing freelance consultations all over the US. I never know when I'll see him these days.

"God knows I would have welcomed a shoulder to cry on. I love my job! (Ex-job, that is.) Ever since I've been made Systems Manager I can hardly wait to get to work in the morning. And Colin's would have been the perfect shoulder, we've grown fairly – *quite* – fond of one another. *Very* fond in fact. I *could* be falling in love with him! Maybe not *the* grand passion, but more than passing fancy. And quitting had left me feeling empty, in need of comfort."

Brenda's ambivalence isn't lost on Penelope. Brenda is grasping, if not at straws, at something equally ephemeral: her human need for comfort. Translating yearning into a signal from an as-yet-unrecognized bliss, willing herself to believe it is nascent love. As if mere volition has a hope of bringing about that luminescent state! Wouldn't we all grab at it if we could! Penelope chuckles. Grief is grief, she could have told Brenda, and, big or small, it is quite capable of manifesting itself in gradations from minor (quitting a job) to overwhelming (failed love, death).

"I blurted out my bad news to Colin," Brenda continues. "I had had extreme provocation, I said. I launched into a litany of the wrongs done me by the creep who calls herself a head librarian, and whose response to my decision to quit has left my morale in tatters. ('Oh fine, thanks for letting me know, we'll start to advertise immediately. Three weeks notice is mandatory, but don't bother to come in unless you want to.' Can you believe it?)

"Colin did not seethe with indignation, nor did he say 'poor wronged and misunderstood you,' not even 'I knew she was an unregenerate witch the first time I met her,' nor any of the thousands of other comforting pleasantries that one might have expected to spring trippingly to the tongue. What he did was bellow, 'Quit your job! Don't you think you might have checked with me first?'

"Now I ask you, Mother, why in hell should I consult with Colin?

"He went on to explain that he was out in the world (not in Plumper Cove cooped up in the cloistered atmosphere of a tree house), and how the job situation is zilch out in those big-time centres where the action is. 'Zilch!' he kept saying. Does his mother keep a card-file of time-worn expressions? He said it wasn't like ten years ago when any librarian with even basic computer training could set herself up as an expert. Everybody has the basics now, but in systems management, he kept repeating, as though just knowing the phrase put him up there with Bill Gates, you have to be top-notch. 'Your average run-of-the-mill library systems manager is damn lucky to *have* a job, any job.'

"I asked him what made him think I was your average run-of-the-mill systems manager? and he said, hey I know you're smart, well above average, and opined that I quite probably would beat the hell out of him. Of course he doesn't believe that for one second, I'm not that naive. He also said in this job market, if you run up against the sort of thing I ran up against, then you just have to count your losses and make the best of it.

"So, I said, what if I'm not willing to make that kind of compromise?

"That's when he started staring at his shoes and asked me what I was going to do, go back and live with my mother? After which Colin jumped up so quickly that he sent his chair toppling with a thump that sent an entire branch hurtling through the air."

BRENDA DOESN'T TELL HER MOTHER THAT THE FALLING branch was aided and abetted by the first quick gust of the kind of deadly March gale that sometimes sweeps in from the Pacific and, like a clear-cutter gone mad, tosses giant trees into hydro lines and as often as not plunges Vancouver Island into darkness. Then slams into the mainland and dims the glitter of the wealthy in British Properties with the same democratic fury that it douses the homeless on Hastings Street. Out on the ocean it teases herring boats that, in their race to be rich, ignore the radio warnings and are on the open sea past the Queen Charlotte Islands. It plays like a cat with the mousy humans scurrying about on their toy boats, tossing them up on giant waves, ten metres, twenty metres, thirty metres high, and – with a fine disregard for their relative worthiness – drowns some and lets others go. One terrible spring in the seventies thirteen herring boats went down.

The falling branch hit the roof of Brenda's bedroom with such a thump that she and Colin were silenced for a moment, and then the wind abated and Brenda said, "Perhaps it's time to examine our relationship, Colin." She was beyond caring, felt she'd had it with this crap and didn't give a damn any more.

"Bren," he mumbled, "I've told you, I can't take on any responsibilities right now; it wouldn't be fair to either of us. I'm damn near thirty-eight...." and a small ripple, like a mini-earthquake, shivered the floorboards. Brenda didn't care that Colin was younger than she was, but for the first time she wondered if he cared. Or if perhaps his mother did. "...and I either devote every waking moment to my job or risk losing out to one of those bright kids that grew up on computers. Hell, Bren," and he looked up with the sort of look that boys learn before they get rid of their Pampers, "this new crop of twenty-year-olds doesn't think like you and me, they think like computers. They've learned them the way kids learn a second language, with the undeveloped brain. Believe me, I have to work my butt off to stay ahead of them."

And now the rain began to come down in a deluge that penetrated even the leaves of their giant cedar, and a little stream was pushed under the shakes on the roof. The roof began to leak in heavy drops that landed with a splat on Colin's shiny shoes and then drummed a rapid beat on the floor. A great gust sent the tree house rocking so wildly that for the first time since she'd lived there Brenda was afraid. "Maybe we'd better go downstairs in case Jason wakes up," she said.

The spiral staircase had no railing and the rocking was so violent that they both turned and crept backwards down the steps. Colin fell the last two and landed with a thump in Jason's bedroom, but Jason slept on, oblivious. They made their way into the kitchen.

Colin huddled on a stool while Brenda put the kettle on the hot plate. The rocking wasn't as fierce at this level, or maybe the storm was just having a rest.

Colin, eyes examining his fingernails, blurted, "I think I know what motivated you, Bren. With women it's different, probably subconsciously you *wanted* to quit because you haven't much longer to have a brother or sister for Jason. But don't you see," and he tossed his hair back and looked pleadingly into her eyes, "I care too much for you to leave you at home barefoot and pregnant while I whip off to the States for weeks at a time. It just wouldn't be fair to you."

The lights went out. Brenda, not unused to this hazard of tree house life, lit candles, but just then a gust of wind sent the tree house flying and riding so wildly that she doused the candles for fear of fire. Pots flew from a cupboard, and in the darkness Colin felt the slight breeze as a heavy, copper-bottomed stainless steel Dutch oven just missed his head and fell to the floor with a crashing that roused Jason. Jason cried out, but when Brenda called that everything was fine he settled back to sleep.

In the sudden white incandescence of lightning they saw branches flying in every direction, and the hemlock next to them began to sway dangerously and then crashed into the ground ten feet in front of the tree house. Falling, the branches swept across the door and took a plank out of the balcony. Another flash showed them the hemlock's great roots stripped, clinging here and there to bits of soil and poking up past the window. In a sudden lull they could hear the ocean booming and crashing against the headland, as though it were trying to get at the land dwellers and add them to those now swaying downward to the relative calm of the ocean floor.

They relit the candles and for a few minutes it was calm. Brenda thought the storm might have blown itself out, and Colin looked at his watch and said, "God, Bren, I arranged for the water taxi in five minutes, I've got to get to L.A. tonight. Look, I'm sorry to rush off like this just when you need me, but that's what I mean; my life is like that at this point in time."

Is it different at some other magical point in time? Brenda was about to ask, but Colin was out the door so fast the wind scattered the words into the night. Brenda knew that no water taxi in its right mind would brave that storm, but by then she was so mad all she hoped for was that Colin would forget the ladder and break his neck. He did fall over the uprooted hemlock, but she doesn't know to this day where he spent the night.

THE LETTER GOES ON TO SAY THAT BRENDA HAS DECIDED to sit right under old Hatchet-brain's good eye for the notice period and surf the Net. She offers to do a bit of research for Penelope on Time, or whatever it is she's working on now. She signs it, your loving and sort of destitute daughter, Brenda, and then adds a P.S. "Heard from Gord lately? He said something about coming out for spring skiing. Oh, and Jason and I will be coming for school break. I'd like to get in a bit of skiing myself while 'between jobs.' Be fun if Gord and I end up going skiing together. Hope a houseful isn't too much for you."

Penelope floats around the house planning where everyone will sleep, then looks out the window to urge the bursting buds of the white camellia into full bloom in time for the visitors. She spots a slug lurking beneath the bush.

Mildred surprises Penelope on her knees under the camellia, doing battle. "Take that!" Penelope is shouting, as she scoops the hapless slug onto her shovel and catapults it into the steep gully at the back of her yard.

"Penelope, dear," Mildred says, and Penelope jumps.

"Oh, sorry. Did I startle you?"

Penelope forces a smile. She will be seeing Mildred Thursday at the potluck dinner, in Tom's lovely West Van mansion which the ghost of his dead wife forbids him to sell, and Penelope wonders what it is that couldn't wait. Mildred is dressed in a too-summery pantsuit that envelops her short plump legs in flowering silk forget-me-nots. Semi-formal attire. Serious stuff.

Mildred is already talking as she walks past Penelope into the kitchen. "I hope you don't mind my dropping in like this, but it's so lonely," she is saying, her still pretty face settling into its quivering mode. "I don't know how you've coped, Penelope, all this time, by yourself."

"I haven't been by myself, Mildred," Penelope says. She motions her into a chair.

Mildred's eyes widen. "You mean — I didn't know you were religious."

"No, no, I don't mean that. What I mean is, I find myself good company."

"But that's still being by yourself," Mildred points out, reasonably. "You aren't two people."

"Haven't you ever talked to yourself?"

"Well yes, but...."

"Then you must be two people," Penelope says, although not without a twinge of guilt. "Otherwise, who have you been talking to?"

Mildred is, at least for the time being, silenced, but Penelope knows it won't last. She tries to figure out what Mildred wants and girds herself to do battle, although she isn't sure whether the battle will be with the Mildred that Penelope thinks of as "really Mildred" or with the other one she met on the trip to Arizona ten years ago, the unseen Mildred whom Penelope has not yet named.

"Now, Penelope," Mildred says, getting to the point, "I know you can be touchy and I hope you won't take what I'm about to say the wrong way."

Penelope has a mad moment where she sees herself scooping Mildred up with a giant shovel and sending her flying into the nearby mountains. But she merely wipes her hands on her gardening jeans and puts leftover coffee in the microwave.

"I *might* take it amiss," Penelope warns, pouring coffee into big mismatched mugs. "I won't know till I hear it."

"It's for your own good, Penny — ah, Penelope."

"You're only thinking of me," Penelope says, but sarcasm is a foreign language to Mildred.

"Now, Penelope, if I didn't say this I wouldn't be a true friend. You were shouting away to yourself when I got here...."

"Not to myself. What makes you think that? I was saying goodbye to a slug. Sensitivity. Slug's last farewell."

"That's even — ah — more bizarre. You know, George actually said to me, before he died...."

"As good a time as any."

"...he said, I think Penny's getting a bit nutty, living there alone like that. Of course, that's the way George talked — but you *are* getting on you know, Penelope." (Mildred is a good ten years younger than Penelope.) "And the other day Mrs. Moore phoned me, said she was concerned about you, she hears you shouting and banging around the house at all hours, she says."

Penelope resolves to shoot the next slug over the fence and into Mrs. Moore's geraniums.

"You wouldn't want someone — like maybe your doctor — to — ah — say something, would you, Penny?"

"Who would he say something to?"

"Well, Brenda...." Mildred regrets the words before they are out. Nuttiness, Mildred thinks, runs in the family.

She changes tack. "How should I know, who to? The authorities, I suppose. But what I'm trying to say, Penelope, is maybe you *are* going to need help, and I'd be willing to take you in." Mildred begins to talk more and more rapidly until she sounds like a TV huckster flogging videos. "We could pool our resources. Sell this place — it's way too much for you to manage by yourself anyway, and my house is plenty big enough for two, and we could share the housework, it would make it cheaper for both of us...."

Before Penelope can utter a sound Mildred is on her feet,

gathering up her purse and looking for her car keys. "Now don't say a word," she says, her staccato, rapid-fire delivery blocking out whatever Penelope is trying to say. "This is a major change I'm proposing, no snap decisions, I'll call you tomorrow," and when Penelope does manage, "Mildred," she holds her hand up and runs out the door and up the path to her car.

Penelope lopes after her and shouts, "It wouldn't work!" just as Mildred slams the car door.

Mildred starts the oversized metallic blue Buick, George's cherished toy, and lowers the window on Penelope's side.

"You still owe me, remember?" she says, then guns the motor, lays rubber, and leaves Penelope coping with this unexpected low blow.

IS PENELOPE ECCENTRIC? IF SHE IS, SHE IS NOT IN THE same league as some of the more extravagant British eccentrics. John Slater once walked the length of the British Isles in pyjamas and bare feet, accompanied by his sensibly shod dog (two pairs of suede booties). He lives to this day on a remote part of the Scottish coast in a cave that floods up to his knees at high tide, and when faced with an ultimatum from his (third) wife he tried living in a cottage but in the end moved back into the cave.

Eccentricity has been defined as setting one's own rules of behaviour. One person with a shaved head, wearing nothing but a toga and chanting and jigging to some incomprehensible mantra might be classified as possibly insane; four people doing the same are dismissed as the odd but quite legitimate Hare Krishnas.

Balzac wrote that eccentricity is a word the English have coined to describe behaviour in members of distinguished families, not ordinarily used of the socially unimportant. And it is true that if the rich and powerful display signs of eccentricity we forgive them; in fact we praise their nonconformist peculiarities, as though these are the manifestation of some superiority, the prods of society, pushing it in the direction of progress (or possibly regress). Glenn Gould's preoccupation with gloved hands, his distracting voice accompaniment to the Brandenburg Concertos, Van Gogh and his infamous self-surgery.

Solitary, then, but definitely not mad. Unlike schizophrenics, who are terrified of and at the mercy of their vivid mental images, eccentrics delight in them but stay in control. Eccentrics are not necessarily even neurotic. Neurotics hate being different; eccentrics revel in eccentricity. In fact it is said by those statisticians who believe they can measure such things that eccentrics are happier and healthier than the norm, perhaps because they find joy in the pursuit of whatever interests them.

Penelope, if asked, would say that she hasn't become as eccentric as she wants but she is working on it.

THE BIGGEST DIFFICULTY BRENDA ENCOUNTERS IN DOING research is finding out what Penelope, in her quest for the "Meaning of Life," is currently exploring.

"Here's something I saw in this morning's *Globe and Mail*," Penelope says when Brenda phones, and she reads it out. "In 1995 on a flight from Milan a UFO buzzed a British Airways Boeing 737 at 6:48 p.m. With good visibility at the four-thousand-foot level of its descent, Captain Roger Wills reported that a wedge-shaped UFO emblazoned with small white lights came so close to his jet that co-pilot Mark Stuart ducked. Although it made no impact on ground radar, an independent observer, Mark Lloyd, near the airport, saw it and phoned the control tower. The Civil Aviation Authority conducted a year-long formal investigation but could come up with no explanation.

"Another authenticated sighting was made by the crew of the Apollo space mission when an object tracked the spacecraft for some minutes, then moved off at high speed. The astronauts told Houston they were being tailed."

"UFO's?" Brenda says. She can't keep the scorn out of her voice.

"No, no, I'm not trying for *The X-Files.* That's just an example. What I'm searching for are odd events that don't fit into the scientific scheme of things, at least the way the theories now stand."

"Ahh. Synchronicity."

"Synchronicity?"

"A Jungian concept. You have to read Carl Jung, Mother, it's right up your alley. I'll bring you a book about him."

"Synchronicity," Penelope repeats. She likes the sound of it.

And Brenda does come up with an instance. On the World Wide Web. "I stumbled on this," she scribbles. "Synchronistic events. Referring to a single time period."

Figaro *and* Le Monde *reported that, in the summer of 1958, three women and one man, in a five-minute period, saw tears falling from the stone eyes of the Virgin Mary at Lourdes. None of the three seemed to be particularly quixotic nor to be seeking publicity, nor had they been acquainted with one another prior to the sighting, and all were resolute in sticking to their stories.*

Penelope quells a slight disappointment. Not much to go on, but then she tells herself to use her noodle and not expect some-one else to do the work for her. She examines the date: summer, the year Brenda and Gordon were six. What would she have been doing then?

She searches through boxes in the basement until she comes up with her old travel journals. That was the summer they rented the house in Roujan. She skips through the entries and there it is, her odd fainting spell. Her excitement mounts as she notes that it was within a five-minute period, at least according to the ancient testimony of the *patrons* of the *boulangerie* and *boucherie.*

She wonders if that was the same five-minute period of the Lourdes phenomena. Although, if she were unconscious at the time she wouldn't have noticed anything.

She had jotted something in the margin about crimson, although the word may have been a private shorthand. At the time she had been paranoid about anyone reading her diary in case they concluded that her "nervous troubles" were worthy of expert attention (Penelope didn't want *anybody* messing around with her head, especially some misogynistic psychiatrist). She sits motionless, burrowing into the places in her brain where memo-ries are filed, trying to remember what could have been crimson as she fell to the sidewalk, and then recalls that the crimson came from behind a house and looked like flames, or maybe streamers. And later, when she is no longer thinking about it, she remembers the name Truffault, and knows exactly what Brenda's next step must be. Find someone in France whose name is Truffault and who lived or still lives in Roujan.

GORDON AND BRENDA WITH JASON ARE GOING TO ARRIVE on the same day, and by the time she makes the trip to Horseshoe Bay to pick Brenda and Jason up (Brenda manages her life without a car) and gets through the excitement *that* generates, Penelope's energy is beginning to flag. The airport is much further than Horseshoe Bay and the traffic will be fierce by the time Gordon's plane arrives.

But Brenda anticipates her fatigue and insists on going instead. "Jason can stay with you. If you want a rest I've rented a video he's only seen twenty times before, it keeps him so focussed the place could burn down around him and he'd never know. Does the ski rack fit your car? I'll put it on for Gordon's skis."

Penelope tries to object although she knows she doesn't have a leg to stand on. She hoped to drive to the airport by herself to pick Gordon up, but Brenda, when she heard Gordon was coming, caught an earlier ferry. Penelope longs to know how Gordon's auras are doing. He hasn't (wouldn't) talk about that on the phone.

Penelope squelches an unworthy wish to be the first he tells, and then she faces squarely the fact that Brenda has always planted herself between Gordon and Penelope. Not that Penelope was being singled out — Brenda also planted herself just as solidly between Gordon and anyone he might care for more than Brenda. In the field of sibling rivalry Brenda got off to an early start, bawling more loudly and fiercely and vanquishing her feeble opponent even before his first apologetic whimper. In elementary school she monitored his friendships, cutting out those that were too captivating, co-opting those she could boss.

As they grew older and Gordon tried to assert himself they became rivals. If Gordon swam across Okanagan Lake, Brenda swam over *and* back, and had to be hauled out forcibly midlake by Grover. When Gordon made the ball team, Brenda practised so assiduously that she sprained her arm and had it in a sling for two weeks. Their skiing exploits in high school became legendary.

Brenda was indefatigable. After school dances she would tease Gordon so unmercifully that Penelope would sometimes intercede, and Brenda would turn on Penelope with accusations of favouritism until even passive Grover was roused to reprimand.

And under the fireworks? Something fierce, strong, unrelenting, something more like submersion than love. Twins, Penelope muses, bound by the strong force, electromagnetic in its intensity. Rip it apart and one might die.

Penelope veers away from that thought and reminds herself that these two aren't children any more, they aren't even young adults. They are in their forties, for heaven's sake, and Gordon can surely look after himself by now — although she knows Brenda better than to bank on it.

AS THEY DRIVE IN FROM THE AIRPORT, GORDON DECIDES to tell Brenda something about his auras, doing it in a humorous, offhand way to disguise the centrality they have assumed in his life.

His sightings, he tells Brenda, started on a Sunday much like any other, except that he had decided to tackle, in a series of three sermons, something a little dearer to his heart than the usual Unitarian mix of humanism and environmentally sound self-help: Jung and the collective unconscious.

He had just dealt with the ways in which the unconscious projects its messages into the conscious brain when he looked up and saw Camilla Clark's head (which Harbit-Jones had once described as a beautifully-decorated empty vessel) shimmering in a whitish haze. Blinking rapidly, he shifted to Cyril Foggarty beside her. Around Cyril was a reddish blur (perhaps he had been to Hawaii? Gordon couldn't remember) which, though startling enough, paled in comparison with Camilla's whiteness, so intense now that the gold of her hair was turning the shade of sun-bleached grass.

He did his best to conceal his shock. Carefully, because of his trembling hands, he rearranged the notes in front of him, though they had little to offer other than constancy. He wondered if he were dreaming and tried to test the feel of reality, but somebody was interrupting, demanding an answer in a voice whose slightly plaintive pitch disguised insistence. Without looking up Gordon knew that the fringes of hair lining the bald pathway of Smith Harbit-Jones' head would be quivering, as though fanned by the activity within.

Gordon rubbed his eyes in a vain attempt to clear the air and, if suitable, awaken, then asked Harbit-Jones to repeat his question.

Harbit-Jones, who was short and nearsighted and dedicated to ridding the world of God, half-turned so the congregation could escape nothing. "In your opinion," he repeated, enunciating clearly, as though Gordon's failure had been one of hearing, "is the collective unconscious merely an elusive, perhaps hypocritical, substitute for God? After all, Jung was the son of a minister and may have been guilty of circuitous rationalization in his need to justify a father figure."

Gordon held onto the solid edges of the lectern. The air had worsened, especially around Harbit-Jones' head. He concentrated on pinning down the exact shade: emeralds, or spring leaves, or a lake of many colours he had seen once on a trip into the interior of British Columbia.

Harbit-Jones was waiting, triumphant now, for clearly he had rattled the Rev, as he persisted in calling Gordon. Gordon closed his eyes as though he might find enlightenment in darkness, but for the life of him he could discern no acceptable response to Harbit-Jones' question.

Rescue, whose source at any other time would not have been entirely welcome, came from Camilla. Gordon opened his eyes and saw that her white brightness was facing Harbit-Jones' green shimmer squarely on. "It doesn't matter how you name it," she was explaining, rather gently, as though to an aging child, "since God isn't a description, He's...or rather, *She's* (laughter)...an experience."

Gordon pretended not to see Harbit-Jones' expression of pained sensibility, which Harbit-Jones then turned on the congregation. Gordon heard Harbit-Jones explaining to Camilla that, while her experiences were undoubtedly profound, they could scarcely form a basis for scientific discourse. Harbit-Jones was pretending dispassion, but the disguise was thin and the congregation restive.

After that there was a space which Gordon must fill. Desperately, he essayed a quip about the unassailability of Camilla's position, upon which, to his immense relief, the unlikely radiance around her head began to fizzle out, leaving the air empty, as though something had been lost.

BY THE TIME THEY GET TO PENELOPE'S GORDON IS ALREADY beginning to regret his candour. He knows that Brenda won't just leave it at that. But he will, he tells himself, be careful about what else he says, especially on the long drive to Whistler Mountain later in the week for the spring skiing.

BRENDA AND GORDON AND JASON VISIT WITH PENELOPE for a couple of days, and then Brenda and Gordon make their plans for skiing at Whistler Mountain.

Penelope can't stop her big mother-mouth from saying, "For heaven's sake, remember that neither of you are as young as you were when you used to do that – hamburgering...."

"Hot dogging," Brenda says and Jason shouts "Hamburgering, hot dogging," and falls over in helpless five-year-old mirth, which he revives periodically during their stay.

"I'll be lucky if I can still snowplow," Gordon says, and sighs.

There was a time when Gordon and Brenda formed the formidable Stevens Duo, when they whizzed down nearly perpendicular slopes at speeds that would have snapped their necks if they made a false move, soared off cliffs into empty air, somersaulted and regained their balances in perfect tandem, became local celebrities. "Those days are gone forever," Brenda says, a longing in her voice that exactly mirrors what Gordon is feeling. "Now, Jason, do you want a different video, or do you want to keep on with the dinosaurs for another millennium or two?"

Jason opts for dinosaurs, and Brenda and Gordon load their equipment and hug Penelope and reassure her of their prudence, and then they are on the Upper Levels Highway and feeling an unfamiliar excitement, as though years are sloughing off them like old skins.

"These colours you were seeing from the pulpit," Brenda says, before they even leave Horseshoe Bay and begin the twisting and sometimes perilous drive to Whistler. "You say they matched their owners? This red...."

"Cyril Foggarty. Yes, he's often angry." Gordon explains about Harbit-Jones' green aura, the cold emanation of logic....

"And the white one, this Camilla?"

Gordon thinks for a moment. "No!" he exclaims, with a sense of discovery. "In fact, Camilla Clark's aura bears no relationship whatsoever to her personality!" Gordon is vehement, and, now that he thinks of it, relieved, to discover this small randomness.

"You dislike this Camilla, I take it."

"Oh no, I don't *dislike* her." Dislike is an unsuitable sentiment in a church committed to the caring and nurturing of ecosystems. Gordon is trying, quite diligently, to find a role for Camilla in his planetary vision; in fact, as he explained to Dr. Weinberg (although he doesn't tell Brenda this) he made a list of her negatives so that he could balance them against her positives. So far the only positive that has presented itself is – to his chagrin – "golden hair." He didn't mention that to Dr. Weinburg. Nor does he to Brenda.

"You say this Camilla's aura was a brilliant white. What would such an aura denote to you, in terms of a person?" Dr. Weinburg had wanted to know.

Gordon wasn't sure, but he thought he knew what Camilla's *should* have been. "Sixties psychedelic patterns," he told Dr. Weinberg. Like the posters plastered on the walls of the commune where Brenda had crashed, the time in California when he went to try to rescue her. He doesn't mention that either.

He is silent for a few minutes, concentrating on a particularly bad patch of road made trickier by a nervous youngster in a Jeep who is tailgating him. Finally there is a place to pull over and Gordon lets the kid pass. Brenda gives him the finger.

SUDDENLY GORDON REMEMBERS SOMETHING HE HAD managed to forget: Brenda entwined in a bundle of muscular arms and legs, jerking and grunting, her long black hair flopping rhythmically over the bed's edge. The joined bodies had seemed to him disgusting, like oversized white grubs mating in the open air, and he had fled, sickened, to the bathroom, and gone on flee-

ing until he settled finally on the ministry. The Unitarian ministry, since he didn't believe in God, certainly not in the anthro-
pomorphic sense, although he was an agnostic and not an athe-
ist (as was Harbit-Jones, who decried agnosticism and accused
Gordon of hedging his bets).

Gordon hadn't mentioned any of this to Dr. Weinberg – it
was too soon for regression therapy – but in response to Dr.
Weinberg's question he said that yes, the auras had returned after
the first time. On the second occasion, there had been an increase
in the intensity of Camilla Clark's aura during the meditation
music. "I do know she loves Mozart," Gordon admitted,
"although with Camilla, who would suspect it? She *hates* Freud
for his anti-feminism, but hasn't read a single word in the original. And she *just loves* Shirley MacLaine."

"In the original?" Dr. Weinberg asked, with a sly grin.

Gordon laughed, pleased with the rather good rapport he felt
they were establishing, and made an appointment for the following Thursday. "Shall I bring dreams?" he asked, holding out his
briefcase as though it already held them.

Dr. Weinberg was cautious. "We'll get to dreams. For now,
auras are enough."

BRENDA DROPS THE SUBJECT. SHE HAS UNDERSTOOD ENOUGH,
even if Dr. Weinberg hadn't. A sense of loss comes and goes so
quickly that she scarcely notices its passage, and just then they
come around a bend in the road and see, quite suddenly, the
peaks of the high-rises of Whistler Village, and she is so busy

responding to Gordon's awe at this ultramodern cityscape that has risen fairy-talelike in the depths of the Coast Mountains that she is diverted, at least for the time being.

On their first fairly cautious descent Gordon is delighted that not only can he snowplow adequately, within half an hour he can ski with confidence and with something approaching the old expertise. Brenda has had more opportunity to ski in the intervening years, but by the third run before lunch they are subtly daring one another.

In the afternoon they even try some of the gentler of their old routines: skiing in tandem around moguls, each in such perfect control that by the third run they don't miss a beat. Nevertheless no one now would take them for the famous Stevens duo of their early high school years. They were about the same size then – Gordon got his growth late, Brenda early – and Brenda was as slim as Gordon. They are, of course, fraternal twins – Gordon is fair and Brenda dark – but Gordon's delayed maturity and a strong family resemblance made them "as alike as two peas in a pod," as Grover was wont to say when striving for some small rapport during their bewildering adolescence.

At sixteen Gordon began to grow, eating so voraciously that Penelope would despair of ever adequately stocking the refrigerator. He grew to over six feet, and towers over Brenda, who is a respectable five feet eight inches. Gordon works out (the Running Rev, he is known as) and although muscular, is still slim, while Brenda had some difficulty in finding a pair of stretch pants that stretched enough for her to ski in.

As they ski the second run after lunch, Brenda can't resist: she slams into the base of a particularly solid mogul that tilts her, unexpectedly, to a forty-degree angle. She comes within an ace of losing her balance but doesn't; almost topples onto sheer ice but in a split second is standing straight again, looking over her shoulder at Gordon with the old triumphant, daring grin.

Temptation flashes like a shooting star through Gordon's brain and is as quickly extinguished.

"Lose your nerve?" Brenda taunts, as they line up at the lift.

"Do you have some sort of a death wish, Bren?" Gordon asks. He thinks he has won a battle of sorts, and again Brenda has a fleeting sensation of loss. She doesn't try any more tricks.

By four o'clock they are exhausted. They bask in a companionable silence on the way home.

IN NORTH VANCOUVER BRENDA TAKES THEM PAST Carson Graham High, and nostalgia wafts over them like a dislocation of Time. The football field and the physical joy of muscles at their peak of perfection, the beauty of unmarred skin and the need to highlight hair with just the right shade of henna, the crushes on boys, on girls, the pains, the triumphs, the boredom of quadratic equations. Betty Grosvenor, who set the standard for dress and behaviour. Ivan, who worshipped and waited on boys and girls alike and who, unbelievably, married Betty. And who is dead. "Wasn't he the same age as the rest of us?" Brenda asks.

"Yes." Gordon says, and then after a moment, "They moved in next door to me, you know."

Brenda hadn't known. "I hope you didn't find that too distracting," she teases. "Remember the crush you had on her?" When Gordon says nothing she goes on, "I couldn't figure that marriage, could you? Betty with every boy on earth panting after her, and Ivan, the class nerd, who couldn't even get a date for the prom."

Gordon nods, and then says, almost fiercely, "He wasn't a nerd, you know. *We* were the nerds."

They turn into Penelope's driveway and Brenda doesn't get a chance to ferret out whatever emotional chord she has struck this time.

APRIL

GORDON STAYS A WEEK AND BRENDA TEN DAYS, and Penelope tells Jason that she is on cloud nine the whole time. Then has to explain that cloud nine is an expression meaning to be extra happy. "Is cloud eight a grumpy cloud?" Jason wants to know, and Penelope thinks that is pretty smart and wishes the potluck crowd didn't have a rule (which she herself proposed) against doting grandparent stories.

Penelope is on cloud nine because of the proximity of her loved ones, of course, but also because she has had what she thinks of as a vital talk with Gordon. (In spite of Brenda's having got her licks in first.) Brenda will eventually tell Penelope all about the auras — although second-hand news (now there's a contradiction in terms!) is never as revealing as getting it from the horse's mouth, so to speak. Well, she got plenty of that from Gordon and she won't be sharing any of it with Brenda for the simple reason that Gordon has asked her not to. "Don't say anything to Bren, okay?" he mumbled, as they finished their cocoa and stumbled off to bed.

After the day he and Brenda went skiing, Gordon fell into a

deep sleep in the tiny room where, in his adolescence, and in common with eighty percent of the boys in his class, he wakened moist and shamed from his nightly rendezvous with Betty Grosvenor. Betty who had married Ivan Petrovic, the least likely boy, the one willing to forego booze in order to qualify as designated driver, the team player who seldom made it past the sidelines but lustily cheered those who did.

The Rev. Gordon Stevens no longer dreams of Betty, but that night he dreamt of Ivan, dead Ivan who, years after marrying Betty, became his neighbour in Etobicoke.

In the dream — one of those that seem too real to be a dream — it occurs to Gordon that he might be dreaming but he discards the possibility. Reality is as present as it was on the cold top of Whistler Mountain, although the density in the air is unlike the ephemeral lightness of mountain air, as though the oxygen that had been missing up there had coalesced and become heavy at this lower altitude and is pressing on his head.

The boundaries of the room begin to dissolve into white arches that push back the walls, which Gordon now sees are indented with small nooks. Delicate cascades of tiny pale yellow and pink roses in urn-shaped vases sit in the nooks, and he sees that he is in the funeral home where, in a custom still prevalent in eastern Canada (one which Gordon regards as somewhat bizarre), Ivan had been readied for viewing.

Gordon is standing in a line behind two women he doesn't recognize, one of them with fairly generous flesh. *Corseted against death*, Gordon thinks, and even in the dream is rather pleased with his imagery. In university Gordon was deemed to have a poetic sensibility (in spite of his failure to produce so much as a rhyming couplet), a belief that reinforced Gordon's own. He chooses words carefully, with a certain flair; he even chooses the words that comprise his thoughts carefully, and the more literate among his congregation are sometimes baffled by what they think must be a quotation they should have recognized.

The dream woman's companion has hair the colour of dead flames. In the dream Gordon thinks he should write this down, but just then the woman whispers to him, "He looks so natural."

This strikes Gordon as so funny that he laughs and is about to turn and point out that Ivan won't be offended if they speak out loud, when the other woman says, "They use cosmeticians." She says cosmeticians with a sort of grandeur and both women tremble, and then, as if on cue, they both gasp and begin to sob.

"Who are they?" Gordon asks Ivan, companionably. "Are they from the office?" He sits on the edge of the coffin. "You can't blame them," he points out. "Magical cosmeticians! They've made you look haughty, as though you should be draped in flags and saluted with cannons." Ivan couldn't have managed haughty on his own. It was the last thing he ever looked when his eyes were open.

In the dream Ivan gets up and stands beside Gordon and looks thoughtfully at his face in the coffin before settling back into his body.

Gordon woke with his heart pounding and fear shattering the night. The fear of annihilation, the three a.m. frenzies as Penelope called them. Gordon got out of bed and put on his robe and went down to the kitchen and switched on the TV without the sound.

He was flooded with the memory of the feeling he'd had at the funeral, that Ivan was watching. That he hadn't left the church yet. About the last thing a Unitarian (a skeptical bunch, especially about any dogma of the supernatural) would be likely to believe. Yet Gordon had felt that; had heard a whisper, a sort of sibilance sighing between the electric chords like the sweet lament of a forgotten oboe, sliding into the swift silences of rain lashing the stained haloes of dead saints. Sorry – sorry – sorry – it would be just like Ivan to apologize for putting them out; if it had been up to him he would have arranged to die in better weather. Ivan wouldn't have expected them to struggle out in the rain.

But we did, Gordon muttered at the talking head on the TV, which was dissolving into Ivan's apologetic face. Everybody did. Those strange wailers from your office, the other neighbours, your bowling team, *her*, and about a hundred people I didn't even know.

It was the kind of church that Gordon had once described – in a sermon scorning the superstitions of established churches – as a "contained and vaulted space designed by Goths to trap the unsubstantial spirit." Coffin in the front, below the altar. Betty sitting in the front row, head bowed, face hidden. Her hair, a heavy night-black coil seemingly designed for mourning, pinned today against levity. Her shoulders shaking under her coat.

Her shoulders shook like that when she laughed, too. Oh, the way she'd laughed, the way they'd both laughed, when she first told him! And the half-smile of surprised sophistication that, ever since their adolescence, had united her and Gordon and excluded Ivan. When she told him, about how Ivan had apologized when he walked in on her and her lover, screwing in their fifteen-year bed, hers and Ivan's. She told Gordon that. She smoked a cigarette, the blue of her eyes mocking the light in his, and inhaled the grey smoke as if she were arming herself. She said Ivan apologized. That was when they laughed. They laughed to cover their rage.

PENELOPE WALKED INTO THE ROOM AND FLIPPED THE TV off. "I thought you'd sleep the sleep of the dead after all that exercise," she said.

"Actually it's because of the dead that I can't sleep. Did you ever suffer from belated guilt, Mother? No, I suppose the kind of life you've led...."

"Don't make judgements, Gordon, about anyone else's life," Penelope said, a trifle sharply. "I can do guilt as well, perhaps better, than you."

"Okay, what I meant was that the sins over which you guilted were probably not as awful as — as present day sins."

"That remains to be seen. Who or what are you guilting about?"

"Remember Ivan Petrovic from high school, the one we all called Ivan the Un-terrible? Who always looked so apologetic?"

Penelope remembered a quiet, eager little boy who sometimes helped Gordon carry his gear home from hockey practise. She supposed that eagerness could, probably would, turn to apology with age, since eagerness was the antithesis of cool, and she gathered that cool was making a comeback.

"I did him a great wrong which I don't think he ever knew about, and until tonight it scarcely bothered me — I mean, we became friends and that meant a lot to him, I guess I thought my friendship was such a beneficence that — well anyway, suddenly I've had this dream and now — now I can't get over feeling guilty."

"You know what they say about the three stages of maturity, Gordon. First of all you blame others, then you blame yourself, then you forgive yourself. Sounds like you're at stage two."

Gordon was heartened somewhat to think he was past stage one, although he found it a bit incongruous that his mother should be dishing out comforting clichés when his own career was based on passing along exactly this kind of stuff to others.

"Do you remember Betty Grosvenor? You must remember her."

Yes, of course, Penelope remembered her. Betty was one of those girls who are sophisticated at fifteen and beautiful at every age. Betty's heavy, thick, shiny, black hair was carefully combed to half obscure her perfect features, and Brenda and Connie spent hours dying and stiffening their hair with gel to make it sweep down over one eye, like Betty's. Brenda's frizz refused and Connie's straight hair hung limply over her face. Betty walked with a distinctive, saucy swing of the bum, and Penelope used to fear that the two girls would put their backs out aping it. Betty found a simple fashion — A-line skirt, cashmere sweater — that set off her attributes to their best advantage, but the cashmere sweater made Brenda look all bust and the A-line skirt made Connie look fatter than she was.

"I suppose you knew that in spite of having her pick of every boy who ever saw her, she married Ivan." Ivan, who could scarcely believe it, and whose face Gordon had seen after she accepted him. Light reflecting from hundreds of crystals.

"That would seem to have been an unlikely match," Penelope murmured. She busied herself with making cocoa.

"Nobody could get over it. I knew her before Ivan did. I half-despised him, I mean, she was one of us; what could she see in him? We were amazed." *Jolted from the insulation of our assumptions.* "They moved next door to me in Etobicoke."

Penelope was careful to keep her voice down so she wouldn't wake Brenda. "And how did it work out? Was he still un-terrible?"

"No, he was — well, I guess sweet isn't the word you use for a man, but he was like that, a terrific father, they had three kids. But she got bored in suburbia — I mean, Etobicoke wasn't exactly a swinging city back then, backyard cookouts weren't her thing. She had an affair, and he walked in on them, and get this, *he apologized!*

"He was the one who moved out when she asked him to. He would sneak around the back every day after work to see the kids. I was furious with them both. When it rained I made him come inside. That was when growth experiences were enjoying a resurgence. She grew, he shrivelled."

Penelope thinks of Anne Lewis and The Spoiler. "Did he stick around — the new one, I mean. Three kids?"

Of course the "lover" had vanished. "She didn't really want to leave Ivan anyway, I could see that, she just wanted a bit of fun.

Everyone isn't a goddamn saint."

"And who would want to live with one anyway?"

Gordon grinned. "He moved back and they reverted to cook-outs. He used to wear these crazy aprons, Mother," and Gordon's voice broke for a second. Penelope resisted the urge to put her arms around him and pat his back, the way she used to when Brenda's teasing got too fierce. "Over 40 and Still Cooking, Wok Master, I May Not Be Efficient But I Look Cute, all those corny mottos – he would stand out in the backyard and cook ham-burgers for the kids, their friends, *her*, half the neighbourhood. He'd throw frisbees up into the blue, he'd make a face of mock horror when one sailed into my garden.

"I put up with it; that's how I felt. Condescending. When he used to call to me to come over I would condescend, when I brought beer he would thank me. I shouldn't have, he'd say, that's not why he asked me, was I sure I could spare it? – You'd have thought I'd handed him champagne in a great golden loving cup." Gordon's voice wavered again, and hurriedly Penelope poured the cocoa into mugs.

"I wish I *had*."

Penelope handed Gordon his cocoa. "You came to care for him," she said, respectfully. "Deep friendship is not a thing to be taken lightly."

Was that what it was? Couldn't anyone say "love" anymore? Gordon sipped his cocoa and thought of the long hot after-noons when he and Ivan had chatted, how the high sound of bees droning around them lulled them with lazy joy.

"Sometimes I wish we'd never watched the playoffs and that

I'd never won a single bet." He picked up the cocoa again and after a moment said, "Anyway, water under the bridge. The oldest boy had an accident on his motorcycle – a stupid thing to let the kid have, I'd never believed in it in the first place, that bloody, shiny, pagan, jazzed-up tribute to – who knows what? Ivan was so proud when he was able to buy it – after all, *she'd* backed him, I would hear them talking about it in their backyard. There were plenty of other things he could have done with the money.

"He bought the motorcycle in the middle of November. He stopped driving, parking was getting too expensive, he took the bus. It rained a lot. He bought a waterproof tent that covered the kid's body and left his head exposed." Maybe the motorcycle gave him more pleasure than a ride to work, maybe he felt himself fastening the white artificial cranium that looked like a baby's improbable head towering over jeans, maybe when the boy roared down the street Ivan flew with him – Gordon wouldn't have suspected Ivan of harbouring such passions.

"The bloody things are unbelievably treacherous – there was an accident, the kid looked dead when they brought him in. Like a girl, thin body, long yellow curls decorated with red...."

Gordon had called the ambulance. Ivan cried and so did Betty. Gordon had put his arm around Betty and quieted her, called a neighbour to take the girls, then waited with them until the ambulance came and Ivan went with the boy. Not forgetting to thank Gordon, of course. He was sorry to trouble Gordon, but would he look after her?

Gordon was silent for so long that finally Penelope ventured, "And did you?"

Gordon stared into his cocoa and nodded.

"Ivan phoned from emergency that the boy was fine, nothing to worry about, he would just wait there while they sharpened their saws. He didn't say that of course, didn't mention that the boy would lose a leg. He made it sound casual, minor, light-hearted, almost chatty.

"I saw the boy at the funeral for the first time in about five years. You'd never mistake him for a girl now, he's got a beard and you can't tell that he has a metal leg."

"I'm sorry about Ivan," Penelope said. "He was too young to die," although she wasn't sure if there was any age when you weren't too young to die. Suddenly she felt inadequate, as though she were poorly prepared for this role that had been thrust upon her, that of "a wise older person." There were lessons for moth-ering and divorcing and even dying, why not for this one?

"The doctors said it was a vascular accident, myocardial infarc-tion, said we couldn't have stopped it. When *she* said he'd died of a broken heart they could hardly keep their faces straight."

"What do you think?" Penelope asked.

"I think — what *do* I think? I think Ivan was one of those rare mortals who couldn't seem to protect himself. We all protect ourselves, you know that, Mother; we use whatever is handy to shield ourselves. Even ministers. He didn't understand that."

This was an interesting insight to Penelope and she thought about her own shields. Against, for instance, the likes of Mildred. Sarcasm? A feeling — perhaps not too well hidden — of superiority?

Gordon got to his feet. "I go on weekends," he said. "On Saturdays, the day we did our visiting. I take an extra beer and I spill it over his grave." Over the sad-faced pansies and the whispering wild flowers that grew in the sunny places of the cemetery. "I try not to forget."

Gordon didn't explain about why the dream had awakened a dormant guilt, but Penelope thought she had a pretty good idea. After all, she'd been there, hadn't she? – at least in spirit. She knew exactly the feeling of emptiness in the pit of the stomach and the shame of betrayal, and then she wondered why any Creator in Its right mind would ever have allowed the beauty of love to be so inextricably linked to the terror of sex.

BRENDA WOKE UP JUST AS GORDON AND PENELOPE WENT back to bed and cursed herself for having slept through whatever was said. But she'd get it out of Gordon – and then she reminded herself that Gordon was no longer the blushing adolescent that came tiptoeing into the house at four a.m. after the grad dance. Brenda had waylaid him in the hall and threatened to wake the household if he didn't tell all. (Grover had been adamant about a three a.m. curfew, although of course he meant Brenda and had fallen asleep the minute she dashed in the door. Grover was, truth to tell, somewhat relieved when Gordon was "showing a bit of spunk" by being late.)

Poor Gordon, with his fumbling half-admission of that first sexual encounter! When Brenda whispered that she just hoped to hell he hadn't gotten Connie – who, after intense badgering by Brenda, he had asked to the dance – pregnant, a red-faced Gordon denied even the possibility so emphatically that Brenda was unsure whether or not their carefully calculated stratagem — hers and Connie's — had succeeded. (Later Connie had explained. As planned, she had snuggled up to a disapproving Gordon — she'd had too much to drink. He couldn't take her home in that condition, and so Gordon drove her up Lynn Valley Road to the parking lot, where he could walk her around in the air. As he was coasting to a stop Connie reached over and unzipped his pants. The car jolted forward and a humiliated Gordon shot his share of the romantic encounter straight up onto the roof of Mr. Smythe's new Oldsmobile.)

A lot of water under the bridge since those days, Brenda mused. Today's sophisticated Connie — Brenda had called her the day she arrived and was answered by a strange voice, a young woman's with a heavy Chinese accent. "I don' know Con — who you ask for?" and there was giggling and an exclamation, "Jeem!" silence, and then Jim Tran answered.

"Brenda, hi!" he said. "Lovely to hear from you. Connie will be so sorry to have missed you. She took Tommy down to Palm Springs for school break and they're staying on an extra week; I *was* hoping to join them but I have clients who've flown over from Hong Kong, you know how it is." Brenda almost believed him.

"Tell her I called, okay?"

"Oh absolutely. And you're keeping well, are you?"

Brenda said yes, and hung up abruptly.

PENELOPE ISN'T ABLE TO DISGUISE THE FACT THAT SHE'S feeling blue that Brenda's and Gordon's visit will soon be over, and at the potluck dinner Mildred is quick to pick up on it. "My, my," she says. "Aren't we quiet tonight. Well," and here her voice takes on the rough edge of martyrdom, "nobody can tell me anything I don't know about loneliness. Nobody to talk to...."

Old Tom peers at her speculatively. "Sometimes that can be an advantage. I get a lot of reading done, that for some reason I never used to find the time for. I still miss Nell even after ten years, that's a given, but I'd rather be lonely occasionally than go with any of the alternatives that have presented themselves." Tom's next-door neighbour, Lydia, has tried more than once to "take him in hand," and Tom's children have hinted broadly at the social advantages of a senior's lodge.

"I'd have gone potty if I hadn't met Dick," Nancy volunteers, and Penelope can't stop herself from wondering if Dick got there in time.

If only Brenda were to decide to live with her, Penelope thinks as she drives home from the potluck dinner, she would never have to confront Mildred with her decision – but Penelope brings herself up short on that one, reprimands herself, reminds herself that it is cowardly to refuse to confront situations. Even the most distasteful.

BRENDA IS GETTING INTO BED WHEN PENELOPE GETS HOME. Since the skiing she's been tired, and then she caught a cold, then the flu. Penelope tried not to show her unease. "Maybe you should get a checkup," she ventured at last, and Brenda, to Penelope's surprise, said that might not be a bad idea.

The doctor couldn't find much wrong with Brenda, although

there are the results of blood tests and a mammogram yet to be considered. All in all, the doctor thought Brenda had just let herself get run down. "Naturally she thinks I should lose a little weight," Brenda sniffed. Penelope stifled an urge to skip around the house.

She tells Brenda about Mildred's scheme. "That aging Barbie doll!" Brenda snorts. "I can just see you trotting out to get your colours done before buying some cute polyester pantsuit for a chummy Alaska cruise."

"Naturally I wouldn't consider it," Penelope says, "but I don't want to hurt her feelings unnecessarily. It's only four months since George died, you know, she's still vulnerable."

"Hm-m-m," Brenda says. "Let me think on it."

The solution, Brenda discovers in about thirty seconds flat, is a man. "Boy, talk about blindsiding my feminist principles! But Mildred — okay, I suppose it's different with her, she's been set adrift in a world she'll never understand, without a man to look after her."

"M-m-m-m," Penelope says, doubtfully. "I'm not sure who I would want to introduce her to. There are sides to Mildred you don't suspect."

"Iron hand in the velvet glove?"

"More like Medusa lurking in the depths —"

"Shallow depths. Short Medusa."

Penelope laughs. "I'll give it some thought, I could have a dinner party."

"Do you know some eligible men? Maybe you should introduce *me*."

"A mite decrepit for you. Anyway, you've got Colin. Haven't you?"

Brenda sighs. "I don't know. After the way he acted when I told him I'd quit my job I don't know if he'll have the nerve to show up again."

Brenda has a mammogram that afternoon, and the next day she and Jason go back to the tree house.

ON THE PLANE RETURNING HOME, UP AT THIRTY-SEVEN thousand feet, a scene splashes through Gordon's mind with such vividness that it might have happened yesterday.

He was waiting with Betty for Ivan to phone. Gordon had poured them both a scotch, and every now and then Betty sobbed and he put an arm around her shoulders, and still they waited. When Ivan phoned from the hospital to say that all was well, Betty was so swept with joy and manic release that she threw her arms around Gordon and told him what a comfort it was to have him there, what a glorious day it had been when they moved next door. She'd always liked Gordon, more than liked him, maybe if Ivan hadn't come along – she'd been so young, had so little judgement.

Betty needed a lot of comforting, and Gordon, as he always had, tries to shy away from the memory. But, up here in the trapped atmosphere it has taken on a life of its own and won't be sidetracked.

"Gordon, I need more than that weak-kneed hug, I've been through hell tonight, I need *you*." As she said this Betty was tugging at her shirt, and then she took Gordon's hand and laid it across the peach lace of her bra while the other hand felt for Gordon's instantaneous response. (He'd had a reasonable amount of experience by this time, there was no danger of his repeating the humiliation of his adolescence.)

"Aha! The old Rev isn't too pure after all," she said with a laugh, stroking his enlarged organ, and then they were lying on the couch in a welter of cushions and breathing like freight trains, and Gordon was scarcely able to contain the wild joy of this living fantasy.

Reality is seldom up to its billing, though, and by the time Gordon stumbled back to his own house he was in a mood of self-hatred that was quite foreign to him. By and large Gordon felt that he usually, or almost always, behaved rather decently, especially considering the examples around him.

He began a rationalization that now repeats itself. It didn't hurt Ivan, did it? Did it? He never guessed, did he? God, how he wishes Ivan could have told him that, could have opened his dead eyes and sat up in his white satin-lined coffin and said that one thing to him. Said he was sorry for putting Gordon to so much trouble, said he was a wonderful neighbour and friend, said Gordon was a person you could always trust.

Gordon has always blamed Betty, but now, for the first time, sitting there above the occasionally green, occasionally snow-pocked fields of the prairies, he sees his own perfidy with painful clarity.

He wonders if every man (person, that is) has the seeds of evil in him, lying in wait for fertile soil. Penelope would never agree; he can almost hear her indignation as she refutes what she would call "passing the buck." She believes in the potentiality of evil all right, but she also believes a person can transcend and control the evil *if he or she wants to.*

Gordon hadn't wanted to, he admits that now.

Betty never again asked for comfort from Gordon or anyone else. Gordon watched, he monitored their house, he listened through the empty walls. She changed, he could see the change in her. It was as though she saw, as though her eyes opened and she saw and was afraid.

Of what? What did she see? Did she see Ivan press his hand to his heart in the quiet of their ancient room when he thought she wasn't looking? Did she hear him gasp sometimes in the night, and wonder? Or was she blessed (or cursed), suddenly, with the power to see the light around Ivan? Gordon is sure there was light, even though the crystal mask had shattered. He thinks that if his new-found power had come on him sooner he would have seen it.

There are plenty of people in the world who would say if it didn't hurt anyone it wasn't wrong, but Gordon is no longer one of those. Wrong is wrong, betrayal is betrayal, and Gordon feels an unaccustomed humility by the time the plane lands in Toronto. It is only later that he contemplates the strangeness of his having confided in Penelope. He has so seldom done so in the past; but then Brenda had always been there.

Gordon remains convinced that Penelope will never, insulated as she is in the twin cocoons of a sheltered life and advancing age, begin to guess at the dimensions of his wrongdoing; nevertheless he feels a curious relief at having confessed as much as he did to her, as though in some way she has granted him absolution and he is free now to get on with the rest of his life.

AFTER EVERYONE LEAVES, PENELOPE IS FREE TO RESUME her daily walk, and she is surprised that pink flowering plums have already blossomed into the ridiculous shape of the Kleenex flowers Mildred made by the hundreds for her daughter's wedding. Two blue jays are carrying on a mating ritual, darting in and out among the boughs, so that bits of pink blossom fall around Penelope and she feels like Snow White (or Snow Grey she thinks, and laughs) running through the bird- and blossom-filled forest. The paler blue of periwinkle carpets a bit of the forest floor where it borders on the sidewalk. Periwinkle, she repeats aloud, caressing the sprightly syllables, but then she thinks the name is prettier than the flower. She likes the richer blue of the blue jays better.

The snow line is still low on the mountains. There is one place where, if she turns around, she can see Mt. Baker, between the roofline of a house and a tree. The sight of it always fills her with a sort of awe, the way the pristine white cone comes up out of the distant haze, rising serene and aloof as though to protect the city – even though the mountain is fifty miles away, over the US border. There is a mystery here, Penelope feels sure of it. Of things that rise from deep places, from inside the earth, from below conscious thought; things that could, might, reveal – but Penelope has no idea what it is that might be revealed, nor why this particular mountain evokes such answering symmetry in her.

Closer, more mundane, the twin peaks of the nearby Lions cut into the blue like a couple of frozen thumbs, and then Penelope is at the park where early red rhododendrons are already in bloom, and the round bed is filled with tulips.

Two blocks past the park is an elementary school. Sometimes, if she is passing at recess, Penelope likes to listen to sounds reminiscent of her own childhood: *one, two, three a-lary* as the ball bounces on the pavement, the swish of double dutch skipping ropes, the fierce examinations of those markers – the pebbles or little bits of glass, or the special lucky rabbit's foot Penelope used to have – that had landed on the boundary between the heaven of hopscotch and the void beyond.

Today, however, it is past three o'clock and the school has emptied and the playground is silent, but as Penelope passes she hears a sniffle, and then a sob, and then a man's voice.

She stops. The sounds seem to come from a small wooded area about ten yards from the sidewalk. A little path acts as a shortcut between the school and the winding street, a short, shaded path darkened by cedars and hemlocks where only an unnatural twilight seeps through. A mildewing place, always damp, a home for slugs. The ground is worn where children run the little distance through the tiny, scary woods to reach a paved walk on the other side, as though concrete offers a safety that is withheld by mouldering earth.

It is four o'clock, and by rights the children should all have left. Penelope hesitates scarcely a second before stepping off the sidewalk and along the path to the clearing.

A man is kneeling by a little girl, one arm around her waist, hugging her reassuringly while trying to wipe her eyes with a messy-looking handkerchief. "Come *on!*" he wheedles. "You're making a lot of fuss about nothing."

The girl has long blonde hair and doesn't raise her head, and at first Penelope doesn't recognize her, but then she sees that the man is the one she has dubbed "The Spoiler," so she knows it must be Kate.

The man looks up and sees Penelope peering through the trees. Later she wonders if something more than mere surprise crossed his face, but before she can hone in on it the beautiful features settle themselves into everyday annoyance.

"What the hell do *you* want?" The harshness of the voice is incongruous, as if Michelangelo's *David* had begun to scream "Fuck off!" at a crowd of fervent tourists, and it startles Penelope so that she mumbles as she tries to explain that she thought she heard someone crying.

"Nothing to concern *you*," and then, grudgingly, "The kid's lost her mother's locket, she borrowed it without asking."

"Oh, Kate, that's too bad," Penelope says.

A giant windshield wiper might have lowered itself from the sky and swept over The Spoiler's face, the way the classical features suddenly clear of all belligerence. "Oh, you know the kid?" he asks politely as he stands up.

"Oh yes. We know one another, don't we, Kate?"

Kate nods mutely, but doesn't look up.

"Maybe I can help —" Penelope starts to say, but The Spoiler is too quick for her.

"We've given it a pretty good going-over. I don't think she lost it here — she thought some kid might have picked it up, then dropped it. Probably in the schoolyard. Anyway we gotta go or there'll be hell to pay — Mom's home with Mikey, he's got a cold," he says. "Honestly, kids!" and he rolls his eyes heavenward, then makes another attempt to wipe away the tears, but before he can dab at Kate with the sticky cotton she slaps his hand away.

He sighs and stands up, and Penelope thinks how very nice he is after all, a little rough and ready perhaps, but decent and obviously caring.

"The Lost and Found...."

"Oh, Jeez, of course, I never thought of that. Hear that, Kate? We won't say anything to Mom for a few days. Give it time to turn up. Well," he nods to Penelope, "thanks. See ya." The Spoiler puts the wadded-up handkerchief into his pocket, then tries to take Kate's hand. Kate yanks it away as though his touch might scorch her skin.

Penelope watches them leave, The Spoiler striding along, Kate, her head still bowed, shuffling along beside him. The child is being difficult. But Kate is bound to resent him, Penelope thinks, this man who has detached her father from the stability of his lawnmower.

MAY

THE LANGDALE FERRY IS NOT ONE OF THE MONSTERS that ply the water to Nanaimo; it is smaller, more companionable, and as often as not when Brenda and Jason cross they meet someone they know from Gibsons, from Jason's kindergarten class, or an habitué of the library who recognizes Brenda.

On the trip back from North Vancouver after their recent visit, the mother of one of Jason's friends persuades Brenda to let Jason stay overnight for a sleepover. Brenda isn't too reluctant; she is a person who enjoys both crowds and solitude, and in spite of the length of time she has lived in the tree house still feels a sense of daring and shivery excitement when she stays there alone, swaying lightly by herself in the blackness of the deserted night.

So she isn't entirely happy when she gets home to find Colin asleep on her little couch. No wonder Goldilocks got so sniffy, she thinks, but when she says, "Colin," he looks so guilty that she stifles her slight outrage.

"I'd just like to talk a bit," he says, plaintively, and she bites off an urge to tell him he's had his chance. In a word she is civilized, even pouring him a drink from her precious dwindling scotch supply.

Colin is too big for the couch, with the result that his knees are pressed primly together below the level of his chin. Nevertheless something about him touches Brenda, and she manages a fairly neutral, "So, Colin, how is the city of angels?" resisting the temptation to add, "managing without you?" Anyway, she is too tired for one of their one-sided fights, where she argues and Colin listens.

Considering that the question is not exactly hard-hitting, Colin reacts as though she's accused him of pirating programs for distribution over the Internet. He stretches his legs out, accidentally touching Brenda's foot in the process, snatches his foot back as though foot contact spreads AIDS, cracks his knuckles and finally semi-whispers, "Tell the truth, Bren, I haven't been there."

"Oh? I thought...."

"Something came up here that I've got to talk to you about." He sounds breathless. "What would you think about my applying for your old job? I mean, would you be upset?" He rushes on to explain that he is getting tired of being on the road, thinks it is time he tried to put down some roots.

What he doesn't say is that Brenda's boss has contacted *him*. Brenda guesses as much. Ever since Colin installed their library's computer system she has suspected that Hatchet-face is sweet on him.

Which poses a dilemma for Brenda. Mean-spiritedness versus magnanimity? It is no contest. "It's a free country," she says. "Help yourself."

Colin then leans over and takes her hand between his. "I have something important to tell you," he says solemnly. Brenda thinks of disasters. An earthquake in Vancouver? A meteor on its way to destroy the planet?

He blurts out that he's been thinking about what she said about their relationship and he realizes he's been somewhat self-ish, and if he does get the job would Brenda marry him?

To say that she is intrigued would be an understatement. She is thunderstruck as well. What Brenda most emphatically doesn't feel is joy, or breathless anticipation – dread would be a more accurate description of what she feels.

Dread is an emotion Brenda isn't prepared for – in the context of marriage, that is. Aircraft hijackings, Bosnian killing fields, tsunamis, terrorist bombs – but not marriage.

Quite definitely not what she would have expected. After all, she'd thrown down the challenge, hadn't she? Why did she do it, if she didn't want to get married? Because she thinks all men are shitty, and now he's called her bluff? If Colin is willing to marry her, penniless and child-encumbered as she is, owning nothing but a tree house, then she is going to have to start revising her jaundiced view of the male – not to mention any number of other things rattling around down there below consciousness.

Colin is going on about how baby boomers may be overly cautious, although he perhaps isn't technically a Boomer (Brenda is but doesn't mention it) and about how he should be willing to take a bit of risk and how much he himself would like to start a family, and he hadn't thought about time running out for her.

Brenda, perhaps for the only time in her life, is tongue-tied.

Finally she says he has taken her by surprise and she is a bit —
overwhelmed — and needs time to think.

Colin treats this load of garbage seriously. He says by all
means, Brenda should take her time, it is a major decision and
not to be taken lightly.

He suggests dinner, but Brenda makes an excuse about fatigue.
He doesn't push it. He doesn't fancy the water taxi late at night,
and besides he needs to update his c.v.

After he leaves Brenda goes almost immediately to bed, but
for once there isn't a breath of wind, and the tree house fails to
comfort her. She can't sleep until a soft morning breeze makes
the pattern of cedar boughs on her wall shimmer in mesmeriz-
ing light. As she explains to Connie later, all she can feel is an
enormous blankness, as though the power has gone off in her
head.

PENELOPE, ON THE LAST LAP OF HER WALK, NOTES THAT IT
is very warm for May. She slows down. After all, she *is* seventy —
no, seventy and a half. *Tempus fugit!* she shouts at a startled dog.
May is exactly six months later than November, already halfway
through her year of exploration. She'd better, she mutters, pull
up her socks.

There is a letter from Brenda in her mailbox. A surge of anticipation — but Penelope brings herself up short. Handle with
care, she warns. If she is to progress she knows she must be on
her guard. Her own children, Gordon and his auras, but especially Brenda, can knock her off the track just by looking pale,

she knows that from experience. Brenda has always been able to take centre stage no matter what; she can and does focus attention on herself. Brenda's goals become everyone's goals.

Although she doesn't know it, for once Penelope is doing Brenda an injustice. Brenda doesn't mention Colin; she has decided to sort her life out a bit before confiding in Penelope or anyone else.

Somehow Colin's proposal has complicated things; it has called up a softness in Brenda that she is, obscurely, afraid of.

An official notice across the envelope accuses Brenda of shortchanging the postal service, another forty cents is due in postage, and Penelope sets the envelope aside to remind herself to pay it. She isn't surprised – the letter is so thick Penelope wonders when Brenda finds the time, and then remembers that time is something Brenda has quite a bit of now.

As it turns out it is not a letter, it is a thick enclosure printed out on computer paper. "Hey, I found something interesting for your research," Brenda has scribbled. "Hatchet-face is away and actually extended my time for two weeks, so I was able to put out a call on the Internet about Roujan and Truffault (that *was* the name of the people you rented your place in France from, wasn't it?) and I got an answer from – you'll never guess where – *Brazil!* Not in Spanish – name is Clarke. Contacted her yesterday and here is the material she sent."

IT WAS FIVE O'CLOCK IN THE AFTERNOON, THE TIME OF the day when Mme. Truffault watered the *jardin* behind her stone house in the village of Roujan, twenty kilometres north of the Mediterranean in the Languedoc area of southern France. Today's meagre offering, unfortunately, scarcely stained the earth, for the dry and cracked soil was thirsty beyond the possibilities of Madame's battered watering can. She sighed and bent to pinch a dead leaf from a geranium, then rested her eyes for encouragement on its single crimson flower.

As she did so, the colour seemed, suddenly, to flare outward like the flame of a candle when wax is dropped into it. Hesitating, she drew her hand back. Before her wondering eyes the unlikely illumination intensified until crimson began to leak from the flower in small banners of colour, curling outwards in hesitant tendrils, venturing further and further, seeping into the cracks in the earth, and finally vibrating in a dizzying borealis around the geranium core.

As the crimson began to intrude into the pores and interstices of a body unused to housing even temporal delight, Mme. Truffault was surprised by pleasure – an emotion now infrequently encountered, but dimly remembered in association with girlhood and a field of poppies. Then mere pleasure slipped away and she was wracked and lifted up by something akin to exultation.

She dropped the watering can and straightened, holding her arms to the sky. Crimson flares emerged from her fingertips, powerful streams of light that could ignite the world. She stood, sending flames into the blue for what seemed an eternity, but was in reality only five minutes. At the end of that time the colour began to retreat, from her fingertips, from her body, then from the earth, and finally settled itself into the everyday crimson of its rightful owner.

Mme. Truffault gathered up her gardening tools, and after supper she went to late Mass where she thanked the Blessed Virgin for exalting her for a little while into a state of grace. At the end of her prayer she whispered, and truly believed, that she was now ready for Heaven, whenever it should be God's will.

She did not mention the incident to M. Truffault – M. Truffault was not on good terms with the Virgin Mary – since she wanted to nourish the memory in the privacy of her soul, where he couldn't get at it.

IN SOME WAYS IT WAS TOO BAD THAT MME. TRUFFAULT, after the ecstasy had left her and she had straightened her watering can and hurried back to her duties, didn't say anything to her husband. M. Truffault was not feeling as affronted as he usually did at any mention of the "former virgin Mary," as he had taken to calling her. He called her that to show how little stock he put in virginity, hers or anyone else's. He was barely able to recall that at one time, in a field of red poppies, it had inspired him *vis-à-vis* Mme. Truffault – now, for the life of him, he couldn't remember what all the fuss had been about.

What he did know was that, as a source of enduring satisfaction, the poppy field had failed him, as had most other things in his burdensome life. And now, when he should be reaping the rewards of a lifetime of work and self-sacrifice, he was afflicted with the injustice of failing lungs; quite possibly, he was dying. Yet he, Roger Truffault, had done everything that could be expected of him. Had he not given up tobacco, one of the few tiny pleasures left to a man bent from the toil of years of supporting two ungrateful women? And then – to turn off what he thought of as the ceaseless nagging of Mme. Truffault (and also to snatch at a slim sliver of hope) – had he not made an expensive pilgrimage to Lourdes? To bow before yet another useless woman? A small favour, that was all he had asked.

Nothing had come of it; he hadn't expected anything would. Lost elasticity in the tiny bronchioles had not been restored; their deterioration had, if anything, accelerated.

Now M. Truffault sat all day in a cloud of irritation: at the TV for failing to divert him, at the foreigners with their expensive clothes and atrocious accents and excessive *bonhomie* who had rented his *gite* next door, at the dog for its stubborn failure to recognize the postman, at the postman for his failure to bring a letter from his daughter, at his daughter for living in a foreign land (Canada, where the foreigners in the *gite* also came from, a coincidence that didn't surprise M. Truffault) as well as – double transgression – for falling in love with a lout who did nothing but plant trees. But most of all, and most pervasively, his outrage was directed at Mme. Truffault for escaping to her garden.

He pushed himself to his feet to fetch the inhalator for the second of the daily sessions that, for a brief time, would send steamy droplets of potent chemicals into the rigid pathways, allowing pointillist molecules of oxygen to seep into his starving bloodstream.

Returning with the apparatus and puffing in tight, panicky, angry gulps from an exertion he shouldn't have had to undergo, he glared into the garden. What he saw made him drop the inhalator. A female figure – no doubt about it, the Blessed Virgin Herself! – was standing, bathed in a halo of vibrating crimson, her arms outstretched to heaven.

Roger Truffault fell to his knees and closed his eyes tightly against the light. He crossed himself and began a rapid string of Hail Marys, and shoots of hope uncurled like new ferns in neglected wastelands of his brain.

He stayed bowed down until he remembered about his breathing. Cautiously he peeked under one eyelid. The vision had solidified into the quite inglorious shape of Mme. Truffault. The sun that had for a moment bathed her in deceptive illumination dipped behind a cloud, and as he watched, she dropped her arms and bent to pick up the watering can.

Nevertheless, when Mme. Truffault came in he didn't ask why she had been lazing about with her arms up in the air, at the hour when he had been needing his treatment. What he did – to her astonishment – was smile at her. Then – to the dog's equal astonishment – he patted it and praised it for finally recognizing the postman, whose relieved back could, at that very moment, be seen hurrying down the street.

And not once, throughout the entire evening, did M. Truffault complain about a daughter who couldn't take the time to write to her poor dying father, nor did he berate Mme. Truffault for her failure to instill filial virtues in said daughter,

nor mention his son-in-law's laziness and instincts for the sub-
tler forms of corruption.

It had been a good day in the Truffault household.

PENELOPE'S ANCIENT JOURNAL GIVES NO HINT THAT
Mme. Truffault possessed any of the physical characteristics one
might expect from a receiver of grace; tall, Penelope had written,
angular, black hair streaked with grey and pulled back into a bun,
black stockings, plain, straight, unadorned, dark dress, grey spotted apron that pinched her in half at the waist. As for M.
Truffault, she had written, "Is there truly a M. Truffault? If so,
where does she keep him?"

Yes, an unlikely vehicle one would have thought, for – whatever it was – and Penelope would be inclined to question the
whole thing as a daughter's reconstructed and overly fond
remembrance if it weren't for her own sighting those many years
ago as she fell to the ground. Crimson flames.

She sees that this is serious stuff, exactly the kind of thing she
is looking for, but she is forced to set aside the necessary contemplation for the time being because there are more pressing
things to deal with, namely bad knees.

Last night at the monthly potluck the knees were fine. Same
time, Nancy's place, more or less the same menu except no Rum
Baba. Nancy whispered to Penelope, jerking her head very
slightly in Mildred's direction, that she'd been afraid Rum Baba
would bring back memories, after all it was the Rum Baba that
George had fallen into on the fateful night, Nancy had always

felt just a tiny bit guilty? Nonsense, Penelope reassured her. George had been a prime candidate for a heart attack if ever there was one, another dollop of whipped cream would scarcely have had time to drop its load when he was stricken.

"Oh Penelope," Nancy said, not sure whether or not this was reassuring, "you really do look at life – in a positive way." Nancy was reading a tattered, annotated copy of *The Power of Positive Thinking* that had, Dick claimed, turned his life around as a young man.

"I just hope poor Mildred – well, I hope she can make such a good adjustment."

They both glanced at poor Mildred, who at that moment was chatting animatedly with Edwin (whose performance at Gimli had given him permanent status). Mildred had not, as Penelope feared she would, seized Penelope's arm when she came in and asked her when she was going to make up her mind; in fact, at the moment, she was showing no signs of intractable grief. She was, in fact, looking quite pink-cheeked and pretty, and Penelope had a moment's sneaky hope that Edwin....

But it didn't seem likely, since just last week Edwin had phoned and asked Penelope if she would like to go to the symphony with him, he seemed to have an extra ticket (materialization? an errant poltergeist?) and Penelope had accepted. With misgivings. She didn't want any romantic involvement; this year had been set aside for the Meaning of Life, and towards that end Penelope had already signed up for a course in anthropology.

Nancy then expanded on tonight's dessert ("It's called cream broolay and you have to make this caramel on the top of the stove and then you drip it over the whipped cream, and that's what gives it that funny bumpy look") and just then Tom exclaimed, *"Crème Brûlée!* My, my, who do we have to thank for this?" and in the adulation that ensued Nancy forgot any embarrassment she may have felt over her unfortunate French.

Mildred and Edwin had chosen chairs next to one another. Who knew? Maybe Edwin would have another miraculous ticket materialization — although Penelope knew that Mildred hated classical music. But she loved k.d. lang "in spite of — you know," and after all, a k.d. lang concert was not to be sneezed at.

PENELOPE'S KNEES BEGIN THEIR TREACHERY AT THE SAME moment as she makes the decision to go for her daily walk. The streets are heavy with multicoloured rhododendrons, shameless azaleas, wilting magnolias, and Penelope has, with some fractiousness, been waiting for the philandering sun to stop its quixotic comings and goings. Twice she's hobbled out on the back step and shouted, "You Elvis, you!"

Mrs. Moore, next door, can't be expected to guess that Penelope is hurling the ultimate opprobrium, that of a fleshy, golden-sequined, periodically resurrected Elvis, at the teasing sun, and so she adds that to the list she and Mildred are compiling. Mildred introduced herself one day when she called and Penelope was out, and Mrs. Moore — Elizabeth, Betty to her friends — recognized her at once as a kindred spirit and made tea, used her best bone china with the lovely roses, Royal Albert. Mildred appreciated such things. Mildred, she soon realized, was a fine woman, willing to make the greatest of sacrifices and take Penelope in. In Mrs. Moore's opinion Penelope should be down on her knees giving thanks.

They are forecasting a Pacific low that will come howling in over the Strait of Georgia tonight, packed with several barrels of rain, but for now Penelope thinks the clouds have conceded the battle, and it's when she gets up to put on her runners that the knees suddenly send out needlelike slivers of pain in both directions.

Sabotage. "Get a grip," she cajoles, and while she massages the aching joints she thinks of the pilgrims in India or somewhere who go up all those steps on their knees. (The thought makes her quite faint.) But she doesn't give in. For if there is one thing Penelope has learned to recognize in her three score years and ten, it is a psychosomatic illness when she meets it. An ache that springs up here, a palpitation there: unequivocal signals of below-stairs conflict.

Below-stairs stuff can be tricky. When, out of the corner of her mind's eye, Penelope catches the shape of something black and heavy rising up like bread dough, she often finds it wiser to simply stomp on the trap door. But sometimes, if the conflict is severe enough, it is risky to leave it unattended. It can lead to something worse – at her age, possibly something much worse.

A judgment call. This time the knees aren't giving her much choice; she laces up her runners and starts out, wincing at nearly every step. She almost crawls up the hill to her bench and then collapses gratefully onto it, and, as she settles back, says, "So what's with my subconscious, Sigmund?"

Sigmund is Sigmund Freud. Penelope knows it is impertinent, but she calls him Sigmund to reduce him to human proportions. "Freud" alone sounds too much like "God" — a confluence that would not have displeased him (Freud, not God) — and Dr. Freud sounds like the old boy establishment, too sequestered for meaningful interchange. She toyed initially with "Siggie," but there are limits. One could scarcely expect someone of his stature to acknowledge flippancy.

Penelope became a fan many years ago after the fainting spell in Roujan, when her darkening dreams led her to the edge of the unsuspected. She read *The Interpretation of Dreams* and was heartened, although in time she came to suspect that Freud's interpretations did not work for her, that a diversity tied up with sexual instinct alone does not encompass all of a woman's spiritual life. (She can't speak for men; she just wishes Sigmund had been similarly circumspect.) But you have to hand it to him, he identified and labelled the subconscious, and Penelope has stumbled over enough of its resident detritus to know that it can't simply be dismissed out of hand.

She braces herself sideways on the bench so that her aching legs can be stretched out, but nothing in the way of a specific worry surfaces. Brenda? Certainly Brenda and her fractured love life do give her concern, but Penelope doesn't think that perturbs her unduly. Brenda has never been easy; she is an intense person — as Penelope had been — caught up in the present, unable to take kinder comfort from the long view.

Typical of Brenda to love someone like that encumbered Gil so passionately. Whereas Gordon — has he ever been in love?

Slept with anyone, even? Of course he has, Penelope knows perfectly well what Gordon's guilt regarding Ivan was all about.

But she is quite sure he has been circumspect, and once again Penelope marvels at the way her twin children seemingly divided the spectrum of human internal resources in the womb. In their shared space it was as though Brenda vetted the situation and cornered all the warm and impulsive genes while they were up for grabs, leaving Gordon with the cool and cautious and cerebral leftovers. Even at birth she refused to give way. Instead of being curled head to toe as twins usually were, their two heads were side by side, so that the birth was long and arduous while the doctor attempted to turn Brenda, whose head was closest to the exit. But Brenda had refused to come second into this world, and he had been about to do a Caesarian when Gordon unexpectedly and obligingly reversed himself.

Perhaps Brenda's erstwhile love, what's-his-name — Gil — was a substitute for some unfulfilled need. For Brenda's dead father perhaps? Brenda had excoriated poor Grover during her adolescence, then as an adult had loved him (perhaps more than Penelope herself had done? She doesn't need to know that). Brenda mourned his death with a fervour that left Penelope shaken and marginally guilty.

Brenda will get over Gil, in time. And over Colin too, at least Penelope hopes so. Surely Brenda won't go into a loveless marriage. The *Globe and Mail's* Social Studies page this very morning quoted Bertrand Russell: "Civilized people cannot fully satisfy their sexual instinct without love." Should she send the clipping along to Brenda? No, better not, there are some things that can't be taught, that must be learned the usual, hands-on way.

Brenda's love life definitely doesn't account for the knees. Nor her joblessness (Brenda won't put Jason at risk, Penelope knows that). Although she is somewhat concerned over Brenda's health (she has the flu again). But not enough to be causing this.

"Sigmund!" she calls, more loudly this time, not because she thinks a disembodied Freud would be hard of hearing — a directed thought, when visiting with the great but dead, would probably do the trick — but just in case their communication is limited to sound waves. And because spoken words help to focus her thoughts.

Usually Penelope is careful to hold such conversations in the privacy of her own home, so that she jumps and almost falls off the bench when a man's voice says, "Sorry, I didn't quite get what you said."

It isn't Sigmund Freud of course, nor God either for that matter, it's just The Spoiler. Penelope is struck, as she always is, by his unlikely beauty, if that is a term you can use for a man, waving flaxen hair, pink and white skin, Greek-godlike features. Penelope can see why any woman, Anne, would — what's the word? — flip, yes, flip over him.

He is standing on the sidewalk grinning pleasantly. "Sorry," he says. "I thought you said something."

"Just talking to myself." Penelope feels quite daring, although she wouldn't be so foolish as to say, "Talking to Freud."

The Spoiler laughs, perhaps more heartily than necessary. "Hey! I do that all the time too. Kids think I'm nuts."

Those would be Anne's kids.

"It's when you start answering yourself, that's when you

should start to worry." The brilliant blue eyes attempt a twinkle. "Well, nice talkin' to you, see ya around," and then, an afterthought, "Oh, hey, the kid found the locket, no sweat. I'm just off to the school now."

He strides off, his six-foot-something, leather-jacketed, athletic-looking body balanced gracefully – wouldn't you know? – on the balls of his loafer-enclosed feet (he doesn't grub about in sweats and runners), his head thrown back as he whistles something that sounds like the Phantom of the Opera.

KATE MUST BE TEN OR ELEVEN YEARS OLD NOW, "poised between childhood and womanhood," as the romantic novelists would say. Penelope shoos a cat off the bench and recites this aloud, laughing with delight at the plummy, fruity sound of it. "Trembling on the brink," she declaims to the indignant cat, "her hair like spun gold shimmering in the slight breeze, silken, or how about weblike? Weblike against the sun, highlighting the spider within." Penelope lets out a yelp, then glances furtively around to see if anyone has heard.

The cat stalks off and the grounds seem safely deserted, and Penelope thinks of the story that went the rounds when Brenda was a teenager, about the girl who refused to wash or comb out the beehive tower on her head and was bitten to death by the nest of black widow spiders it was hosting.

The story was apocryphal, had to be. Nevertheless it has left her feeling slightly agitated, and, forgetting her knees, she jumps up and is blasted with pain.

She must be zeroing in. Something she was thinking about. Black widow spiders? – hardly, she isn't even afraid of spiders. Garter snakes, that's something else. Anyway, they (black widows) don't live around here.

In the distance she can see Vancouver's outer harbour, sheltering six or seven container ships swinging at anchor, their rusty hulls low in the water, waiting, like dispossessed immigrants, for the bureaucracy to let them in. And sailing past them, its bow in the air as though fearful of contamination, the Love Boat, as whitely virginal as its TV image, jaunty with its cargo of frisky seniors searching, if not for love, at least for the lobster Mornay.

Beehive hairdos? Most people wouldn't know one if they were clobbered with it, much less live in dread of meeting one. It was only a hairdo, for heaven's sake, and even when they were popular they had no death-dealing properties that Penelope has heard of, short of a tendency for young women to be top-heavy.

Cautiously she stretches her legs out and gazes at the bright red salvia in the round bed, set off by blue flowers whose name she forgets, and then reaches out to touch the great Douglas fir beside her.

Its comforting solidity, she knows, is deceptive.

Until lately she saw trees as tall and stalwart, friendly, shedders of leaves or needles, shade givers, threats to hydro lines, oxygen suppliers. But the Science for Seniors course has forever altered her perceptions, and to some extent Penelope regrets this loss of innocence. Now she is afflicted with a vision of trees as tightly clustered agglomerations of cohesive atoms and molecules, vibrating at dizzying speeds, held together by a fierce magnetism.

She stands up cautiously and tries to remember what she had

been thinking about before beehive hairdos. The family The Spoiler had spoiled. A warning jab. Anne? The Spoiler? Kate?

The left leg flashes a red alert from knee to ankle, and she is forced to prop herself against the bench.

"Back to you, Sigmund," she says. Or perhaps Carl Jung would be more appropriate. Brenda has just sent her *The Portable Jung*, and Penelope likes what she's read so far, since he isn't all sex.

CARL JUNG CAME FROM A LITTLE SWISS TOWN, WHERE "there were dreams which foresaw the death of certain persons, clocks which stopped at the moment of death, glasses which shattered at the critical moment."

After Jung's first published works he and Sigmund Freud became friends, then master and disciple, but by the time they had their famous confrontation over what Freud came to call Jung's "spook complex," Freud was already sulking over Jung's defection from the true path of sexual repression.

In 1909 Jung visited Freud in Vienna and asked Freud what he thought of precognition and parapsychology in general. Not much, apparently. Freud finally asked Jung point blank to promise never to abandon the sexual theory, and, in Freud's own words, to "guard it against the black tide of mud of occultism." Jung, however, could not agree that sexual trauma was the basis of all ills, and stubbornly insisted that there was something greater manifesting itself in the spirit of man. (And possibly woman.)

The disagreement led to one of the most bizarre encounters in the annals of psychology. This is how Jung described it: "I had a curious sensation. It was as if my diaphragm were made of iron and were becoming red-hot — a glowing vault. And at that moment there was such a loud report in the bookcase, which stood right next to us, that we both started up in alarm, fearing the thing was going to topple over on us. I said to Freud, 'There, that is an example of a so-called catalytic exteriorization phenomenon.'

"'Oh come,' he exclaimed. 'That is sheer bosh.'

"'It is not,' I replied. 'You are mistaken, Herr Professor. And to prove my point I now predict that in a moment there will be another such loud report!' Sure enough, no sooner had I said the words than the same detonation went off in the bookcase.'"

BY THE TIME SHE HAS HOBBLED HOME PENELOPE FEELS drained. Her usual method for restoring lost energy is to go out into the garden and kneel beside the pink rhododendron where there is a patch of ground with no periwinkle, and press her palms down on the warm earth. When she does this she feels the warmth rising up through her, a sort of reassurance, as though the earth itself were some kind of human extension, as though it harbours a thick brown energy that once buoyed and comforted primitive people, long before the cerebral cortex began its distracting chattering.

But the knees are not yet able to bend, and so Penelope brews some raspberry tea and tries to meditate by clearing her brain of distracting thoughts. Usually she is unsuccessful, either vetting a dozen errant thoughts or else falling asleep. But today almost at once a scene rises before her eyes, and she is quite excited as she hurries to nail down the memory.

In the tiny village on the Canadian prairies where she lived as a child, her closest friend was the daughter of the station agent (a job of some prestige, bringing with it a red-shingled two-storey house by the tracks), and one evening when she was about five and the children were playing a wild game of tag in the little woods of aspen poplars and saskatoon bushes near the station, Mr. B. played right along with them, just like one of the kids. (Penelope can't remember their last name, *that* must be Freudian. She can only remember the first initial and then she thinks perhaps it's just as well, the times being what they are.)

She was "It", and they were coming after her! Suddenly Mr. B. swooped her up in his arms and ran through the woods to a small clearing, she giggling and excited from the wild run and the close escape. As he set her down he said, "Let's play pretend married, I'll be the Daddy, you be the Mommy." He smoothed the leaf-strewn patch of ground. "We'll lie down here, and I'll show you what Mommy and Daddy do," he whispered.

Oh, children have a built-in radar. It was as though alarm bells went off in her head, as though every sense stood at attention, as though she had met and was now in mortal danger.

This is what surprises Penelope now, that she knew peril when she met it, even then, even though it appeared in such affable guise. She can still feel the coolness of the darkening evening, the springiness of the mouldering leaf-bed, its smell of damp decay. She can look up still, in her mind's eye, at the leering giant — a slim, shadowy, pale man in braces and a hat, whose breath smelled, not unpleasantly, of booze — and who was reaching and trembling with his enticing hands.

Are children pre-wired against sexual predation? Or is it the function of fairy tales, with their wicked giants, their ogres, their gap-toothed, leering witches, to implant a necessary message, that there are some inhabitants of this strange new world who will do us irrevocable harm?

She broke free and ran. She tore through the spindly, closely spaced aspens on her sturdy brown legs as though the monsters of nighttime terror were breathing down her neck. Branches reached out to pluck at Mr. B., at his clothes, his grasping arms, while she slid through below branch level. She outmanoeuvred him, and she didn't pause for breath until she got back to the others.

Penelope knows now that she was imprinted, during that wild run, with a caution that has stalked her throughout her life, and that will never leave her now. Looking back she sees that it started then, for even at five she knew enough to never again let herself be in a situation where she was alone with Mr. B. — nor, in the years since, with his fellow travellers.

THE MEMORY HAS LEFT PENELOPE WITH A DEEP, UNSHAKABLE conviction of what it is she must do. She settles herself on her hard kitchen chair, back erect, feet planted on the floor, eyes tightly closed.

She pictures her table, her chairs, *herself*, the way she imagined the Douglas fir in the park, as a great mass of infinitesimal, brightly coloured, whirling galaxies. Every now and then some rogue molecule, escaping the swirling whorls of its binding, perhaps rocketing from her own pitted flesh, comes along and in its chaotic freedom slams into the table's edge, bursting the bonds of a table molecule and sending it flying.

Wear and tear.

She concentrates on The Spoiler, picturing his personal molecules whirling, vibrating, dancing with the speed of light. Then her own head, from which dart little particles of energy, particles that have no mass, neutrinos perhaps, that can fly through air and steel and concrete and the centre of the earth, searching out the vast tunnels between the orbiting electrons of atoms and all the other detritus of space. She aims the concentrated stream so that it hones in on its target, knocking off the single electron of a hydrogen atom here, taking out the lumbering nucleus there, cutting the magnetic stranglehold between two hydrogen atoms and the single oxygen atom in a molecule of water, shearing these and everything else she can corral into The Spoiler's head. She directs this energy (exteriorizing) into all the tiny interstices of his being, and she pictures the rogue particles agitating his thought processes, travelling along wispy grey neurons, leaping the deep canyons of synapses, carrying the single message passed on by the neutrinos, "You have been weighed in the balance and found wanting." (A biblical phrase that Penelope has long admired, and is glad to have found a use for.)

This is exhausting work, but Penelope is buoyed up as she imagines how the bombardment begins to induce paranoia in The Spoiler until he becomes convinced that someone knows, and then she imagines how a flood of fear washes through his brain like a great tsunami as he remembers that Penelope may have heard something.

For The Spoiler — if her knees haven't misled her and her assumptions are correct — will have done this before, and will perhaps have been caught. If he is guilty the turmoil in his head will send him away. His leaving will be proof.

Of course there's always the possibility — Penelope isn't one of those people who think they are infallible — that she may have misjudged The Spoiler, in which case no harm done, merely one of those mild, inexplicable uneasinesses common to all of us from time to time, and which he will shrug off in a day or so.

She isn't surprised when she hears, later, on *Quirks and Quarks*, that scientists in Australia have found that the brain's electrical impulses can be trained to switch on a light. In fact she marvels that they took so long to catch on.

Her knees begin to improve.

JUNE

Brenda's occupation, or former occupation, has made her acutely aware of the dearth of women's stories in the history books. Wars! she exclaims. Fought by men! Started by men! Men killing men! And what were the women doing while the men sliced one another up? Hah! Sitting at home sawing off chastity belts would be her guess. She has been urging Penelope to write down some of the things she remembers from her childhood.

This would be a good time to start, Penelope thinks, while her knees are bothering her. There are plenty of spare pages at the back of the notebook she uses for Science for Seniors. For the hundredth time she resolves to buy a computer, even though — the stumbling block — learning it would take up precious time. But Brenda assures her that in the end it would help her enormously, especially with her science assignments.

Where to begin? She searches for something defining, and comes up with the "dirty thirties," as those depression-ridden years came to be known.

The summers of the "dirty thirties," she writes, *were long, oppressive,* grasshopper ridden, and, at least on the Saskatchewan prairies, hot with the bright, protected clarity that must have been the norm, all those millions of years since the dinosaurs, before we started messing up.

So, today's question: what did we do with ourselves, we who were children, hour by hour, minute by minute, in the great hush before television?

She was going to write, "in the innocent years," but on reflection she thinks that innocence may dwell only in the eyes of the nostalgia-beguiled beholder. Innocence is about much more than street smarts; innocence and its loss are at the very core of human tragedy and comedy, and then she reflects on how true this is, that when we meet up with the facts that set our preconceptions on their heels the experience is both liberating and imprisoning. "What you don't know won't hurt you," as her mother always said.

Of course we were innocent in ways that are not offered to today's children, insulated compared to them, muffled in cotton batting against the unharnessed electronic universe, yet we knew something was up. Children can always tell. Even though the dimensions of our world were defined by the fairgrounds on the east, the highway on the west, the tracks and the giant red grain elevators rising on the north, and the distant bluffs of trees on the south, inside those boundaries we may have had a better crack at losing at least one kind of innocence than children in the middle of large cities today, because we weren't watched. We were turned loose in the mornings of the great daylight and encouraged to "stay out of our mothers' hair," until hunger and sleep gathered us in.

Small prairie towns were hotbeds of childish shenanigans — at least ours was. Barefoot boys and girls of four and five were easily hidden by the low bushes, and in tiny clearings we explored our orifices and appendages with mutual giggling curiosity, well aware that such explorations were forbidden;

aware that our parents knew something and did something they weren't talking about; curious, as all children are, to find out what it was.

I remember, when we were very little, trying to figure out where my brother's tiny penis could possibly be inserted to cause such loaded silences, but I never understood it; as for him, he hated being the subject of experiment.

Penelope wonders if she should write a thing like this, perhaps one can be too open, or as Brenda would say, let too much hang out. She has always felt some guilt about her brother, remembers quite clearly urging him to try to separate the puffy labia of a younger three-year-old in an attempt to settle once and for all whether or not this bizarre rumour had any truth to it. At that time, Penelope was almost five and the ringleader/instigator.

She can scratch it out later if that's what she decides.

Certainly we gave our versions of original sin more than passing thought, but no more than we gave to the building of tree houses, the late dusk challenge of hide-and-seek, the tantalizing reward of a Sunday trip to the lake.

Not that we didn't have adult child abusers; they weren't sprung unheralded into modern times, and then she tells the tale of her own near trauma with Mr. B., whose name still eludes her.

Children live in a network only vaguely apprehended by the adults around them, Penelope remembers that clearly. As time went on, all the kids came to "know" about Mr. B. – or at least they knew "something," a personal experience, a bit of hearsay, some wildly inflated, titillating tale, unlikely amalgams of invention and partial truths. *We giggled and exchanged gossip,* she writes, *about how he had driven his other daughter (not my friend) and a companion to a lonely road and persuaded the companion to "do it,"* although we were still unsure of what "it" consisted.

I don't know where the truth lay. I know now that Mr. B. drank and that his wife covered for him. She was a stout German woman who could throw the heavy switches on the CPR tracks, and she learned to send telegrams in Morse code in a language that would remain forever clumsy on her tongue. The adults in the town treated him with ill-concealed contempt, but they tolerated him; they knew nothing of the Mr. Hyde hidden beneath the bumbling, good-willed exterior.

Years later Penelope had finally told her mother. "But why didn't someone tell?" she gasped.

A good question, to which Penelope doesn't know the answer. All she knows is that the children, every one of them, knew about him, and that not one ever told an adult.

Penelope puts her pen down. She isn't quite sure why these recollections are making her uneasy but she feels a strong need to get out, knees or no knees. She puts on her runners and thinks she can always cut back at the halfway mark if the walk bothers her too much.

WHAT IS SO RARE AS A DAY IN JUNE, ANNE LEWIS IS thinking sarcastically. The sparkling day is doing nothing to alleviate a heaviness that has attached itself to the soles of her shoes, the hem of her skirt, as though lead coins had been sewn into the buckles and seams and are weighing her down.

She is in her front yard, listlessly pushing an ancient manual lawn mower over her small patch of grass, trying not to let herself wonder why Richard won't take hold and do these sorts of domestic jobs. That was one thing about Don, the husband from whom she is separated — you could hardly pry him loose from his electric lawn mower, the only possession he seemed to care enough about to take with him when he moved out.

She stoops to smell a single flamboyant peach-coloured rose on a scraggly rose bush — old Mrs. Stevens says it doesn't get enough light, thanks to the overgrown bloody hemlocks.

Think of the devil. In the distance she sees Penelope and notes that her hands are flying about in an uncontrolled sort of way and she is muttering to herself. She seems to be having difficulty walking.

Anne stifles an impulse to go inside. Richard says he's sure the old girl's lost her marbles, that she accosted him with some wild tale about Kate losing a necklace, that it made Kate cry. Anne knows Penelope has a small streak of eccentricity but she has always liked her, found her small singularities amusing, her feistiness reassuring, likes the way she enthuses about blossoms and rhododendrons and how new bushes must be shaped, fertilized, watered, sheltered, like wayward children needing guidance.

But for the last year Anne has been tempted to hide whenever she sees Penelope approaching. She feels a kind of shame, or no, not shame, shame implies wrongdoing, more like embarrassment, when she meets her. Penelope disapproves of Richard; Anne saw it in her eyes the first time she and Richard encountered Penelope on her walk, in those early, knee-melting, joyous days of that lost, mad spring.

But it's already too late. Anne stands her ground. "Hello Mrs. Stevens. Is your leg bothering you?"

Anne is surprised that Penelope doesn't respond, that she stops in her tracks, seemingly at a loss, almost as though she doesn't recognize Anne, and finally seems to focus, then blurts out, "How is Kate?"

"Fine, fine thank you," Anne says, although this isn't entirely true. She's been worrying about Kate. Lately Kate has been withdrawn, acting strangely, not doing well at school. At first Kate loved Richard so much she was like a rival to Anne, all over him with the innocent abandonment of a child, but now.... "She misses her father, I guess," Anne says, without intending to.

"Only a parent is capable of the kind of disinterested love a child needs to thrive on. Anyone else may be suspect."

Anne is surprised. She wonders if Penelope is chastising her, or merely trying to have the kind of conversation Anne would expect to have with a contemporary, although not usually with an older person. She doesn't know how to respond, and then as the remark takes hold she has to bite her tongue against a sudden uprush of anger.

"It troubled me to see her crying," Penelope goes on. "I can't imagine that the locket was that valuable." She turns away abruptly, as though she has said more than she intended.

For a long time Anne stares after her receding back. Suddenly she glances at her watch and runs for her purse and car keys, even though Richard phoned to say he would pick up Kate on his way home, that he was leaving the office early.

SUDDENLY PENELOPE FEELS A HEADINESS, A JOYOUS lightness that makes her want to skip down the sidewalk — although the knees will scarcely let her walk. The mountains are shimmering in a slant of light that traces the outline of distant firs against the intense blue of the sky, and the scent of roses from a passing garden takes her back to the wild rose country of her youth. "My heart leaps up when I behold a rainbow in the sky," she says, flinging her arms wide, and thinks this is what Wordsworth meant, this bursting hymn of praise, this "Hallelujah Chorus" in the head. Thanking the Lord (or Whoever) for Its bounty.

But no sooner does she begin to scrutinize her joy than a childish belief slithers in, that if you indicate to God (or Whoever) your appreciation, He/She or It will, in some way, reward you. She scorns the half-hopeful wish, but as the unadulterated joy retreats before analysis, she thinks that introspection is not an unmixed blessing.

When Penelope gets home she sees her journal still open on her table, and wonders whatever happened to her friend, Mr. B's daughter. Oh what a friendship that first one is! The fulfilment in discovering a kindred spirit, a being who thinks as you do, who can confide her longings and terrors and meet instant resonance and understanding, who loves to build forts as much as to play with dolls, who brings an imagination that reinforces and supplements your own. Little girls feel a bonding for years with such a friend, a different kind of attachment than that afforded by parents.

Her friend had, Penelope remembers, been a self-possessed child. She never hinted that she knew anything of her father's predilection and Penelope would never have considered asking her.

She married and moved away. She and Penelope exchanged

Christmas cards until she died, very young, at forty, in a faraway country, in Africa. Penelope has never heard what happened to Mr. B. Probably he sank into a boozy old age and died, mourned, she supposes, by those who thought they knew him.

Gordon and Brenda, as children, had never felt the need to go outside their charmed twosome to find a soulmate, as Penelope had. They were self-sufficient, and Penelope feels some pride about this.

PENELOPE'S PRIDE WOULD SUFFER A SETBACK IF SHE KNEW that Gordon has come to decry the insularity of a childhood that centred around his and Brenda's companionship, because when one of them – Brenda – grew older and defected, Gordon was left with an interior space that was scarcely acknowledged, but felt like loss.

Gordon begins to comtemplate the ramifications of his loss. Ordinarily he doesn't go in for this kind of delving, but not only Dr. Weinburg but Penelope herself has given him the needed prod. Penelope applauded his love for Ivan. Prior to that Gordon was cautious about defining his affection (Dr. Weinburg hinted at elements of sexuality), but Penelope's praise has left him reassured. And relieved – Gordon has, at times, suspected that his own nature might not be privy to the grand passions.

And if, as Dr. Weinberg believed, the roots of his aura affliction were psychological – buried trauma, not to mention guilt – the large dollops of guilt Gordon has now unearthed surely meant that he is, finally, cured.

And so he is caught off guard when the auras return on Sunday during meditation. Gordon often uses meditation as a time to look out over the congregation and remind himself of those he should seek out, the backsliders who aren't doing what, in the heat of altruism, they have pledged to do, and who sometimes leave the church rather than cope with their guilt. Gordon gives them absolution, if not love.

Meditation also affords an opportunity to review the shifting tide of "relationships" in the church, an exercise that usually leaves him ruminating sourly on the complexities of the sexual revolution. Gordon's great-grandfather (Penelope's grandfather) was a Baptist minister. Penelope has often recounted how the old devil — who lived to a devilish old age — believed in God and monogamy and his wife's holiness, and Gordon can remember how, in the old man's dotage, he would expound, to the embarrassment of those around him, on the way his wife's holiness had manifested itself in a natural and commendable distaste for intercourse. Victorian times, Victorian beliefs. Sometimes Gordon envies him.

He closes his eyes as Mozart's twenty-first symphony begins, and tries to let it soothe his turbulence. Penelope has always claimed that music (by which she means Mozart, Beethoven, and Bach, and perhaps a thin slice of Stravinsky) is an ancient language wired right into the brain, and that it is capable of delivering subliminal messages — although she has never confided, at least to Gordon, their content.

Gordon raises his head to examine the silent congregation and is dazzled by an entire church alight, blazing and shimmering a foot above the heads of the meditating people. Quickly he closes his eyes, covers his face with one hand, then peeks through his fingers. The vibrating mass has not dimmed; if anything, it has increased in intensity.

Reminding himself that scintillating lights are among the commonest of migraine auras, Gordon forces himself to uncover his eyes and, invoking the cross of science that will keep the devil at bay, observes carefully. He avoids Camilla Clark and concentrates instead on Smith Harbit-Jones who is, as always, directly in front, and again sporting bright, shimmering, leaf green.

Next to him Janet Livingstone (she and Harbit-Jones have a relationship that has been the subject of intense analysis by the Living Relationships group) shimmers under a kaleidoscope of colours, mostly blues, almost no green, and an occasional flare of red that is dampened immediately by the blue. Now that Gordon thinks of it, without Cyril Fogarty there is very little red. Cyril has left the church in a huff over what he calls its pseudo-intellectualism, and because Camilla has spurned his money along with his advances.

The familiar *andante* signals the end of meditation, and involuntarily Gordon looks at Camilla. He regrets it immediately. Camilla's features are even and tranquil, yet when she catches Gordon's eye he remembers, suddenly, an old black and white photo of Marilyn Monroe that he, as an adolescent, kept under the mattress. (Penelope found it and stared at it for five minutes, trying to understand what it was that men saw to worship in that pale and baffled face. In the end she smoothed it out and returned it.)

Camilla doesn't look like Marilyn Monroe, yet on occasion there will be a glint in her blue eyes, a cross between innocence and sexuality, that has led more men than Cyril Fogarty to make fools of themselves.

The clear light around Camilla isn't white as much as it is dazzling, and as the music steals into the room the light becomes so intense that her features seem to merge into the shimmering mass, and Gordon has to look away. At the same time he is aware of sexual disturbance in his groin, and he surmises that the auras may be causing a hormonal upset.

Evading Harbit-Jones, Gordon slips into his tiny office and closes the door. He needs to get a grip, if not on himself, at least on the face he shows the world. Not, as Gordon has himself explained countless times, that a malfunction of the brain is any more shameful than a malfunction of the heart, but he has to be pragmatic: he is there to succour, and one can only succour from strength. He sits down and assumes the meditating position, which the congregation substitutes for prayer – head back, eyes closed, hands resting on his knees and cupped upward to receive whatever there was to be had of tranquility.

At once an image of Brenda intrudes itself and his cupped hands form fists.

When, in that time long past, he flew to California and Brenda's rescue, she claimed she was seeing auras. He said flatly that she was lying. (Brenda was given to exaggeration.) He said she was a victim of her bizarre environment, California T-groups and primal screams and communal living. She laughed at him and bragged that she'd seen her lover's aura – magenta, it was – at the moment of ecstacy.

That shook Gordon severely – he and Brenda were only

seventeen at the time – and he shouted that Tom, the barefoot
Hare Krishna who jigged along after her, was no more her lover
than the man in the moon. She tossed her black hair over her face
and peeked out at him with a superior, teasing smile and he
retreated, the anger fading before a kind of grief that welled up
from the soles of his shoes and enveloped him like heavy air, so
that he had to strain against it as he went on about his life. It came
to him only later that he didn't know what colour magenta was.

He phones Dr. Weinburg and makes an appointment for the
following week.

JUST AS PENELOPE IS ABOUT TO HEAD OUT THAT EVENING
for this month's potluck dinner, Brenda phones to say that she
and Jason will be arriving the next day. She says she'll explain
when she gets there, and Penelope picks up a low-key worry, as
though electricity can transmit bad vibes via telephone wires.

It is handy, though, to be able to mention the fact casually as
Mildred greets her. "How do you stand it, a child around the
place like that?" Mildred asks querulously, and Penelope notes
that No-name Mildred, who has been in hiding for some time,
is front and centre tonight.

Edwin, she notes, is not gracing their little get-together. "No
Edwin?" she asks, casually.

"Disappointed, are you Penny – ah, Penelope?" Mildred asks
loudly, with just the trace of a leer.

There isn't much Penelope can reply to that. A denial would be
interpreted as a *blushing* denial, so she just smiles and turns to old

Tom and asks what he's reading. Before Tom can answer, Mildred snatches the book away from him and reminds him that this is a social occasion, for heaven's sake he can read at home the rest of the year.

This doesn't appear to faze Tom at all, but it bothers Penelope. She is tempted to stick one foot out and trip Mildred, the way the girls did back in Grade Six when someone got too big for their britches.

THE FOLLOW-UP MAMMOGRAM BRENDA HAD IN GIBSONS requires more tests, she tells Penelope, and as that will mean babystitting for Jason she thought she'd have the tests done in Vancouver.

"They're almost certain it's just a cyst, apparently very common at my age, but they always make a big deal where breasts are involved. Sometimes I think they're a curse laid on women, don't you? Men see them before they see your face, and as for your brains, big deal! Boobs beat brains any day."

Penelope laughs, and the taut strings of fear loosen somewhat, although from now on, like a virus that feeds on tranquility, fear will never quite disappear.

Penelope and Brenda settle themselves for a companionable cup of tea, and Penelope gets out the new jigsaw puzzle she has bought for Jason. Jason wishes she had a computer.

"A serious question, Mother. Should I marry Colin?"

Penelope holds herself very still. "I thought he hadn't popped the question."

"How do you pop a question?" Jason wants to know, and

Brenda tells him it's an old-fashioned expression meaning to ask someone to marry you. She shoos him into the den and shuts the door firmly on his cries of "Pop! Pop! Pop!"

"He has. But there are complications," Brenda tells Penelope.

"Such as?"

"Well, for starters, would I want to be sitting at home jobless while he tears off to L.A. and points east?"

"What does he say to that?"

"Believe it or not, old Hatchet-face has offered him *my* job, although Colin didn't admit that to me. He says he's considering applying for it, since we both want family and we'd need to start right away and he wouldn't want to leave me home barefoot and pregnant. No, he doesn't say it like that, but that's the gist, more or less."

"It would be hard not to resent his having your job."

"You're damn right, especially since I loved my work. But I did quit of my own free will."

"I wonder."

"Whether I quit of my own free will? Of course I did...."

"No. Whether or not we have free will. But that's another question. The important one here is, do you love Colin?"

"No. Yes, in a way, but...."

"Not truly, madly, deeply."

"No. But it seems to me if we're compatible and surprise! his mother likes me, that should be enough. Were you madly in love with Dad? Yes, I'm sure you were, that was a real love match."

Is that how it seemed to Brenda? Penelope chooses her words carefully. "I was only twenty. There wasn't much to compare it with. And yes, I would say we had a good marriage."

Sometimes. For in any marriage there is a twisting and tearing going on beneath the surface. Penelope envisions little polarized tentacles, like charged strands of spiderweb, that wave around each of us searching for attachments. As the years go by two people will acquire an invisible, impenetrable forest of these interwoven strands, a tangled fishnet binding them together. Fierce attractions, fierce repulsions, easygoing linkages, disparate viewpoints, strengths, failures, approvals, disapprovals, some tentacles disconsolate and flapping when Time's Up and others that won't let go. For a long time after Grover's death Penelope felt as though the severed tentacles were in such pain they might never heal. "But would they have grown in the first place, without that passionate binding?" she asks aloud, and Brenda, exasperated, says, "Mother! I come to you in need and you tune out."

"You ask a hard question, you have to wait for the processing. Yes, I was in love..." Penelope doesn't like people to make little quotation marks in the air, although the two words tempt her "...when I married. I think you need that – passion – to get you over the hard parts that come later."

Brenda is intrigued. "Did you have hard parts?" she asks, but Penelope isn't about to let herself be trapped in that quicksand.

"Just my children," she quips, and then, "Back to you. Why do you want to marry this man you don't seem to love?"

"I respect him, I want a family, we're compatible...."

"How compatible? I suppose you mean sex." She sighs. "Does he have a sense of humour?"

"Not big."

"Does he like tree houses?"

"No, but we wouldn't live in one...."

"Approve of tree houses, then?"

"No. He loves Jason."

This throws Penelope for a moment, because it *is* important. "That's a big plus. But Jason is not exactly unloved without him."

"Do I get the feeling you aren't in favour?"

"I wouldn't marry someone without love, or passion, or whatever you want to call it. What if you then met your true love, like that Gil of yours, the red-hot star-crossed focus of your life?"

Good point, although Brenda doesn't expect lightning to strike twice. Still, she nods thoughtfully and is marginally happier, although she shouldn't be, she really *wants* to be married. She thinks Gordon would approve of marriage, although, trust Gordon, he hasn't tried it yet. She wonders what Connie would think.

BRENDA HASN'T SEEN CONNIE SINCE CHRISTMAS, SO the next day she leaves Jason with Penelope, since Tommy will be off to kindergarten, and heads for West Vancouver.

Connie opens the beautiful carved door as though its weight is more than she can manage. "Hi, Bren," she says, the words thick on her tongue. As she ushers Brenda into the sunroom she explains that she went back to work for a month but "couldn't take the rat race," and then is so silent and withdrawn that Brenda babbles feverishly about Colin to fill the silence. She can't be sure that Connie is even interested.

"Colin's mother is away, so we went back to her apartment last night. I think Colin felt very wicked, making love in the maternal nest."

"Love?" Connie asks. "What has fucking got to do with love?"

Brenda is taken aback. "Hey, that's the point of *my* story. By the way, why do you ask?"

"Sorry. Academic curiosity I guess." Connie opens a bottle of wine. "Go on. What happened?"

"Afterwards, you mean? While he had his shower I drank some wine, then fortified myself with a liqueur. His mother keeps a well-stocked cabinet, I'll say that for her. Anyway, when I heard the water stop I went in and blurted at the shower curtain, Colin, are you in love with me?"

"A fair question, considering." Connie pours the wine into tumblers and forgets to say "Cheers." "Go on," she says.

"It took about two minutes, but finally he sort of mumbled, Bren, I think I answered that question. Uh-uh, I said. You asked me to marry you. You didn't say you loved me.

"He finally came dripping out and proceeded to dry very thoroughly – I'm sure his mother taught him well. Gave the hair a real going-over, toes one by one, behind his knees, kind of cupped his balls carefully in one hand and blotted them with the towel. He didn't answer at first, and when he did he was kind of sniffy. I'd think that would be a foregone conclusion, he said. I pointed out that maybe he just thought we were very compatible, or that he might feel responsible for our long-term relationship, or grateful for my job, or maybe just sorry for me. Perhaps, I expanded, he just thought it was time to get married since his mother might like some grandchildren before she's too old to enjoy them?

"He didn't think much of the motives I was attributing to him, said they aren't motives he'd want to think he has. I ended up assuring him that I didn't have a low opinion of him, and I promised never to ask again if he'd just answer that one question and say he loved me."

"Let me guess," Connie says, pouring more wine into her glass. "He got dressed and left."

"Right on. He said he thought we wouldn't tell his mother just yet about our marriage plans. I reminded him that I hadn't said yes, and here's the part that really burnt me. He was very sweet and quite patient, and he asked me not to take it wrong if he gave me a word of advice."

"Cut out the booze?"

"How did you know?"

"I've been there."

"What he actually said was that I shouldn't drink liqueur, especially after a lot of wine. God knows *I* know that, and usually I have enough brains not to, these days."

"Does he love you, do you think?"

"I don't know."

"Do *you* love him?"

"I don't know.

"When you don't know, then you don't. That should make your decision easier."

"Right. What it shouldn't do is make me feel shitty, undesirable, worthless. It does."

Gil didn't make her feel that way, even when he left.

Connie is holding the almost-empty wine bottle as Brenda grabs her handbag to leave. Connie doesn't get up. She waves and says, listlessly, "Don't do it, Bren. Not worth it." It occurs to Brenda that the tic has disappeared.

But as Brenda starts down the steps Connie pushes herself out of her chair, and, still holding her glass, follows Brenda to the door. "I can't believe you don't remember Madam Pele in Hawaii," she says.

"Afraid I don't. Why, what did she see in my future?"

"She wouldn't say. She said she couldn't, that you hadn't decided."

"Not to worry. Survival of the fattest, as you know," and finally Connie laughs and stands in the open door waving until Brenda is out of sight.

THE NEXT MORNING PENELOPE'S KNEES HAVE CLEARED UP.

So! The Spoiler has gone. "No thanks to you, Sigmund," she begins to shout, then stops herself so as not to waken Brenda and Jason. Although, give him his due, Sigmund was partly right; he and Jung were like the blind men and the elephant, both were partly in the right and both were in the wrong.

Just as well, though, that Freud didn't cotton on to catalytic exteriorization. It's a powerful tool and not for everyone, especially those (like Sigmund) with a lot of enemies.

Penelope feels both humble and proud to be the possessor of such knowledge, and, addressing the picture of Carl Jung on the cover of his autobiographical book, *Memories, Dreams, and Reflections,* she swears a vow to use her gift sparingly and only in the service of womankind.

Later, when Brenda and Jason have gone to the Science Centre, Penelope goes for her walk. She lingers in front of the Lewis house. There is no one to be seen and finally Penelope ambles on. But just before she turns the corner a minivan stops, and a stocky man gets out. He walks around to the passenger side and slides open the door, then leans in and begins to wrestle with something.

Penelope's heart quickens. From this distance she can't make out who it is or what it is he's struggling with, although it must be heavy. Finally she sees what looks like a long handle emerging. The man continues to pull, and a large object follows the handle. He wrestles it out of the van, and he holds it in the air for a moment before setting it on the sidewalk.

Penelope, with a surge of joy, or triumph, or vindication, can see exactly what it is.

A lawn mower.

July

"**H**I GORDON" (BRENDA WRITES),
"The surgeon wanted to do a mastectomy but I said no dice, lumpectomy. They're my boobs, I said. 'I can't guarantee —' but I said I know you can't, who can? You aren't God, although I think this was news to him. Then, after they got the lump out, they did a mini-Chernobyl on me and I felt wilted, and Mother insisted I wasn't well enough to leave the comfort of her house, and besides I have to go in every week for six weeks (I chose the quick and dirty rather than the slow and tottery) and have stuff dripped in that makes me feel super lousy and is also making my hair fall out in big, furry clumps.

"Mother seems to like having me stay, even though I haven't been a bundle of laughs lately, facing my own mortality and all that, but she didn't exactly have to twist my wrist. Makes for continuity for Jason while I'm being bombarded and poisoned. And there's one small advantage for her that even I admit — keeps Aging Barbie (Mildred) away. Mildred can't stand children. Never babysits her grandchildren ('I raised mine, that's enough'). Probably why Jason always acts up when she comes snooping around.

"Did some snooping myself in the new Roman forum downtown which is laughably called a library. Aren't libraries supposed to be big, silent, studious places? This one has an indoor street and Cappuccino Unlimited. Came up with something new for Mother's research. Thank God. Mother's behaviour when I'm sick gives new currency to the expression 'spaced out.' She goes around being forcedly cheerful and muttering little pleasantries like "it's an ill wind that blows nobody good," and doesn't even laugh, in fact seems to take it seriously, when I counter with that old saw about an oboe being an ill wind that nobody blows good. All it does is remind her that she likes oboes, and she puts on the first movement of Schubert's 'Unfinished' with its downbeat intro that is reminiscent of things I'm trying not to dwell on.

"Anyway, I copied this ancient (sixties) news item from a microfilm of old *Arizona Alternatives* the library is keeping, God knows why. It has lifted Mother, at least for awhile, out of whatever dimension I've sent her into."

Galaxy-wise it was a good day, for which the Children of a Minor Galaxy claimed the credit. The Children had gathered, one hundred strong — the men in robes printed with swirling galaxies and tied with hemp, the women in gowns embroidered with rainbow-ringed Venuses, their hair laced with cactus flowers — on a slab of red shale at the dizzying top of a rock outcropping near the town of Sedona in Arizona, which as faithful readers know is the locus of four energy "ley lines." The confluence of the ley lines is marked by shiny pieces of jewellery, bright bits of glass, multicoloured agates, and the faces of discarded wristwatches, which form the circle of an Indian medicine wheel.

At sunrise The Children meditated on the raising of planetary consciousness. Nothing happened. By nine o'clock ("Brenda! That would have been five o'clock in France! The very time!") the sun in Arizona had been up for some time. The Children, after feasting on tofu and sunflower seeds, were beginning to stretch out in the sun for a nap when they were all, each and every one, overtaken by a sudden and delicious happiness. For no discernible reason they began to chuckle and giggle and roar until tears coursed down their cheeks, and it was only later, when they read of the several recorded events that found their way into the newspapers, that they understood.

Under the heading, "A Good Day On A Minor Galaxy." The Divine Galactic Light was interviewed for this newspaper (see page 12). He made it official: there was a five-minute burst of heightened consciousness on the planet Earth. Thanks, of course, to The Children of a Minor Galaxy.

"So it seems that those five minutes which Mother has dubbed Truffault-time did make some sort of stir here and there throughout the world, a news insert here, a magazine article in some astrological magazine there, and while she prepares nourishing meals for me that would leave me more pleasingly plump than I was in the first place, were I not frequently upchucking, she muses on the meaning of it all.

"She can't get over the synchronicity of the thing: 'Those Children of a Minor Galaxy were the same people we bumped into in Sedona when I was there with Mildred and George!' she keeps exclaiming.

"'Can't be the same ones,' I point out reasonably, 'unless

they've found the Fountain of Youth. This Arizona newspaper is thirty-five years old. Wasn't the Sedona trip just after Dad died?'

"Logic, at the moment, is not her strong point.

"Speaking of things weird and unlikely, what's with you and your auras? Did they depart? If not, why not? Keep me posted, I need distractions. Desperately.

Your battered twin, Brenda."

PENELOPE'S BRAIN HAS GONE INTO SOME SORT OF HOLDING pattern, as if even the automatic act of breathing requires the mustering of all available grey cells.

She is afraid to hope.

Now, though, she begins, tentatively, to inspect the garden with more than perfunctory interest. Begonias are settling in, impatiens doing well, especially the Korean Impatiens with their glossy leaves and pale pink and purple flowers. She admires the subtle blending of colour, congratulates herself for putting them beside a trailing purple geranium, although that's looking a bit straggly. Not enough light. Will the dahlias bloom before September now that she's moved them to a sunnier location? She sighs and wishes the Douglas firs weren't so gigantic, in spite of which she loves them, whirling molecules and all.

Brenda has gone over to Keats Island, between poisoning schedules as she puts it, to collect her computer and other necessaries, and to tell the post office to forward her mail. She needs a separation certificate from the library and application forms for Unemployment Insurance, (or Employment Insurance as it is now euphemistically called), necessary stuff like that. She phoned to say the tree house was well except for traces of some small furry thing – she supposes she should sell, except that tree houses are not a hot real estate item at the moment. Also she says there is a fat letter from Brazil, and Penelope feels the first uplifting of spirits she's felt since – since the surgery.

Penelope takes Jason to the park every day, although he ignores the swings and slides and jungle gyms and insists instead on crossing a small creek on carefully placed stepping stones, falling in the shallow water as often as not and squealing with delight as the water seeps into his runners.

Penelope tries not to play the heavy with him. She knows he isn't himself these days, since Brenda has been sick. He has been told, of course – Brenda is much too modern a mother to keep the child in the dark – but Brenda has also assured him that the doctors now have powerful medicines and she will get better if she just takes the stuff they pump into her. But Jason picks up on the unstated fear, especially Penelope's. He loves Penelope, but not in the visceral, connected way he loves his mother. A low-key unease swirls around in him but he is too young to identify its source. Instead he focusses on perceived threats, losing his beloved tree house, not starting at the Gibsons school in the fall. He isn't even aware that he is acting out, especially at times like the present when Penelope is looking after him.

Penelope now lets him go barefoot in the park but makes him wear the shoes for the walk home.

"Didn't you ever go barefoot, Grandma?" he asks, and she has to admit that she never wore shoes from summer's beginning to end.

She explains that there weren't any concrete sidewalks in the little prairie towns. "The sidewalks were wooden and things fell through the cracks, and beyond that there were no houses or high rises, just flat green, then yellow fields. When I was older I learned that the population on the prairies was one person per square mile, and I used to think about each of those squared miles which I knew were the size of a section of wheat, and wonder which one was my personal section, and whether I would ever live on it."

"Do I have a square mile too, Grandma?" Jason asks, and Penelope doesn't have the heart to tell him that he'll be lucky to have a square foot by the time he's grown.

"After the wheat was cut in mid-August the year I was your age, my feet grew too wide to fit in between the cut rows. The sharp stubble hurt. And rusty nails could kill you, before antibiotics. My Dad would soak and soak a sore foot, and he'd add hot water until I would squeal that he was burning me.

"Later we moved to Lloydminster, which looked like a metropolis to me." Jason is no longer listening, he runs ahead, but Penelope goes on talking as he dances along the sidewalk fifty feet ahead of her. "School and new friends filled my head, and summer freedom was enough of a novelty to sustain my brother and me through the heat of July. But just like you, as surely as July melted into August, novelty melted into boredom. 'There's nothing to do,' we whined, and our mother would pause, in the midst of canning fruit in a kitchen as hot as the seventh circle of Hell, and wipe her glistening brow. If we didn't get out of her sight, she would murmur ominously, there might not be money enough for....

"But we would be gone before the words could become form. You'll find out, Jason, when you get a little older, that words, once uttered, may harden and set like cement. Of course we knew what she meant. Posters everywhere, in the Drug Store windows, flapping in the breeze on telephone poles, nailed to weather-beaten board fences, proclaimed the Big Event, August 15, 16 and 17, the jubilant three days when the fair would 'hit town.' That was the way people said it, as though the fair came at us like a tornado and smashed the whole place sideways with its tinsel and lights, its raucous barkers, its tinny music, the practically bare-naked ladies, the shooting galleries, the noise, the dust."

Several people pause as they pass Penelope, thinking she is addressing them, and Jason, who is nearly six now, waits for her and takes her hand protectively.

"My brother and I lay tingling and wakeful the night before, and in the morning my father dug deeply into his pockets among the nails and staples and candy wrappers. Maybe it was because his father had been a Baptist minister that Dad so actively courted small pleasures of the flesh. He loved sweets and was generous about sharing. The kids all followed him like the Pied Piper, and he found two whole dollars for each of us."

"I have two dollars...." Jason begins.

"Two dollars was a lot of money then. My brother and I ran to the fairgrounds so fast that my heart pounded and I had to slow down, and my brother got there first."

"I could have beaten him," Jason says.

"Except for a weather-beaten grandstand and wooden stage, the area was a barren tract of ground, a breeder of whirlwinds, a home for wandering tumbleweed and purple Russian thistle, usually deserted, but now magically transforming itself — for they were still setting up, we were so early — into a metropolis of Ferris wheels, Tilt-a-Whirls, an Octopus, candy floss and hot dogs and Crown and Anchor and (gasp) prizes!"

Penelope pauses and her eyes shine as she throws her arms into the air to indicate the height of the magical machines and the diversity of the entertainment.

"Oh, I tell you Jason, you've never seen anything like it! Cuddly teddy bears, fake-fur rabbits, beautifully packaged 'toiletry sets,' and even — oh, how my brother's eyes flashed — a twenty-two, a beautiful, shiny, wooden-handled rifle."

"Mother says guns are bad, I can never have one."

"They are, Jason, they are, but oh, in those days, those early days, twenty-twos were revered by boys and tolerated by men; they were great for gophers, and for practising — before the manhood-confirming acquisition of a shotgun — on the swarms of wild ducks that stirred the dark surfaces of prairie sloughs.

"I'm going to win that!" Penelope shouts the words so that a passing dog barks at her, and Jason has to shout even louder to get her attention. "What? Grandma, what are you going to win."

"Not me, it was my brother who was going to win the twenty-two. He was ten and I was thirteen...." and then Penelope's voice falters as she remembers what he was like as a boy, how she loved him.

Penelope speeds up until a plaintive, "Grandma! You're going too fast," brings her up short. Jason tells Brenda about it that evening, when she phones to say she will be one more day and she is fine. Brenda doesn't mention Colin, even though Penelope knows perfectly well that Colin works in Gibsons now.

COLIN HAS BEEN WONDERFUL WHILE BRENDA HAS BEEN SICK, funeral-arrangements of flowers during the week when he's away, lots of visiting on weekends. His mother even came to visit, although she still doesn't know about the marriage proposal. Now it's Brenda who won't let Colin tell her. "What's to tell, Colin? I haven't said yes," she points out, but he just sighs and tries to be patient. The Big C hasn't impaired my brain, she feels like shouting at him. On the other hand she supposes the impairee is the last to know.

They've agreed to meet in Molly's Reach in Gibsons, and Brenda gets there before he does. She watches him loping along with his neat, organized, jogger's springy step – Colin has always been attentive to his body, has never smoked, and eschews red meat.

"Been waiting long?" he asks. She shakes her head and orders a glass of wine – she's allowed one glass a week – and he orders mineral water (never drinks on the job, he says, then chokes a bit as he remembers that this could be construed as insensitive).

When the wine comes she lifts her glass and says, "Here's to your success, Colin."

"You really are a brick, Bren," he says, taking her hand, "and with all you've been through on top of everything else. It must be damn hard for you, seeing me take over a job you really liked, even though you did quit of your own free will."

"It *is* hard," she admits, and blesses the waiter who appears at that moment and causes Colin to drop her hand. Having one's hand held by a kindly, handsome, six-foot-three man who wants marriage could make a brain seize up.

"You folks okay?" the waiter — whose name they have been told is Rick, (Hi, I'm Rick, your waiter) — asks.

"Us folks sure are," Brenda says. Colin looks embarrassed and Rick hesitates, then laughs. They order, and Brenda mucks around with the gooey pasta for awhile until Rick brings coffee. The time has come. She gives up waiting for inspiration and says, simply, "I can't marry you, Colin."

Colin gawks, recovers, and says, "Brenda, just because this — awful business —"

"My cancer?"

Colin squirms. It's not a pleasant word, Brenda knows that. It's not a pleasant thing. Naming it won't make it go away any more than not naming it.

"No, Colin, it's not that. Or perhaps it is in a way. While stuff was dripping into me I had a lot of time to think, and I know it wouldn't work."

There is a long moment while Colin stares at her and then another long moment while he stares into his coffee cup. "I don't get it, Bren," he says finally. "You gave me to understand that you wanted to get married."

"I know," she says miserably. "I should have thought things through first, but I did think I wanted to get married and that it was you who was just — oh, I don't know, just out for a relationship. Not a commitment."

Colin takes his hands off the table, wipes them with the napkin, scrunches in his shoulders and holds his arms tightly against his midriff, hands clutching the opposite elbows. "I'm sorry your opinion of me is so low," he says. Very stiffly. Glancing sideways at the bill as though he is about to bolt.

"Wait, Colin," she says. "Look, it's not like that, I didn't mean to make it sound that way. My opinion of you is not low, in fact the very opposite, but you have to admit you never really said anything that would make me think you really — cared for me like that. So naturally I assumed it was just a good friendship."

"Friendship! Bren, do you usually — well, you know — with your friends?"

"Fuck, you mean?"

Colin glances over his shoulder to make sure no one has heard.

"Sorry," Brenda says. "I didn't mean to offend you. Of course I don't, at least not after reaching the age of discrimination, but you never actually got around to mentioning what your own habits are."

"I am not in the habit of treating the affections of women lightly."

Brenda doesn't feel remotely like laughing. "I'm sorry, Colin.

I guess what I was trying to tell myself was that because you and I are very compatible, and I like you very much and I like your mother, that I cared for you in the marrying way. I tried to convince myself that mutual affection and respect are enough."

"It seems to me that they're enough, Bren. What more do you want?"

"Love," and then Rick, with impeccable timing, repeats, "You guys doing okay?" Brenda shoots him a glance that sends him scurrying to take the bill and Colin's credit card out of her reach.

Colin clears his throat and says, "I didn't think you'd be tied into romantic ideas like that, Bren, but I think it goes without saying that we — ah — love each other, at least that's certainly the case with me, and anyway, it — ah — love, that is, is the kind of thing you expect to achieve during marriage. Mother says she and Dad found that their affection grew and deepened through the years."

"I mean the kind where you have to write love poems and shout them at the world. The psychotic kind."

He looks puzzled. "I'm afraid I'm not following you, Bren."

"Sorry. I guess I'm not explaining myself very well. All I know is that if you start a marriage without — whatever the hell it is — you put it at risk. I mean, your muse or anima or some cute young or even old thing might come along later —" She stops, aware that she isn't getting anywhere. "Oh the hell with it. I'm doing a lousy job, Colin, but what I'm trying to say is, I can't do it. Not right now, anyway."

"I think I know what's bothering you, Bren, and I respect you for it, except that I'm going to have to talk you out of it."

"What's that, Colin?"

"Same thing that was bothering me. You don't want to enter a partnership when you can't carry half the load. Listen, forget it. I'd like to start a family anyway, and I know you want that — as soon as you're well, that is. Plenty of time for you to get back in the workforce later."

She doesn't tell him that she is probably sterile now. He'll think that is the reason. It isn't.

"Thanks Colin, but honestly, that isn't it."

She hates the way his face closes, but she can't take on his hurt; she has enough on her hands. He will have lots of help from her ex-employer.

"I'm sorry, Colin," she says again. Meaning it.

"Don't worry about it, Brenda," he says stiffly. "Well." He stands up. "No doubt we'll see you around."

"I hope so Colin."

She really does hope so. They say goodbye at the door of the restaurant and shake hands in a civilized manner, and she catches the ferry back to Vancouver and feels lost and sad, but as though at least one thing has been put right.

PENELOPE IS ENCOURAGED WHEN BRENDA TELLS HER. She thinks it might jump-start the healing process, although she isn't leaving it entirely to chance. After her initial success with catalytic exteriorization Penelope spends at least a half-hour a day concentrating on any rogue cells in Brenda's body that have evaded the chemicals, annihilating them with streams of the most powerful electrons she can lay her mind on. Glowing, they are, sparkling white arcs like the ones that snuffed out the life of the fireman just last summer, so potent it seems that the physical universe itself could crack and split before them. She beams them into Brenda's body like miniature cruise missiles programmed to reduce the demonic rebels to dust.

Brenda gives her a letter. "Ta da! Brought to you from Brazil by the magic of worldwide communication, from Mme. Truffault's daughter."

Penelope admires the exotic stamps, one of which shows an angel with arms upraised and white lines radiating out behind her.

She hopes this is a sign. Brenda's illness has stalled the Meaning of Life research, and she needs a sign. Mme. Truffault's moments of ecstacy have begun to assume enormous importance in her mind. Catalytic exteriorization may have flushed out The Spoiler, but it doesn't feel to her as though it is working for Brenda. Although she can't afford to take the chance of giving it up.

"I'M SO HAPPY THAT YOUR MOTHER IS INTERESTED," Claire Truffault-Clarke has written, "since what my mother experienced changed our lives."

"My husband Tom and I were living near your Whistler Mountain – perhaps you know about it? – and it was a lonely place many years ago. We had a kind of house like a trailer that big trucks could move from one tree-planting place to another, and it was long and thin like a road."

Claire wrote that she remembered the day clearly. She woke at 7:20 and lay perfectly still. If she moved, the waves from the wake of the minuscule tadpole racketing around in her womb – the motion transmitted by some kind of perverse bodily harmony – would flow through her and make her sick. She thought it must be something akin to the tuning fork the teacher in her science class used to use, whose harmonic frequency set up sympathetic vibrations in a crystal glass and shattered it. She sometimes wondered if the tiny life would end by shattering her.

She didn't want Tom to notice her *mal-de-mer*, because that would start the pressure again. When he first found out that she was pregnant Tom wanted her to get rid of it. Now. In the first trimester, before it was too late. Oh sure, he would explain, I want kids when the time comes. Not now. We can't afford it. I'm planting *trees*, for God's sake. To get me through medical school. At such times Claire pretended that her grasp of English was inadequate.

Now, when Tom came in, rosy from the shower, she calmed the sea with an effort of will and said, "Plant one for me!" and when he answered, wryly, "I'm afraid I already did," she laughed far beyond the strength of the joke.

After Tom's pickup truck had roared into the distance she slid carefully from the spine-cracking pullout bed and ran for the bathroom.

Throwing up left her weak. She sat on a hard chair and obediently nibbled a cracker (Tom had told her, grudgingly, that she should keep something on her stomach for now) and wished for her mother. Her mother would have a remedy. Tom could scoff, but modern medicine didn't know everything. Her mother knew things he didn't; secrets were passed down in a land with centuries to draw on.

Not like this raw, new country with its frail wooden houses. In Roujan the house was built of stone, thick, cool, durable. At this moment — five-to-eight in the morning — her mother would be hanging the laundry in the cool morning air. No. It was — daylight saving, add nine hours. Nearly five p.m. in Roujan. Her mother would be watering the garden.

Suddenly Claire saw her mother standing in the garden. The brilliance of geraniums mingled with the green of lettuce, the tangle of peas, the scent of thyme. Her mother had her arms outstretched, and Claire imagined healing crimson flares pouring from her fingertips. Claire felt suddenly happy, an uplifting of her spirits beyond the pleasant seductiveness of nostalgia. She thought of scenes scarcely remembered, herself as a little girl wriggling her toes into the crumbling reddish earth as she followed her mother — young and thin-waisted — to pick the fat red raspberries. Squashing the plump fruit between her teeth. Feeling the sun resting on her thin bare legs.

"The image of Mama lasted for about five minutes," Claire wrote. "Afterwards, for the first time in days, I felt better. I made toast and smothered it with butter and jam, and I still remember how it tasted, better than truffles, and I drank milk that was like the finest Merlot, and put coffee on, and while I waited for it to brew I knew what I must do. There was a battered old table we ate on, and I wiped the crumbs away with my sleeve and pulled open the drawer and got out a pen and an airmail form and started a letter. *Chere maman. Cher papa*, I wrote. Would a little one be welcome in the *famille* Truffault?"

To Claire's surprise, her husband Tom, when he got home, was in complete agreement. Something had happened to him, too, that morning.

WHEN TOM STARTED OUT IN HIS BATTERED PICKUP AND careened around the mountain curves with his cargo of seedlings, he thought to himself that he was at the end of his tether. He formed a mental picture of being at the end of a tether, a long rope that was fastened about his neck and attached to a two-pronged stake whose tines had been hammered all the way down to solid rock. Each day an invisible and still microscopic hand looped the rope in. It would take about six weeks more of developing fetus to strangle him, unless Claire could be made to listen to reason.

He parked the truck and unloaded the first batch of Douglas firs, picked up his spade, and started "heeling" in the seedlings. Dig a hole, grasp the small tree firmly at the top, push the roots into the hole, kick back the earth, then press hard with the heel of his boot all around it. Tom was conscientious; some of the gang didn't give the earth more than a perfunctory push with the sole of the shoe, but Tom liked to think of the small green forest that would spread over the ugly scar of clear-cutting, and so he stamped down with all his strength.

By eight o'clock he was just about ready to put in the first tree when he thought he felt it move in his hand. Startled, he dropped it, and as he did so he imagined he heard it cry out for help. Suddenly it seemed to him that all the seedlings were imploring him to hurry, telling him they were drying out, crying out that they needed to wind their roots into the nourishing soil, and in the distance he thought the forest bent toward their cries. He imagined small threads, like shimmering cobwebs, stretching from the distant trees, and he thought they were catching him, too, in their net. He thought of the shining filaments rising over the mountain and enveloping Claire and the tiny life she was carrying, and he felt something well up in him, like love, or joy, knowing that he was connected to the trees and to Claire and to the tiny tadpole in its concealed ocean.

He fell to work with such vigour that all his seedlings were in before noon, and when he raised his head he saw that his tether had fallen away. He hurried back to have lunch with Claire, leaving the distant trees to watch over their young.

"AND THAT'S WHY OUR DEAR SON WAS BORN," CLAIRE finished off. "I cannot now imagine how our lives would have been without him, and sometimes I think that that is the reason Mama had this special visitation, because hers was the biggest happening I ever heard about."

As if to prove her point, Claire had appended some articles which she'd found among her father's papers. The tabloids, it seems, had had a field day. (*Aliens Zap Earth; New-born Says Hi, Mom.*) Eventually, and because a lot of people had felt *something*, or remembered having felt something after they read about it, tiny articles appeared in *The New York Times, le nouvel observateur* and *Der Spiegel,* and crept apologetically onto the back page of *The Times* of London.

PENELOPE'S SPIRITS LIFT. MME. TRUFFAULT'S IS THE MOST direct confirmation she has had of an invisible universe whose filaments of energy may be woven among the photons of light, or may alternatively be surfing the crests of its waves, should light turn out to be waves instead of particles. A continuing enigma in the world of esoteric physics.

Penelope knows she must work hard to extract whatever meaning is to be found in the Truffault saga, and she is encouraged by the P.S. Claire appended. "Papa spent his remaining years working out scientific theories that may have accounted for – whatever it was that happened. If I can find his notes I will send them."

JASON DOESN'T LET PENELOPE FORGET ABOUT THE TWENTY-TWO. "Did your brother win the gun?" he wants to know. "You promised to tell me the rest, Grandma," and he dances impatiently around the room.

"Wait," Brenda says. "Why don't I get Grandma to write the rest of the story in her journal, and then tomorrow I'll read it to you." Brenda is exhausted; she took Jason to the park earlier because she is determined to keep her muscles from wasting away while she's getting her treatment.

"A bit of writing every day, that's all it takes," she urges Penelope, and then the clincher, "I get a kick out of reading it while I'm being dripped into."

"Okay, I promise I'll work on it tonight if you'll promise to go to bed now. I'll make you a nightcap."

Penelope prepares cocoa: mix a teaspoon of cocoa and a teaspoon of sugar together, stir out all the lumps, add a cup of hot milk, the way she made it all those eons ago every evening after skating at the local rink, the swish of the speed skates that were all the rage, the clasped fist of the boy who was wearing hockey skates and thus likely to skate out of sync with her, his short sharp strides trying to accommodate her long graceful sweeps. Penelope heats the milk in the microwave, that's different anyway, and thinks that journals are all very well, but they are hard work and likely to induce nostalgia.

But they serve as a distraction. To Penelope, who can't dismiss a foreboding. To Brenda, who seems to enjoy this ancient stuff.

"I'M GOING TO WIN THAT," MY BROTHER SAID.

He was ten and I was thirteen. The organizers of the grandstand show had recruited the local high school girls as their chorus line, and by the time I had seen my brother firmly ensconced in front of the little shooting gallery where he was going to win the twenty-two, several of my classmates were already being fitted with their outfits: tight electric blue satin briefs and matching bras. I remember that my bra was loose, the slight swellings that passed for breasts insufficient to fill the wired curves, and below the elasticized satin of the briefs my thin white thighs would not meet unless I bent my legs slightly at the knee. We were given cursory training, which none of us believed we needed.

There were two grandstand shows a day. I stood there, before the uncritical farmers and townspeople and their families, knees slightly bent, occasionally straightening the balancing leg when a frayed line of us kicked more or less on cue. Afterwards my mother said, "For heaven's sake stand up straight. You look like a stork with your knees bent like that." My father just snorted.

What did parents know? In our hearts we were the Goldwyn Girls, the Ziegfeld Follies, and R.K.O. Radio Chorus all rolled into one, high-stepping and pirouetting in our shiny satin on a magical stage under glittering silver spangles and a decor of bluest crepe paper, riveting the eyes of the talent scout from Hollywood who would surely have found his way to our little northern town.

We were – at least as far as I was concerned – handsomely paid: a pass for all the rides. I spent hours swinging in a chair on the Ferris wheel, rewarded with an occasional stop at the very top, surveying below me the plains of waving golden wheat which I thought must be like the ocean, and out of which rose skyscraping red elevators, Alberta Wheat Pool, Saskatchewan Co-op, Federal Grain, where my father worked, and one other whose name has been buried in the cells of dead neurons.

And then I would look inwards from the sea to the island of the fairgrounds, and watch the mad gyrations of the Octopus, and laugh at some of my bolder classmates clutching one another in the Tilt-a-Whirl; usually I saw, almost directly below me, my brother, standing in front of the shooting gallery where the twenty-two was displayed, hoarding the dwindling change from his precious two dollars, determined to win, in spite of the greasy barker who kept urging him to get lost.

I was supposed to keep an eye on him but the responsibility didn't weigh heavily with me. He was always in the one place, counting his money, weighing his chances. He was a cautious boy, and yet, gazing down on him, the euphoria of the Ferris wheel was momentarily stilled by something I thought I saw, something at the corner of my eye that I couldn't quite catch, a stealthy shape, a dark-

ness that seemed to settle around him, even then, even there in the harsh August sun whose glare could penetrate and backlight the deepest shadows.

I shrugged it off. What could happen to him? In those days the things that could happen to boys were never mentioned; certainly girls knew nothing of them. We knew almost nothing of what could happen to girls for that matter — and yet, I suppose I did know. How many years had passed since our childish explorations? At some level sex is known early, and then forgotten.

THE PHONE RINGS. MILDRED. "WHERE ARE YOU, Penelope?" she asks. It is potluck night. Penelope has forgotten.

"Oh well," Mildred says. "Edwin is here, he'll take your place." Penelope thinks she detects a tiny note of triumph.

She tells Mildred to go on without her, she is too tired to go out now. Besides, there is still work to be done.

She sits in her meditating chair and directs wobbly neutrinos at any rogue cancer cells (ugly blobs of slime) in Brenda's body, and is ashamed when her own chilly, stiffening body wakens her a couple of hours later.

AUGUST

WHY WOULD OLD PEOPLE WANT TO KNOW MORE about the earth they are about to leave? To Barry Manly, Ph.D., the proposition seems self-defeating, gratuitous, almost presumptuous: a sort of denial. It isn't the stereotypes of aging – forgetfulness, curmudgeonliness, slowing intellectual processes – that give him pause, it is wonderment, bemusement, before this unanswered ('because unasked) question. In the end he has been persuaded to teach, in August, *An overview of the startling changes in thinking during the twentieth century, dealing specifically with Evolution, past (and future?)*, for Capilano College's Science for Seniors.

Barry goes over the list of names – he prides himself on knowing who is who by the end of the first class – and then introduces Lucy. Lucy is a skeletal reproduction of the famous *Australopithecus afarensis* discovered in 1974 in Ethiopia, and, although Barry wondered if beginning with a skeleton might be a bit morbid (considering), evidently it is not.

They make their way to the front of the room, spry ones, slow-moving ones, some who use canes, and even one in an electric wheelchair. (As an enchanted Barry recounts later to an approving Marion Galt – English as a Second Language, Canadian Literature, and the true reason Barry finally accepted the assignment – he thought they were going to adopt Lucy.)

The thin, intense woman with wavy, iron grey hair, sitting in the very front (Penelope), is first off the mark and shakes Lucy's bony hand as though she is greeting an old friend. "How old?" she asks, and when Barry says about three to three and a half million years, one man quips, "Just about right for me!" Another man begins to serenade her with the first line of "Lucy in the sky with diamonds," his voice surprising in its richness. This makes several of the women laugh, rather shyly, as though they are being daring – the Beatles, Barry remembers, were nothing but outrageous adolescents when this group of oldsters were in their forties.

He has just begun to tell them of the intense excitement Lucy's discovery generated when he is interrupted by a shout of recognition from Penelope. "The missing link!" she cries, and all eyes, clear to cataract-cloudy, focus on her. "When I was young," Penelope explains, excitement making her voice quiver, "the biggest headline of all was when archaeologists thought they'd found the missing link."

"Everyone didn't believe in Darwin, back then," another woman offers, and the white-bearded man who sang, says, "They weren't even too happy about it in the United Church." His speaking voice is thin and cracked.

"One doesn't *believe* in Darwin," Barry interposes. "One lets the facts speak for themselves," and with one eye on Penelope – who is semi-crouched to get a better view, although to Barry it looks as though she is about to spring at him – he allows that you might describe Lucy as a missing link, "not in the older meaning of the word as you perhaps understood it – uh...."

"Stevens, Mrs.," and then, remembering that Dr. Manly – Barry – subscribes to the use of first names in his classes (having no idea that this will be deemed radically modern by this group of students) she adds, firmly, "Penelope."

"Yes. Thank you. At one time, Penelope, people thought there would be a single definitive creature between the great apes and *Homo sapiens*. Now, however, we think of *Australopithecus afarensis*," he writes it on the board, "as merely the probable beginning of an evolutionary branch that has ended with us."

"So far," Penelope murmurs.

BRENDA IS FEELING SO MUCH BETTER THAT SHE DECIDES to drop in on Connie while Penelope is at her class. Connie is home all the time now; she is, she says, working from home, and she leaves it at that.

Connie answers the door wearing an old grey flannel jogging suit, her hair, suspiciously greasy, flopping loosely, one side splayed over her shoulder and the other a ragged line two inches shorter.

They go into the kitchen where last night's unscraped plates are piled helter-skelter on every inch of counter space, and the overflow from an open bottle of red wine has splattered the land-scape.

Connie is drunk.

"Bren — Bren-da, what a great surprise. Jus' in time for sheli-bration."

Brenda shoos Jason into the den with Tommy, who is glued to a violent TV program. Brenda switches channels and silences the boys with a look that intimidates even Tommy, then goes back to the kitchen.

"What are you celebrating, Connie?" she asks, surprised and slightly amused by her own overweening disapproval. She, Brenda, who once upon a couple of decades ago scarcely took the time to unpack at Stanford before she hightailed it to the pot-laden streets of Haight-Ashbury.

"Shelebrating cause I'm preggers."

"Christ!" Brenda gets up and snatches the glass from Connie's hand. "Do you want the kid to be born with Fetal Alcohol Syndrome?"

"No shweat — sweat. It won't be born."

"What? Why?"

"Old Chinese saying, only the husband who wears the shoe can tell where it pinches," and Connie giggles and lurches for the glass in Brenda's hand, then sags into a chair and starts to cry.

"Jim doesn't want it?"

Connie shakes her head no, and between sobs says, "There's lots of time yet, he says. Course, he doesn't know."

A fearsome tide starts in Brenda's toes and sweeps up her thighs and makes her genitals tingle in passing, then bulldozes through the density of her still-plentiful hips, through the scarred and battered breast and into her neck and up until her brain feels seared with it. She picks up the wine bottle and hurls it into the sink where it smashes with such a crash that the boys hear it over the TV, then grabs Connie by the shoulders and yanks her to her feet and starts yelling.

"For Christ's sake this is *your* decision! What kind of fucking wimp are you anyway? You want the kid, you have it. It's your life to lead not your goddamn husband's, he doesn't get to lead two lives."

Jason and Tommy creep in from the den and are for once struck dumb. Years later Jason will swear that Brenda's wig uncurls itself and stands out from her head the way hair does when you grasp the handles of the electrostatic machine at the Science Centre.

Connie's mouth hangs open and a drop of wine dribbles from the corner.

"Where's your goddamn bedroom?" Brenda shouts, and Tommy says in a small voice, "I'll show you."

Brenda and the boys tear up the stairs, and Brenda starts pulling out drawers and throwing Connie's clean underwear on the unmade bed, and grabbing shoes and nightgowns and slippers.

Connie, in sober shock, follows. "What the hell do you think you're doing?" she asks.

"You're coming with me," Brenda says. "Until you get your head screwed back on straight. Get me a suitcase or a bag or something, and I won't take no for an answer."

Connie starts to protest, and suddenly, as though a tiny light had switched on at the end of a very black tunnel, she fetches a small suitcase and begins almost frantically to help Brenda pack, and then they go to Tommy's room and throw his favourite videos and a few clothes into a plastic bag.

They are locking the door when the phone rings. "Don't answer it," Brenda says.

Connie doesn't.

BECAUSE IT IS SUCH A HOT DAY PENELOPE ESCAPES THE madhouse after dinner and goes for her walk.

She is happy enough about Brenda's rescue mission. It is giving Brenda a very focussed direction which she can use right now, but Penelope does find two small boys a bit wearing. In addition she can't prevent herself from resenting the intrusion of Connie on her own time with Brenda, a weakness that at one time she would have worked hard to expunge but now is able to allow herself as an acceptable human frailty.

In any case Connie's visit isn't going to last too long, she knows that. She saw, at the birthday party, how proud Jim Tran was of Tommy; he wouldn't risk a custody battle, and she suspects he loves Connie but needs a reminder. And there are cultural forces to be reckoned with. The senior Trans had not been happy about the match. Penelope remembers that they had flown very reluctantly from Hong Kong for the wedding and stayed only three days. Nor had Connie's mother been happy; it was the sort of thing, Mrs. Smythe said in a tight voice, she would have expected from someone like that crazy Brenda Stevens with her weird upbringing. Neither Connie nor Jim will want the "I told you so's" from Mrs. Smythe, nor whatever the equivalent is in Cantonese. (Penelope doesn't know it, but Jim has already phoned and spoken to Brenda. Connie refused to talk to him.)

Penelope is nearly at the Lewis house when she sees the red and blue "For Sale" sign. The house seems to be empty already, and Penelope feels a familiar twinge. Filaments of community severed abruptly, stories lost, tentative friends forgotten.

The aggressive chugging of hovering helicopters is displacing the usual low-key chattering of birds and lawn mowers and neighbours. Annoying, but not all that uncommon; hikers are always getting lost or falling down cliffs. People tend to forget that urban Vancouver is a cement ribbon of modernity, and that if you walk north past the clipped lawns and wilting hydrangeas you will be stopped by rain-forested mountains sweeping down to the ocean in leg-breaking creeks and ravines.

Nature, Penelope likes to think, even in these tamed times, poses the biggest threat to human life. She has always tended to pooh-pooh the dangers of modern urban society, especially as it applies to North Vancouver, and she is fond of pointing out to the more paranoid of the Seniors Centre habitués that for twenty years she has walked the same three-kilometre walk, and the closest she's come to disaster was from a falling branch in a wind storm.

She is close to disaster right now, although she doesn't know it. There is a trail that cuts through the forest just above Penelope's house, carved by Scouts through the treacherous

deadfall and named after Lord Baden-Powell who started the Boy
Scouts. This evening, only a quarter of a mile away on the Baden-
Powell Trail, a brute lurks, a supposedly evolved human dressed
in modern clothes, jeans and T-shirt, ragged and filthy.

His name, she learns later, is Waters, which could be some
sort of cosmic joke, since he apparently never washes. And if you
believe – and she does – that the cosmos has a sense of humour.
David Waters, a murderous rapist who is stumbling along in the
woods just above her house.

Although she doesn't know how near he is, she does know
about the crime. North Vancouver – and greater Vancouver as
well, indeed the entire Lower Mainland, and south as far as
Bellingham, and even Seattle – have been caught up for two
weeks in the horror of the thing that has happened. A man
seized a young girl in broad daylight, went into the video shop at
ten in the morning when the clerk was occupied with replacing
last night's returned videos – Adult Movies, Classics – to their
separate quarters (as though *Hot! Hot! Hot!* might bleed into and
corrupt *The Age of Innocence*). The store is in the very mall by the
Safeway where Penelope buys her groceries. In fact – this came
out later – Waters bought his groceries there as well; the staff
remembers him, oddly enough, by the foul animal smell that sur-
rounds him, like a private zone of toxic pollution.

He forced the girl at fake gunpoint across the adjacent Upper
Levels Highway and into a densely wooded ravine. Penelope
often marvels that a place so urbanized can still have secret places
where one person can keep another bound and gagged and used
as a toy, a plaything, the paper doll of his most perverted fan-

tasies, taking pleasure, presumably, from her terror. Surely, Penelope thinks, children would have found them, children must explore these small hidden clearings. When she was little – but it isn't like that now. Perhaps monsters mutate out of the pollution of modern society.

As a child Penelope was taught that evil grows from a weak character, and that character, like leg muscles, must be exercised to temptation-resistant fitness, but the Science for Seniors course opens up another possibility.

BRENDA HAS ONLY THREE MORE SESSIONS OF CHEMOTHERAPY, and Penelope – in spite of a strong superstition handed down by her grandmother and reinforced by the observations of seventy years, that troubles always come in threes, and so far there have been two, although whether Brenda losing her job counts is a moot point – is beginning, guardedly, to believe things may turn out alright. She even looks forward to the monthly potluck dinner, which should be at her house but, in deference to her problems, is at Nancy and Dick's place.

MILDRED, FROM HER PERCH BESIDE EDWIN, WAVES cheerily as Penelope comes in, but to Penelope's discomfiture Edwin gets up immediately and crosses the floor to put his hand on her shoulder. "Great to see you back, Penelope," he says, and then, reaching into the breast pocket of his summer jacket (Edwin has two jackets for occasions requiring some degree of

formality; a tan summer jacket of linen and cotton, and a winter
Harris tweed), pulls out two symphony tickets and waves them.

"Symphony, Penelope. Your favourite – mostly Mozart."

Mildred doesn't speak to either of them for the rest of the
evening.

PENELOPE NEVER DOES GO TO THE SYMPHONY WITH
Edwin, because the very next day the third blow falls: metastasis.
The dreaded incursions of a few rogue cancer cells that managed
to escape the surgeon's knife and survive the poisonings. Into the
lymph glands. Radical mastectomy, no two ways about it this
time, just lucky that the bone scan shows no signs of it having
spread further.

Connie and Tommy leave immediately – it is understood that
negotiations have gone well. Penelope overheard Connie shout
into the phone, "Get rid of your goddamn concubine and I'll
have you know I'm forty-one, not thirty-five," which shocked
Penelope: she can't imagine a marriage where one party doesn't
know the other's age.

The radical mastectomy, according to the doctor, "Got everything, as nearly as we can tell," and Brenda admits that she should
have had it done in the first place. "Why hang on to it? Who needs
two boobs? I'll still have one, I won't miss the other," she says.

Brenda won't let Penelope give up the course, pointing out that
since she's destitute she qualifies for Home Help. Within a week
she is installed back in her bedroom, with a Home Helper woman
who comes in every other morning to tidy up and make casseroles

while Penelope's at her class. Penelope drops Jason at his playschool on the way to class and picks him up in the afternoon. On alternate days people like physiotherapists and nurses who change dressings come in, so that the place is bustling and cheerful, and the pale ghost of fear that has caused even the elements to whirl into contention is almost but never quite banished.

Brenda phones Gordon to reassure him. Gordon sounds unlike his professionally compassionate self; he sounds distracted and he says it wouldn't be the best time for him to come out, although he doesn't explain why.

"Don't leave it too long, Gordo," Brenda says, ominously. "I need to think a bit about Jason's future – just in case, worst case scenario. Anyway it isn't something to discuss with Mother, at least not at the moment."

Gordon says he'll come in the fall for sure.

GORDON IS SEVERELY SHAKEN, NOT ONLY BECAUSE HE loves his twin, has always thought of her as the strong one and of himself as the fragile one, but because mortality itself is threatening. Connie had been threatened when classmate Ivan died, and even Brenda had found that Ivan's death cut a little close to the bone. But Gordon is now facing annihilation at his right hand, the extermination of his double, his other, the loved one who once, in chaste splendour, had been front and centre. Gordon's focus on Brenda had been far more unswerving than Brenda's on Gordon, although she had accepted his allegiance gracefully and as no more than her due.

After her call Gordon's first impulse is to fly to Vancouver and stop the desecration, which in some illogical corner of his brain he thinks of as Brenda's own doing; but he can't leave Etobicoke because he is waiting, although what he is waiting for he doesn't know and can't imagine.

Whatever it is has to do with the auras. About a month ago they intruded during the Monday night Living Relationships group which, to Gordon's chagrin, Camilla had decided to join. "I'm afraid I don't have a living relationship or even a dying relationship," she said, but didn't explain why she would bother to come.

She has a habit of speaking with her eyes unfocussed, as though she isn't addressing her listener but is reciting lines in a bad play. Not that it matters, for Gordon seldom listens to her if he can help it; she is a part of what Harbit-Jones calls the fruitcake fringe, a group that goes in for past lives and spiritual healing. (Gordon would never call them that himself, but by his silence he knows he acquiesces when Harbit-Jones says it.)

THEY HAD JUST FINISHED THE MEETING, A GUARDED skirmish around the edges of Janet's and Harbit-Jones' guilt (she left a husband for him) when, for no apparent reason, Camilla's head began to glow in the centre of a white radiance around which faint ripples of blue pulsed like some private aurora borealis. Gordon could only stare.

Camilla was fairly used to being stared at. "What colour is my aura, Gordon?" she asked. This was a favourite line, handy at parties with the likes of the unlamented Cyril Foggarty.

"White and blue," Gordon blurted, and then heard himself laugh so artificially that he was quite sure the jig was up, as Brenda used to say. "Sorry, a slight problem I'm having with my eyes."

With which Camilla's shimmering began to fade, leaving Gordon with the absurd sense of loss he'd noted on the first occasion.

Camilla seemed unsurprised. In exactly the same tone of voice she would have used if he'd said it was a nice day, she asked, "Are you left brain or right brain?"

Harbit-Jones snorted. "That stuff is only a theory, or not even a theory, more like a hypothesis."

Of all Camilla's daffy characteristics her failure to acknowledge Harbit-Jones when he spoke was the one that annoyed him most. "Maybe you want to start developing your right brain. It's the seat of intuition and music and creativity," she murmured, as if Gordon had expressed a desire.

It was perhaps the last thing Gordon wanted to do, since he suspected that his right brain was quite well developed as it was. For a brief moment he imagined his own aura as a perfectly balanced prism, and was thus caught off guard when Camilla asked him point blank if he would come Wednesday night to the Living Energy group. So far Gordon had avoided contact with the Living Energy crowd; it was composed almost exclusively of "the huggers," as Harbit-Jones called them, those who, like movie stars, embraced ardently at every encounter, male and male, female and female, and, most trying to Gordon, male and female.

Gordon had been unable to prevent himself from retreating from the males and responding, sometimes inappropriately, to the females — especially those who, like Camilla, were inclined to flatten their unfettered breasts against his chest in an excess of fellowship. On one occasion his reaction had been so sudden and forceful that Margo, the immediately following hugger, appraised him rather speculatively and volunteered to do his typing on Thursdays (work which she had previously scorned as part of the male power structure) when the regular typist was off. Prior to this, in spite of his pleas in the newsletter and even from the pulpit, Gordon had been unable to find a volunteer typist, and he could not prevent himself from thinking, rather wryly, that he was more persuasive below the belt than above.

The week's topic turned out to be The Intuitive in Creativity. Janet had dragged along Harbit-Jones, who said at once, "Let's define our terms," a gambit that silenced everyone except Camilla. She protested that if you had intuition you wouldn't need to define it, and if you didn't, you couldn't. "Like blindness," she said. "How would you describe light and shadow to a blind man?"

Gordon was rather struck by her imagery and that night he had what he thought was a significant dream. There was a woman who was nobody that Gordon had ever seen, although for a moment he thought she might be Brenda, and then perhaps Betty Grosvenor, except that her hair was as golden as Camilla's. In the dream he felt an enormous longing, and when the unknown woman held her arms out to him he was swept with an emotion he could not identify, at least to Dr. Weinberg.

When he awoke he felt wonderfully happy, as though he had dreamed of love.

The dream didn't help. Dr. Weinberg was single-minded, and so Gordon did his best. Perhaps, Gordon suggested, because as an impressionable adolescent he had been exposed to a belief in auras (Brenda's) he was now suffering a sort of delayed suggestibility? Dr. Weinberg accepted this premise as though it had been his own, and offered hypnosis. To the surprise of both of them the hypnosis seemed to work, at least in the three intervening Sundays until Gordon's next appointment. Dr. Weinberg was delighted and Gordon regarded his cure with a mixture of relief and sheepishness.

It was later that the sense of waiting slipped in, preventing Gordon from flying to Brenda's rescue.

PENELOPE'S MIND AS SHE RETURNS FROM CLASS IS FULL OF LUCY, and so she is unprepared when she gets home for the sight of an ambulance and an attendant helping Brenda into it. She jumps out of her car, fear causing her to jam the seat belt, but Brenda waves and calls to her. Nothing to worry about, she says, a weak spell, fainting actually, and the Home Help woman bursts in with explanations, better not to fool around, get in there where they can deal with it, and Brenda reminds Penelope that Jason is to sleep over with Tommy, and she gives Jason a hug and tells him she'll see him tomorrow.

In a blanket of numbness Penelope goes on automatic pilot, hurries Jason into the car, fastens him in and drives the Upper

Levels and takes the twists and turns on the climb to Connie's as though she were trying out for the Indy 500. Jason, sensing disaster, is quiet, possibly frightened, although nothing registers on the robot Penelope has become.

Connie at least looks energized. Her hair is pulled back neatly in a ponytail, her skin is glowing, and the tic has gone (although it has laid a pathway that is ready for resurrection, should the need arise).

Nevertheless when Connie hears the news she can't stop a quick gasp and "I don't like the look of this," but she recovers quickly and says, "It's probably routine. They shouldn't turf people out of the hospital so fast in the first place."

Penelope breaks her former speed record on the trip to Lions Gate Hospital. In the chaotic hype of Emergency nobody notices her, and Penelope runs in and starts yanking curtains back. A wizened man in the first cubicle pulls an oxygen mask off his face, stares at her wildly, throws back his cotton sheet to expose his flabby crotch, then laughs in a rattling wheeze and screams, "Get the hell out of here!" In the next cubicle a fat woman with a nosebleed is startled by Penelope's wild eyes and her hand jerks and dislodges her nose plug, and blood spurts and sparkles high in the air and speckles her blue gown and white sheet, and even Penelope's cotton blouse.

Finally a nurse catches up and glares at Penelope and directs her, frostily, to Information.

Eventually Penelope locates Brenda in a comfortable semi-private room with a roommate who seems to be about the same age. Red, nourishing, AIDS-free blood is running into Brenda's veins. "Nothing but a bit of anemia, not uncommon after chemo *and* an operation," a cheerful nurse explains.

Brenda herself is sleepy. "Relax, Mother, I'm fine. Go home and write some more in your journal and bring it in if I'm still here tomorrow."

THE DARKENING DAY BECOMES A JUMBLE AS PENELOPE drives home (erratically, but the traffic is light and the hospital a mere five minutes from Penelope's house.) Ambulance, Brenda, Jason, Connie, and before that Lucy. Lucy in the sky, Lucy in the savannah, Lucy —

Penelope unlocks the back door and steps into the kitchen, and almost immediately catches a glimpse of a shadowy object that looks like a dark, hairy foot behind the archway into her compact dining room.

She feels no shock, merely a resigned acceptance. Penelope has been this route before — when something burrows deeply enough into the spongy grey machine where the ghost lurks, the disturbance will sometimes people her world with fleeting pictures that are not unlike the hypnagogic images that form on eyelids just before sleep, except that these are hologram-like, three-dimensional, solid, touchable even.

Before Penelope met her real-life childhood friend, Mr. B's daughter, she would have been lonely if it hadn't been for the ubiquitous invisible friend beloved by many children. Penelope's friend slipped in and out of visibility, pink cheeks, curling ringlets, everything that Penelope wasn't but longed to be.

She had had another manifestation while trying to recover forgotten skills at the piano, just after she and George abandoned their liaison. One day Chopin (dreamy, romantic, hauntingly sexy) slid in beside her on her piano bench, his leg brushing the silk of her gown. A third sighting after Grover's death: oil painting lessons ceased abruptly when a broad-brushed, lecherous Picasso, half-man, half-bull, with a left ear askew on his cheekbone, pursued her around the dining table where she worked. (She switched to watercolours. A better class of artists.)

"You might as well come out," she says now.

Lucy walks out boldly – at first Penelope can only see her out of the corner of her eye, but then Lucy solidifies and Penelope is able to look straight at her. A naked, swarthy, hairy creature with apelike features, small by contemporary standards – under four feet – but walking upright with the sureness of a person who is no longer an ape. "An exceedingly primitive being, not even in the *Homo* genus," Barry had said, writing *genus* on the board, then *species*, explaining that closely related creatures belong to a single species, while closely related species belong to a single genus. "The brain of *afarensis* was about one-third the volume of the brain of modern man, but Lucy and her crowd were the first truly bipedal hominids."

Bipedal she may be, but when Lucy sees this (relatively) tall, pale animal, a being unimagined in Lucy's world of mostly four-footed and slithering predators, she falls onto four legs and dashes into the far corner of the dining room, where she disappears.

Penelope, affecting unconcern, wanders about her kitchen. Finally Lucy peeks around the corner, then ventures a foot or two into the room, poised for flight should this strange creature prove aggressive. Penelope decides to gain her confidence as one would a domestic pet, but when she opens the fridge and takes out a T-bone steak, Lucy darts forward and snatches it from Penelope's hands and begins to gulp it down, raw. There is a small tussle, and Penelope learns that size cannot compete with a musculature that has only recently given up swinging from trees. Finally she distracts Lucy with water, which she puts in a bowl and sets on the floor.

How could blonde hair evolve, Penelope wonders? Or red, especially red? Even three million years seems an inadequate time for softening the black bristles that cover Lucy from head to ankle. Imagine Lucy hawking shampoo! Or wired Maidenforms! Or – and the image catches Penelope unawares, so that she guffaws aloud – white lace panties over her bristly, heavy-lipped privates!

Penelope could swear that the look Lucy directs at her is one of injured pride. Lucy picks up the bowl and pours the rest of the water over her black head.

Suddenly there is a fearsome crashing and Lucy leaps into the air. A gigantic, roaring, clanking monster has appeared outside the window. It extends its vicious-looking claws and picks up a big green stump and empties the contents into its cavernous mouth, then chews with a prodigious grinding. As the garbage truck leaves, Lucy hurls herself, trembling, at Penelope, wrapping her arms tightly around her. Penelope is surprised by the allure of Lucy's smooth fur, although at the same time she fears for her seventy-year-old rib cage.

Penitent, Penelope proffers bananas, a fruit Lucy understands.

Lucy begins to strip the bananas just for the peelings, shrieking with (Penelope supposes) amusement as peelings splat on the ceiling, the windows, the shiny linoleum, until the little kitchen is littered with slippery, wilting debris. Perhaps a sense of humour is already emerging, even if it is at the level of the Three Stooges. (It is Penelope's belief that humour is as necessary as oxygen for survival.)

She tries to teach Lucy to say "banana." Ba-na-na, enunciating slowly, holding the fruit just out of reach above Lucy's head. Lucy, delighted, shouts "Na-na-na," and tries to climb up Penelope, who quickly gives her the banana in self-defence. Lucy peels it and wolfs it down and throws the peeling at Penelope, continuing to shout "na-na-na."

Penelope looks out into the garden to rest her eyes, and to her horror sees that Lucy has slipped out and is cradling Mrs. Moore's cat, Basil, in her arms. Basil hisses and tries to scratch (which momentarily halts Penelope in her tracks and makes the hair stand up on the back of her neck. Isn't Lucy *her* hallucination?). Lucy throws Basil up in the air and catches him neatly, then dangles him by the tail and twirls him around and around her head.

"Lucy!" Penelope shouts. She tears out of the house and runs across the lawn and grabs the poor cat and gives Lucy what her mother would have called "a good dressing-down." "Can't you see that you're hurting poor Basil?" she scolds. "I don't care if you are a stupid *afarensis*, you can't just beat up on smaller creatures any time you happen to feel like it...."

It is then that Penelope becomes aware of Mrs. Moore, lean-

ing over the fence. On her face Penelope reads a triumphant confirmation of what she has long suspected, what she'd said to her
husband earlier, that Penelope is getting "nuttier than a fruitcake." "Ever since she got home this afternoon she's been talking
and shouting at the top of her lungs, and you should have seen
her kitchen — splattered with banana peelings from one end to
the other. We'll be murdered in our beds one of these nights,
that'll be the next thing," she declared.

"As good a place as any," was all Mr. Moore said, switching
on the TV.

Penelope draws herself up to her full five feet six inches and
goes to the fence and hands Basil to Mrs. Moore. "I was just
explaining to him that it is wrong to torture mice," she says with
dignity.

"Do you have a mouse?"

"No. Or rather yes, I did have, but thanks to Basil I now have
only a dead mouse. Which I must get rid of," and Penelope goes
through an elaborate charade with a shovel and the garbage can.
Mrs. Moore, she knows, is not fooled, but she can't prove anything.

BY NIGHTTIME PENELOPE IS EXHAUSTED. LUCY HAS SWUNG
from the chandelier, broken a bowl, cringed and cried when the
dishwasher went on, discovered the lights and turned them off
and on for nearly an hour, and finally after repeated tries, learned
to open doors. It was then she discovered the basement.

She appears to love the basement, which must seem to her like a cool cave. Penelope hunts out an old blanket, and Lucy curls up on it and falls asleep immediately. Penelope tiptoes up the stairs; then — feeling a bit guilty, but what else can a person do? — locks the basement door and tumbles into her own bed.

Brenda phones to say goodnight. She sounds cheerful. She has been chatting with her roommate and says a little blood martini was all she needed. Responding to the distraction in Penelope's voice Brenda asks her sharply what is happening. Penelope is on the verge of explaining about Lucy but bites her tongue just in time. She doesn't want the Home Help moving in on *her.*

BRENDA DREAMS THAT SHE GETS OUT OF HER BED AND slips into the corridor, which stretches menacingly and endlessly into a mist-shrouded distance. Doors, squarely opposing one another, line its sterile sides. They are all closed.

Suddenly a nurse runs up and Brenda sees that her skin is very brown and her arms are huge, and then she recognizes the fortune teller she and Connie met in Hawaii, Madame Pele. "You can't stay in the corridor, you must choose a door," she says, but before Brenda can ask her why, she pushes her aside and runs past her into the mist.

Gil is behind one of those doors, Brenda understands this. She begins to walk, pausing before the first set of doors, then the second, then the third. Then she sees that the fourth door on the left is open slightly and she pushes it carefully.

At first she thinks nobody is there, then she sees a form on the bed and she sees that it is Gil. He has grown very old, he is wizened, shrunken, and tubes are running into his mouth and his nose and his arm.

She bends to embrace him, but he is sleeping, and she is afraid to waken him. She turns to leave. Suddenly he calls. "Brenny-penny," he says, and she wheels around, but as she tries to run to him her feet are frozen to the spot, and then she is kicking her feet against tangled sheets and struggling through the woolen mist of sleeping pills into the sterility of her hospital room.

The moon is shining in the window, and its cool light reinforces the dream's longing, a love and longing she once felt, in some other century.

PENELOPE WAKENS IN THE MIDDLE OF THE NIGHT WITH a sense of lightness, as though she too has dreamed of love. She looks out the window at the moon-splattered lawn and the crooked apple tree in the back corner. "Silver fruit upon silver trees," she recites aloud, a phrase from ancient times, public school, and then the silver shadows form themselves into two egg-shaped spaceships, huddled together like twin dirigibles, their skins so transparent that she can see right through them to the garden, the birch tree, the brooding Douglas fir. She stands there, shivering, until the great moon slides behind the fir tree and the spaceships dissolve.

Why, she wonders? She knows from experience that such projections are portentous and she is eager for revelation. For the first time in a long time she is hopeful.

LUCY SLIPS AWAY IN THE NIGHT LEAVING NOTHING BUT a trail sculpted in three-million-year-old volcanic ash, two sets of prints side by side. When the giant volcano erupted, Lucy and her companion had not gone far enough. They staggered and pitched forward, felled by suffocating fumes, and were covered by volcanic ash. In the end nothing marked their passing but an ancient trail of two sets of footsteps, in the badlands of Ethiopia. Mary Leakey, who found the trail, said it produced, for her, "a kind of poignant time wrench."

One set of footprints is Lucy's, Penelope understands that when she finds the basement deserted and Lucy gone. She wonders if the other one arrived on the spaceships and slipped into Lucy's cave in the dead of night. Did Lucy recognize him at once? Did she take his hand and desert the small family she had always lived with?

They would have been in love, as much in love as any modern couple, as Troilus and Cressida, as Dante and Beatrice, as — as Diane Chambers and Sam Malone, since love would have been among the first things to set up housekeeping in the primitive brain. (The fact that there is no scientific evidence to support this would not bother Penelope one whit, even if she paused to consider it. She has raised children; she knows full well that no child would survive infancy without love.) Mary Leakey has described how, at one place on the trail one of the travellers stops, pauses, and turns to the left. Perhaps it was Lucy, who thought she'd heard something, and, turning, saw steam from the mountain shooting high into the blue. Perhaps she was afraid. Perhaps she tugged at her companion's arm, urging him to hurry. Perhaps he wrapped his arms around her.

Penelope smiles, and even though she has learned that reminiscence is best avoided, that beneath the seductive surface of memory there is a whirlpool of lost hope and forgotten desire, she cannot stop herself from remembering the bliss of first love. Sometimes it comes back to her in dreams.

AT THE NEXT CLASS PENELOPE ASKS BARRY WHETHER Lucy could talk. The white-bearded man, whose name turns out to be James, laughs aloud, then bows in rather a courtly manner to Penelope. "I'm sorry, Mrs. – ah – Penelope, but isn't that rather like the old conundrum of whether the falling coconut makes any sound when there is no one to hear it? I mean, how could anyone possibly know?"

There is a titter of polite laughter, especially among the women – the widows particularly – who have come to believe that dapper James is intellectually a cut above the rest, and – even more titillating – a widower who must be in need. Penelope, however, sees him as the epitome of the ease with which some males assume superiority over other people (especially women), without in any way being superior.

Barry, forestalling confrontation, interjects smoothly. "Good question. Not speech as we know it, perhaps, but one school of thought believes that *Homo habilis,* who came later, had the neurological equipment for at least rudimentary speech, because the bulge of Broca's area is present. But the flexing necessary for the larynx to drop isn't very developed...." He shows them the spot on Lucy's skeleton, which, at their urgent request he continues to bring to every class even after her place in the evolutionary sun is past.... "and so the full range of sounds as we know them wasn't possible."

Exactly as Penelope was beginning to suspect. She has come to realize that bananas had nothing to do with it, that Lucy shouted either "na-na-na-na" or "da-da-da-da" or sometimes "ma-ma-ma-ma" to everything, just as Brenda and Gordon had done when they were babies. What she was most like, Penelope has decided, was a temperamental two-year old. "Ontogony recapitulates phylogeny," according to Barry, and she supposes this is what he means, that two-year old behaviour was grown-up behaviour in Lucy's time. (Penelope knows a couple of people at the Senior's Centre for whom this still holds true.)

Barry goes on to say that recent research on the bonobo ape suggests that basic language ability developed earlier than we used to believe, but that even *Homo erectus* – well after Lucy – may have lacked the necessary fine control of the ribcage muscles. "Full command of speech probably didn't develop until three or four hundred thousand years ago."

This, to Penelope, is the most staggering of all the news Barry has yet given. She thinks about how valuable words can be when they are treated with respect. We can put words to our experiences. We can say, that is the garbage truck, that is thunder, that is the cry of the loon. Do not be afraid, we can say, I am here, as we push back the terror of the unknown.

That is what words do, she sees it now. They define the past and project the past into the future, they set up expectations;

they may, in fact, be self-fulfilling. But most importantly, they are the pathways by which each of us seeks to describe our lonely, disparate, personal universes.

SEPTEMBER

"'I‍F YOU DON'T KNOW HOW TO DIE, DON'T WORRY; Nature will tell you what to do on the spot, fully and adequately. She will do this job perfectly for you, don't bother your head about it.' Know who wrote that?" Brenda asks.

Penelope shakes her head.

"Montaigne. Is that reassuring, or what?"

Not to Penelope. She feels a painful clutch somewhere between solar plexus and heart, a familiar breathlessness that silences her. Brenda, half in love with easeful death – where did that line spring from? Palgrave's *Golden Treasury*, Penelope remembers, a grey-green volume that could fit in the palm of one hand. She can call up the page but can read only that one line. Wilful Brenda, life-asserting Brenda, the wild woman who ran with the wolves before the rest of them even jogged with the coyotes, the leader of the pack – how has this come about?

Penelope tries to rouse the sleeping healer in Brenda, and one morning finds herself standing in front of the bookcase with Lewis Thomas's *The Medusa and the Snail* in her hand. She doesn't remember how it got there but she takes it as a Jungian synchronicity, and leafing through, comes on one of her favourites, the essay where Thomas recounts how he and another young intern would hypnotize a warty patient and remove the warts from one side of the body only.

But what Penelope wants to get through to Brenda is Thomas's speculation about the power that resides somewhere in the brain. He himself, Thomas admits, wouldn't be able to get rid of the warts even with all his specialized knowledge, and he, like Penelope, figures that if we could just tap into the superintelligence in the unconscious which, he says, exists in each of us, we could access technical know-how that is beyond our present understanding.

All Brenda says is, "Lewis Thomas? Didn't he die? Of cancer?"

"Only when he was old, when his time had come."

"Does a person know when that is?" and then, changing the subject, "Your journal, Mother." Brenda always changes the subject when Penelope gets too close to whatever it is she is protecting. "I want to know whether Uncle David won the gun. God, do you realize how politically incorrect that is? And here I am rooting for him."

Rooting for easeful death.

AT SOME POINT ON THE SECOND DAY OF THE FAIR (Penelope writes) *I did seek out my brother. He had used up nearly all his money, but just as I came up to the little shooting gallery he scored a direct hit and won.*

With the hardbitten cynicism that characterized the swarthy men who "worked" the circus, the operator flung a box at him. "Here ya are, kid. Now get lost, will ya?"

It wasn't the rifle. I don't know whether my brother hadn't scored the points that were needed, or whether the operator cheated him in not awarding him the prize that was the gallery's chief attraction; all I know is that the brute tossed a beautiful blue box at my brother, and the look on his face would have stopped a grown man from protesting, much less a ten-year-old boy and a thirteen-year-old girl.

"Evening in Paris," the box was labelled. The cover was the dark blue of late evening. Silhouetted against the darkening blue was the Eiffel Tower, and in front of it was a woman and a man. The woman was in a long, flowing dress "cut on the bias," something my mother was attempting to do with the dress she was making for the Thanksgiving dance at the church hall. The shiny satin fell gracefully over the perfect hips of the woman as she leaned against the man's tuxedo-clad shoulder.

My brother stared at the box for a long moment while I held my breath. He didn't handle frustration well, even then. Once, when I had tried to comfort his measles-stricken anger with my most precious possession, he had sent the china egg cup hurtling across the room, smashing it against the wall. Alternatively, he looked as though he might cry, an indignity not tolerated in days when frontier life demolished men for less.

"Take it," he said suddenly, shoving the box at me. He hurled his few remaining pennies in the dust, spun around, and stomped out of the fairgrounds without a backward glance. He didn't return; he sat for long hours in his narrow little bedroom, staring at a wall.

I spent those hours with the box and its contents, trying to unravel the mystery that must be concealed in it. To begin with, there was the sophisticated world of Paris and the Eiffel Tower. I knew little of the French. They spoke a foreign *language that we were taught in school because some people in Canada spoke it. I knew they were a lewd lot, because I'd heard of "French safes," which had something in common with "French kisses," "doing it," and Mr. B. It never occurred to me that women who wore dresses cut on the bias and men who wore black jackets and funny ties could have anything in common with Mr. B's besotted fumblings.*

The interior of the box contained parfum, eau de cologne, talcum dusting powder, and huile pour bains. The latter, after laborious translation, I added to the round tub set in the kitchen on Saturday night for our baths. I doled out the oil a few drops at a time over the space of a year. After the bath I patted powder over my skinny body with a voluptuous white puff that had been concealed in the shiny round powder box, dabbed myself with the eau de cologne, saved the parfum, whose secret was surely concealed in the blue box with its blue inset bottles, and waited for revelation.

"NEAT, MOTHER. WHERE'S THE REST?"

Brenda is propped on the kitchen couch, exhausted from trying to pack for a return to Keats Island. She has promised Jason to get him back in time for school which starts on the sixth, she has made arrangements that will allow her to return to Vancouver when she needs to, but fatigue has ambushed her.

"Give me time, Brenda. I'm a stewed-ant, remember?" (Student. Old family joke. Brenda doesn't laugh.)

"Oh yes. Evolution and messed-up genes. I probably got my encroaching enemy from some hairy swinger, except that she was lucky enough not to know what was happening. Ever think about that, Mother, that up until this century people could die with hope?"

"There's always hope. Remissions...."

But Brenda cuts her off. "Tell me the rest. Did *Evening in Paris* change your life? Did Uncle David ever get a twenty-two?"

"When he was nineteen I gave him one for his birthday. It was considered an acceptable gift in those days. By then he may not have cared, although he expressed pleasure."

"It was just last winter he died, wasn't it?"

"Yes. Alone. In a shabby room in Calgary." They didn't find him for several days. The floor was littered with bottles whose contents had become his substitute for the darkened room of his childhood. He wasn't a fighter; Penelope was the fighter. Some of the bottles had contained fluids not meant for drinking — cooking sherry, shoe polish, cleaning fluid. In earlier times there would have been bottles of perfume, of *Evening in Paris*, perhaps.

"They don't make *Evening in Paris* any more," Penelope says. She thinks that perfumes are more realistic now, that we don't have the same illusions. "Even little children know what tongue-kisses are nowadays, and they know the meaning of condom, if not of French safe. TV has spelled out what will happen next. The man will shed his tuxedo and the woman will discard the dress that is cut on the bias. I guess they even know where the man and woman are headed, and most of what they will do."

"Sure. That's why the perfume touted as being the most seductive is called — fairly matter-of-factly, when you think about it — *Obsession*."

"*Poison*," Penelope murmurs. "I thought it was *Poison*."

IN ETOBICOKE EVERYTHING HAS RETURNED TO NORMAL, except that Gordon is still afflicted with his curious sense of waiting. What he is waiting for he can't tell, nor can he tell whether he anticipates or dreads the future event. He thinks that Dr. Weinberg must have left him with a post-hypnotic suggestion. Dr. Weinberg denies it, but to be on the safe side he re-hypnotizes Gordon and removes it. Nevertheless, the sense of waiting slips back and Gordon finds himself becoming apathetic, as though the importance of the future event is so overwhelming that the present doesn't matter.

Later, in a meeting of the Living Relationships group, Camilla murmurs that she supposes most relationships can be rescued by love, and she smiles a tiny smile and looks sideways at Gordon with the enigmatic eyes. Gordon is dazzled by a momentary glimpse of white blazing around her head, only this time instead of dismay Gordon feels a pleasant euphoria, as though he is welcoming back something he had been in danger of losing.

Surreptitiously, he continues to watch Camilla. It seems to him that she makes a certain amount of sense: after all, what is a relationship if not a search for love? Even Harbit-Jones is forced to admit that he has been driven into Janet's care by something unquantifiable; he prefers to call it admiration, since he can't get his tongue around love.

After the meeting with the Living Relationships group, Gordon is able to cross vagueness off Camilla's list of negatives, since the conviction has grown in him that vagueness such as Camilla's may be in the eye of the beholder. His list of her positives begins to grow, slowly at first, and then by leaping geometric progressions. Intuitive, warm, caring, spring from Gordon's pen, followed by giving, kindly, empathetic, sympathetic, and finally, the pen having now acquired a life of its own, loving.

GORDON IS THE LAST TO KNOW. MARGO, WHO HAD volunteered to help, leaves typing and very nearly leaves Unitarianism. As for Harbit-Jones, he is hard put to find a rationale for his anger. Gordon's mind will turn to mush; the non-huggers will feel alienated; Gordon might as well kiss goodbye to his hopes for election in the Unitarian Universalist Association; and finally, his trump card: he, Harbit-Jones, doesn't know if he can remain in a church where a looseness of intellect threatens to become the norm.

Gordon hears but is at a loss to understand, although the words are beamed directly at his left brain from Harbit-Jones' corresponding hemisphere. A left brain may be all Harbit-Jones possesses. He has informed Camilla that if the right brain harbours the kind of nonsense she spouts, then he sincerely hopes his has atrophied.

"What on earth are you talking about?" Gordon asks finally, and Harbit-Jones shakes his head and widens his eyes to indicate disbelief.

"Good God, what a babe in the woods!" Harbit-Jones says, the tone one of pitying contempt, and turns on his heel, rather slowly so that Gordon may pursue him.

Gordon is about to do so, but just then the sense of waiting slips back and he forgets.

That night he dreams he is a babe in a woods of symmetrical Christmas trees that are hung with shimmering sunlike globes. In the distance the golden-haired woman is beckoning to him. (She no longer reminds him of Brenda. Nor of Betty.) He is a young child, and he is filled with yearning and love and joy as he fights the density of his dream to reach her. When he wakens the dream lingers with him all day, filling him with a sense of the marvellous. It comes to him that such a dream might be significant, but he is reluctant to approach Dr. Weinberg again. He wonders if Camilla may be able to divine its meaning.

No sooner has he decided to seek her out than he knows, with a certainty so fierce he feels it searing the right side of his skull, that he is about to find what it is he's been waiting for – although his left brain, for the life of it, still can't figure out what that might be.

PENELOPE WILL NEVER BE SURE WHETHER SHE FINDS THE place by accident or whether she is pushed and prodded by the ghost she has, up to now, believed is in the machine. (Events of late are eroding her faith.) All she knows is that, while making her way to the parking lot after her class, she bumps smack into a substantial and very solid Douglas fir.

She looks about. She is on a dirt path in a small clearing that is rimmed by western hemlocks and Douglas firs and surrounded by blackberry bushes. In the centre of the clearing are the charred remains of a fire. A rag with rusty-brown stains hangs from a branch.

She shivers. The place is dark and clammy and has a peculiar stench, as though foulness is rising from the lone banana slug crawling among the hemlock needles. Bad vibes, Brenda would say, and Penelope has to fight a rising panic. Something evil, a sort of ectoplasmic miasma, an invisible, erratic vibration that is scarcely contained by the rules of harmonic progression, is lurking just out of sight, ready, if it escapes from its prison, to expand and blight everything it envelops.

Penelope turns and stumbles out of the clearing and doesn't pause to catch her breath until she reaches the road, where she sits for a moment on a nearby stump. She feels chilled, even though the bright sunlight reflecting off the deserted pavement is hot. Suddenly the charred remains of fire, the broken ferns and bracken, the tattered rag fall into place – the newspaper photo in the *Sun*. Where the rapist brought the girl, after he hijacked a car.

All living things have memories, or so Brenda says. Even a great towering tree is not exempt and could wither and die from sights too painful to be borne, and only the deadliest of mushrooms will ever again find nourishment in the clearing's foul and toxic earth. Penelope knows this.

She jumps to her feet, then sees that she has come way too far. The parking lot is half a mile behind her and she is on the periphery of the Seymour rain forest, where, if she had continued, she would be well and truly lost.

She begins to run, then stops and scouts the paths and the road carefully to make sure no one has noticed. Deliberately she slows her pace, strolling back and even whistling a bit, as though she had intended this additional jaunt all along. She knows she hasn't quite been herself since Brenda got sick, and Mildred and Mrs. Moore are watching.

BRENDA IS BACK IN THE HOSPITAL. "YOU AREN'T GOING to believe this, Mother," Brenda says, her face alive and interested for the first time since the current bout of chemotherapy began. She is nearly as white as the hospital pillow. Last night she took a turn for the worse; tubes blocked, the doctors mutter, as they replace the bits of plastic that are designed to drain away treacherous liquids that no longer serve as joyous lubricants. Liquids that have turned into poisons. It seems there is a small tumour on her shoulder and her white blood count is up.

"I phoned Gordon this morning and he acted very mysterious. I think there's a woman in his life!"

Penelope quells a little snake of jealousy. "Serious?"

"Sounds possible. Get this. He's coming out the first of October and he says be prepared for a surprise. I think he's bringing her with him!"

Penelope gapes. She almost says, it *must* be serious, Gordon wouldn't live in sin, then remembers that nobody nowadays would know what she was talking about, that living together is what everybody does and more power to them. Penelope often thinks she was born fifty years too soon. The longing, the frustration, the sexual prohibitions whose mythic proportions put pleasure on hold. Sometimes permanently.

"Are you with me, Mother?"

"Oh, sorry. Did you get a name?"

"No. You phone him, I'm feeling a little tired."

Penelope cranks the bed down, fetches water for Brenda, and then hurries off to pick up Jason. She is afraid that her energy is failing but is fiercely determined not to wear out before this is over. Only two more classes, and then Gordon will be here to spell her off. Gordon and – and whoever. She forgets to phone.

Homo habilis WAS DISCOVERED BY LOUIS LEAKEY at Oldavai Gorge and, with a brain half again as large as Lucy's, Barry says, he represented a "quantum leap" over the previous hominid line and was the first to be called by the genus *"Homo."*

Current theory has it that *Homo habilis* left the forests during a long summer of great heat and drought and food shortages, but Penelope knows her departure (all "quantum leaps" were female) was aided and abetted by her inferiors. Penelope has observed this, that the dumber you are, the more opinionated, bullheaded, tunnel-visioned (Penelope has in her mind two or three men and one woman at the Seniors' Centre), the more you'll try to discredit and drive away those who differ.

Barry then distributes an artist's rendering of a big, hairy

Homo habilis, and Penelope wonders aloud why artists' renderings are always male.

The women in the class glance at James to see how he will take this. James, humble before the burden of expected sagacity, hesitates, then offers, rather tentatively, "If the very first *Homo habilis* had been a woman, I doubt that being smarter would have done much for her."

"So what else is new?" Fran asks, giggling, and Marge says, "I suppose what would happen is that the dominant male would — ah — *subdue* her." Marge, very ladylike, can't bring herself to say "rape." "She probably just resigned herself and accepted the traditional ways, which were probably not that much different from the great apes."

"Sort of like women in the fifties," Penelope offers, then snorts as she wonders how Grover would have reacted to being compared to a great ape. The fifties, virtue and virginity paraded as synonymous, so that women who were raped lost some virtue, as though the temptations they presented in the form of perky breasts and shapely legs could have been suppressed if they'd put their minds to it.

"The horror, the horror," Penelope mutters aloud, and the aging students look at her fearfully, afraid for her, afraid for themselves. They have no way of knowing that Penelope is thinking of the malevolent clearing and the girl who was brutalized there. And that she is wondering if some trace memory from that first human to be raped, something ancient inscribed on the old brain, would have reinforced the girl's terror.

Then she thinks that David Waters himself might *be* a brutish forebear, a throwback to *Homo habilis*, or possibly an *Australopithecus afarensis*, sporting some ancient genetic code that is missing a string or two. She remembers a book she read, Lessing, the fifth child a throwback whose presence gradually destroys the civilized family he stumbles into. Well, if 99.6% of our active genes are the same as chimpanzees, why not? (Afterwards, when she has learned something about the social behaviour of chimpanzees, she realizes she's done them a disservice. Chimpanzees don't, as far as she is able to find out, indulge in cruelty for the pleasure of it.)

The girl Waters abducted will never get over it, Penelope knows that. The damage will leach into every pore, puckering her firm young breasts, blotching her hard white belly, erupting in purple blotches on her skinny thighs. Penelope no longer believes the Victorian dogma she was taught, that the soul is distinct from the body and can be sliced off neatly when the body sheds its mortal coil. She thinks now that body and soul are entwined, that infinitesimal soul tendrils, like tiny roots, grow and curl around the bits and pieces that hold us together, so that an outrage perpetrated against the body shrivels the roots and harms the soul.

YOU CAN'T KNOW THE FUTURE UNLESS YOU EXAMINE the past, which may be why Barry's elderly students are still exercised about what has gone on here on earth. Perhaps they all think, as Penelope does, that from the assembled clues they may yet extract meaning, a need made a thousand times more pressing for Penelope with Brenda's encroaching cancer.

Thus, when Penelope tunes in again to find Barry expounding on *The Origin of Species* she thinks she may be approaching some kind of epiphany. Enraptured, she contemplates the eons that have given the brilliance of one butterfly's wing a slight survival edge over its drab cousins, or the minuscule heritable mutations that have resulted in a many-faceted eye, the design of which beats out the honest gaze.

Barry also touches on a newer, somewhat modified evolutionary theory, something called "punctuated equilibrium," which has it that long periods of relative stability are punctuated by sudden appearances of new species.

This leads to feverish speculation. Marge tells of reading about a ten-year-old Alabama boy who has finished his bachelor's degree, but Barry points out that this could be a deviation within the accepted norm. "Bigger brains aren't necessarily the mark of evolution."

Barry regrets the words before they are out.

"You mean to say," Penelope asks, "that sometimes *smaller* brains emerge during evolution?"

"Then evolution would go backwards," Fran, who is round and short and merry, says. "I think that's happening to my husband."

After the laughter dies Penelope points out that if survival is the only name of the game it would make more sense for a species to stay at a less complicated level in the first place.

"Uh oh. I think Penelope is invoking a Superior Intelligence," Norm says. Norm is in the wheelchair. He is also a Unitarian.

Penelope doesn't tell him that her own son is a Unitarian minister, and therefore she knows a thing or two about the limitations of Unitarianism. Unitarians, Gordon says, are open to any and every kind of thinking, but Penelope has noticed that any and every kind of thinking, Norm's as well as Gordon's, doesn't have much use for Supreme Beings.

Barry distracts them with a challenge for the final class: come up with the kind of evolutionary enhancements that might ensure human survival.

BRENDA GOES TWICE A WEEK FOR RADIATION "TO SHRINK the tumours, make her more comfortable," and Penelope has to drive her across Lions Gate Bridge to the Cancer Clinic at the Vancouver General. Connie, who now has a rounded little tummy and the distant, self-communing air that pregnant women sometimes have, takes Jason on these days.

Tommy's birthday is later than Jason's so that Tommy is still in kindergarten and home for half the day. The visits with Tommy help. Jason's disappointment over not starting school is extreme, but Brenda has promised him that when Uncle Gordon comes they will work something out.

Penelope doesn't let on to Brenda that the pressure is beginning to batter her. She doesn't mention Lucy, or *Homo habilis*, or David Waters. Because what Penelope is up against now is randomness, only a different kind of randomness than the kind she had resolved with Chaos theory. What she is up against now is the randomness of death. Whether it is merely an orderly progression of cause and effect as Chaos randomness professes, or whether there is anything Above and Beyond that may be appealed to, or can interject, or in any way dispense some kind of alleviation. Mercy. Some hint of love operating in the universe, something outside the evolved species we have become.

As a child she remembers having a strong feeling of "being watched," and even until recently, if she thought about it, the invisible world about her seemed to be inhabited by at least one Benign Other who had her interests at heart.

Lately, though, nobody's home. She thinks of her attacks of faithlessness as being like tiny fingers of smoke seeping through the cracks of a closed door, and she knows that if she dares to open the door the whole edifice, herself included, will explode into flames, and nothing will be left behind except a few charred remains.

The meaning of life, if any. Set against the randomness of death.

AT THE NEXT CLASS THEY ARE ASKED FOR THEIR RESPONSE to the challenge Barry threw to them in the last class, *Evolutionary enhancements that might ensure human survival.* Fran believes in environmental awareness, Norm in higher IQ's, Marge is for resistance to AIDS, and James sings, "I dream of the genie for the light brown hair," which everyone (except Penelope) assumes is a profound yet lighthearted attempt to bring genetic structure in.

Penelope herself cannot speak because a whirring has started up in her brain, gentle at first, but as it fires up to a shrill whine she becomes frightened. Until, that is, she recognizes it for what it is: the sound of the silver spaceships she saw in her yard, the night Lucy left.

Now she remembers where she first met them. Twenty-five years ago, in a book Gordon had been assigned to read in school.

Silver spaceships were hovering mysteriously above the earth but minding their own business, so that people stopped being frightened and got used to their presence and went ahead with normal pursuits, such as bullfights. But when the bull was gored the pain of the piercing thrust of the matador's sword ripped through the insides of every person in the stands, and a great scream from twenty thousand throats rent the air, and as the blood flowed from the wound and the bull staggered and fell to its knees every spectator writhed and fell as well.

That was the end of bullfights.

It is all Penelope can do to stop herself from covering her ears against the crescendo of sound as she shouts, "Empathy!"

The silence is total, and then Grace says, "Kind of hate to miss it, whatever it turns out to be." Grace is very shaky. Her daughter comes for her after class.

Nobody picks up on empathy – directly. James, who has been uncharacteristically silent since his genie song, glances furtively at Penelope and then says, "I'll tell you one thing, he'll – sorry, Penelope," with an exaggerated bow, "– *she'll* be *a person* who knows instinctively how other people feel."

Fran, Gertie, and Marge are all a-twitter over James and his insight, and Penelope wonders what it would be like to be less evolved, a male *Homo habilis*, say, and simply punch James out.

Although she should be used to people dining out on her insights, God knows she's sat on enough committees in her day to know that reason has little to do with acclaim, while the pecking order has everything to do with it.

WHEN SHE GETS HOME, MILDRED PHONES TO REMIND her of tonight's potluck dinner, and Penelope says she'll have to give it a miss again. "I suppose you're tired after the symphony," Mildred says, her voice dripping sympathy.

"Oh my God!" Penelope exclaims. The symphony was last night, and Penelope had agreed to meet Edwin at the Hyatt for dinner, since she'd be over town anyway at the Cancer Clinic. Brenda would take a taxi home.

She's stood poor Edwin up. He must be very angry – he hasn't even phoned.

Penelope knows that Mildred will call Mrs. Moore as soon as she hangs up, and she herself must phone Edwin. She pulls the phone book towards her, and it is then that Penelope has her inspiration – to invite James to the next potluck dinner. She scribbles a reminder on a piece of paper, because these days radiation is wiping out her memory.

AFTER THE FAREWELL PARTY AND THE PROMISES TO KEEP in touch and the decisions to take another course next semester, the terrible possibility Penelope faced after finding the clearing begins to haunt her, a possibility far worse than that Waters could be an evolutionary throwback. It is this: that he may *not* be a throwback. That he may be the harbinger of something brand new, a tentative new spur on the twisted evolutionary tree, bursting like a boil out of contaminated bark. She can hardly bear to entertain such a thought, but intellectual honesty forces her to ask, why not?

The mysterious evolutionary tree, as Barry so often says, has its roots in the primordial stew. (Barry is very fond of this metaphor, so much so that none of his pupils ever again think about evolution without imagining a tree.) In the roots, then, must be where the great mystery is contained, and Penelope pictures these roots as a gnarled black mass encircling our blue planet at about the height of the atmosphere, the tree spreading over them to form an enveloping canopy. A rather squat circular tree with vinelike branches, the leaves stylized, precisely placed, and fruit scattered among them, something like Penelope's apple tree. She envisages little people growing on these branches like apples, some – *Australopithecus robustus* and *Australopithecus boisei* for instance – the final fruits of a failing branch, and others the half-formed buds of little stick women who, when they are ripe, will fall one by one onto the nourishing earth, carrying the seeds of what comes next.

Then she thinks that it isn't the roots that are the great mystery after all. It is the soil they tap, the nourishment in the primordial stew which, Barry said, is the still-expanding, still-bursting energy left over from the Big Bang, still singing in its celestial rhythms of the end point towards which everything is rushing.

The stew, then, must contain a code, some version of the personal spiral helix that commands each of us to breathe and grow and procreate and die. An ordering force that brings order from disorder; that throws the switch when it is time for Lucy to give way to the upstart *Homos*.

This new insight strikes Penelope with the force of revelation, as though a private personal particle of energy released from the Big Bang itself has honed in precisely on her, as though she and she alone has uncovered the Godlike solvent that will some day dissolve the murderous miasma of the haunted clearing.

She will definitely not share her discovery with Norm *or* James — especially not James, he would undoubtedly write a book and become famous. Instead she phones Barry — forgetting that it is one o'clock in the morning — and wakes him from a recurring nightmare, one in which he loses control of his aged class and finds himself seated in the front row, under the accusing glare of twenty pairs of reading glasses, writing an exam for which he hasn't studied.

THE FEARFUL BUSINESS IN THE SUMMER ENDED WHEN the car Waters hijacked was spotted by an alert citizen.

Waters would probably have killed the girl but there wasn't time. By the time the police and their tracking dogs closed in he was gone. He ran for it, stumbling over fallen trees, slipping on steps made treacherous by recent rains, ducking around the edge of clearings to avoid the peering helicopters, stumbling along the rugged Baden-Powell trail which cuts over the mountain slopes behind Penelope's house, through North Vancouver and West

Vancouver from Deep Cove to Horseshoe Bay.

The girl was taken to the hospital where she was washed and washed, as if it would be possible, ever, no matter how strong the soap or detergent, to wash away what remained.

The police didn't think Waters would get far, although as night began to fall so did their hopes.

The killer evaded them all. He was in the process of strangling another woman when he was caught.

A different fork in the trail and it could have been Penelope.

October

O CTOBER TURNS INTO A MONTH OF IMPROBABLE contrasts. Warm, Indian summer for the first three weeks followed by an unprecedented outbreak of Arctic air that manages to fight its way through Yellowknife, veer west past the Alaska border, skip through Smithers with enough ferocity to freeze Tyhee Lake overnight, turn the Caribou rangelands into frozen food, and howl into North Vancouver with such outrage that a giant hemlock topples and crushes the carport three houses down from Penelope. Rain turns quickly to freezing rain and then to snow, and Grouse Mountain Ski Hill is able to open on a record-breaking October twenty-eighth, before the inevitable November rains will wash down all but the highest peaks.

For Penelope, October goes by in a blurred mix of amazement over Gordon and apprehension about Brenda. Gordon, cautious Gordon whom she has always envisaged tied to an ugly duckling, a bookish woman in tweed suits and sensible heels and mousy hair, arrives with the swan instead. A fairy tale princess with golden locks and shimmering, flowing garments of tie-dyed silk.

And they are married. Gordon! To do something so — well, so

impulsive, so daring, so — so un-Gordon-like. Through her shroud of Brenda-induced misery Penelope is at least diverted by a Gordon so obviously besotted.

At first Penelope can't get a handle on Camilla. It's as though she won't come into focus, as though there are no brain modules in Penelope's brain into which she can be fitted. Camilla is warm and friendly but distractingly vague, and it isn't until Penelope finds her in the living room sitting cross-legged and meditating that she begins to understand. The last thing she would have expected from Gordon, she thinks, as she welcomes this new daughter-in-law with a mixture of diffidence and relief.

Relief because Penelope recognizes at once that Camilla may be just what Brenda needs, that Camilla will take over the catalytic exteriorizing and send out healing energy into Brenda, that she can perhaps create a cosmic convergence that will replace what Penelope has come to regard as her own feeble rays. And indeed, Camilla offers to give a healing almost as soon as she and Brenda meet.

Brenda, however, is curiously obstinate. She agrees to the healing but can't seem to prevent herself from making smart cracks to Gordon over Camilla's bowed head, as though she is trying to enlist him in her dance with death. Penelope surmises that Brenda is jealous, displaced by Gordon's new anima.

Jason has no such hang-ups. He takes one look at Camilla and drags her off to his Super Nintendo, and from then on follows her from room to room chattering incessantly. He insists that Camilla read his nighttime story and he tells her that she looks just like Rapunzel, not to mention the princess who pricked her finger and fell asleep for a hundred years until the prince kissed her (that would be your Uncle Gordon, Camilla murmurs), and Little Red Riding Hood, except for the cloak.

Penelope thinks this should rouse Brenda, the two most important males in her life being co-opted by this shimmering woman, but Brenda smiles a somewhat contemptuous smile and suddenly gets much worse and returns to the hospital.

"You're blocking something, Brenda," Camilla murmurs, in her fey sideways voice that Brenda can *not* take seriously. She is sitting beside Brenda's hospital bed with her eyes tightly closed.

Although Camilla has never been able to *see* auras — a failing that has served to reinforce her admiration for Gordon — she can feel them. A slight resistance marks the edges of Brenda's, something ragged in its outline. As for the main body of the aura, a lack of density tells her that Brenda's energy is not getting through and she places one hand at Brenda's knee and the other at the soles of her foot and feels a fairly good flow there, then moves up section by section, thigh to knee, gut to thigh, gut to neck, neck to forehead, to the sixth chakra, the mythical third eye, the eye of psychic wisdom, and on to the seventh at the top of the head. The blockage, Camilla explains to Brenda, is around the first chakra, the seat of sexuality. Where the kundalini sakti, the coiled power, lies latent and ready to snake up to the seventh chakra and unleash its healing powers.

Camilla concentrates. Something that is white and pristine is struggling to rise from a deep place. "Let go, Brenda," she urges. "Let it come through, don't be afraid. You're wrong to rely on — whatever it is — a sadness, a loss, although it isn't lost, you just think it is. It's blocking your energy around the first chakra."

"I must speak to it," Brenda says, and shuts her eyes and wishes Camilla, whose rantings disturb her in some undefinable way, would just get lost.

Camilla and Gordon beg to take Jason back to Etobicoke with them, and when Camilla asks Jason if he would like to come and live with her and Uncle Gordon for awhile, Jason slips his little hand into the hand of his fairy tale princess, his face alight with the glow of first true love, and says that would be okay. "I did want to start school at home but with Mom sick I could maybe start at your place." Camilla hugs him and assures him that he can, and Jason is so excited about the plane trip that his disappointment is almost extinguished.

Brenda consents because she knows Penelope is wearing out. Privately she tells Gordon that if the worst happens she would like him and Camilla to raise Jason, for, in spite of her disdain, Brenda trusts Camilla. She knows Camilla will love Jason as much as if he were her own (she and Gordon are already hoping), and she knows it isn't the best thing for a child to be brought up by an aging grandparent.

Brenda has never cried throughout her ordeal but she can't prevent the tears that suddenly overflow when she says goodbye to the son she may never see again. Seeing his mother cry sends Jason into tears and he wipes his face with his knotted-up fist and hugs her and says, "Don't cry Mom, I'll come back real soon and as soon as I learn to write I'll send lots of letters and by then you'll be better."

Camilla takes Brenda's tears as a good sign.

THE WEATHER FRONT HITCHES A RIDE ON THEIR AIRBUS
as it flies eastward following the warmth of Camilla, and creates
a vacuum that allows the cold and snow to streak in and settle
over an outraged Vancouver.

Brenda dreams she is in the corridor again and opening Gil's
door. His bed is gone; the room is empty. A window has replaced
the entire far wall, framing the snowy cone of Mt. Baker that
rises over Vancouver as it sometimes does on a clear day, like a
vision, a guardian, a god, the shape like Fujiyama.

The second night it *is* Fujiyama, only this time the window is
gone and there is nothing to stop Brenda from stepping out and
standing beside the cherry tree whose pink blossoms outlined
against the pristine white of the mountain are featured in tourist
brochures.

Each night the mountains grow bigger. On the third night
when she opens the door, Mt. Everest is directly in front of her,
mysterious, inscrutable, the stark crystal summit seemingly inaccessible, a place of failure, a place of triumph, and she begins to
climb through the snow to reach the peak. She notices that she
has her skis on.

WHEN SHE WAKENS SHE KNOWS SHE HAS BEEN GIVEN A SIGN.
In her dream of Everest Brenda was alone. A whitish mist
swirled around her, and then the sun broke through and she saw
that she was on the very top of the mountain, a pure granite,
windswept, knife-edged slab. All about her the sky was a translucent blue and she could feel the sun warming her face, and her

skis so perfectly wedded to her feet that they seemed not alien, but a benign, organic extension.

Poised on the knife-edge she gave a mighty shove with her ski poles, scattering the powder into the blue, lifting herself at the edge of deep abysses, weightless as her body twisted in the air and sheared effortlessly onto the steep slope. She rose and doubled back and touched down again and again, three times, and then there was a moment when she decided not to turn, to leave the earth altogether and soar instead into the blue, up and up into wondrous space, so light, so delirious with forgotten joy that she laughed aloud. And woke herself up.

For one brief moment she stays free, and then the pain ambushes her. Pain is that kind of enemy, bullying, sneaky, despicable, waiting a fraction of a second before pouncing. Or perhaps the dream had driven it off. Once, on an overseas flight, Brenda had dozed just as the sun was beginning to streak the slight curve of the horizon. Somewhere over Ireland she wakened with a start and found herself staring at light glinting off a silver wing and its giant engine. She could hear nothing, no sound, no throb or grind of the mighty turbine. She remembers the heart-clutching moment of terror until the sound clicked in again; now she ponders this apparent lag that can delay her sensibility.

BRENDA CAN'T BE BOTHERED TO OPEN HER LETTER FROM Brazil, it has nothing to do with her now. She gives it to Penelope; it was Penelope who wanted this stuff in the first place.

Brazil, August. Notes from Claire Truffault-Clarke.

Long before the matter of the ginseng had spread to newspapers as far afield as l'actualité, Papa had picked up the first reports that filtered out of China, although much of the "news"— the supposed affirmation of the restorative powers of ginseng on a single night in several hundred marital beds — was anecdotal. Later, thanks to the obsession of the now-fabled "Ginseng Seekers," who were to spend the rest of their lives in the search for the exact brew they had drunk, a social scientist on a Canada Council grant was able to reduce the legendary performances of that night to a five-minute time frame, and to correlate those minutes — plus or minus a fifteen-minute margin of error — with the five minutes of other mystifying reports. Very few scientists were willing to accept his methodology.

For the rest of his life Papa added ginseng to his morning herbal tea infusion.

M. Truffault's devotion to ginseng sprang from a hope that, with the aid of his inhalator and Mme. Truffault, he would be able to re-enact at least a modest version of the mystery of the poppy fields, although Penelope doesn't know about poppy fields. What is clear is that M. Truffault was seeking ginseng's restorative powers in his marriage bed. She wonders if Claire had guessed the obvious, but she thinks not. No child ever wants to contemplate her own parents' sex life. Perhaps this human quirk explains why Freud went hog-wild with his Oedipus complex, and she is about to mention this to Sigmund when she remembers that she hasn't been consulting him lately;

he hadn't had anything useful to say that would help with Brenda.

Claire went on to say that her father began to pore over the myriad newspapers he now subscribed to, perusing each and every anecdote relating to the aberrant five-minute period, discussing the many hypotheses with the postman. (Now that the dog was subdued, the postman accepted a daily *café au lait,* also laced with ginseng.)

The more M. Truffault thought about it — which was a great deal, speculative thoughts of truly heroic proportions having replaced personal suffering as his daily preoccupation — the more convinced he became that he and everyone else (here he tapped the postman's chest with his finger, perhaps to reassure that worthy that his puny five minutes of mere well-being did not exclude him) had been the recipients of *something.* "Zapped," M. Truffault whispered dramatically, pointing an imaginary gun and pulling an imaginary trigger. (The effect was perhaps diminished when he had to translate, the postman not being *au courant* with American slang.)

Trying to retain any vestiges of credibility that remained to him, the postman ventured the popular psychological premise of mass hysteria.

"Throughout an entire planet? In the same five minutes?" The withering passion of M. Truffault's response sent Mme. Truffault scurrying to fetch the inhalator. Risking asphyxiation, he waved her away while he denounced this heresy. He, Roger Truffault, knew from personal experience — his son-in-law was completing his medical degree, was he not? — that psychologists are not considered logical.

To cap his argument and exterminate the postman's misguided gullibility, M. Truffault waved a copy of the Toronto *Globe and Mail* – sent to him by his dutiful daughter, who was about to give birth to a boy, no doubt about it, a boy to carry on the Truffault name – and quoted the *Globe's* resident philosopher. (Claire had appended a translation.)

The philosopher had ventured to speculate, M. Truffault puffed, pointing to the foreign words, that the brain may harbour a tiny receiving set, whose location – given the evidence adduced from epileptic seizures, surgeon's probes, and even CAT scans – might well be the right temporal lobe. Right here, M. Truffault said, tapping his skull, although the postman already knew that. "You see," M. Truffault gasped, just before Madame moved in with the inhalator, "consciousness hurtles through the ether as radio waves do, and those waves, for five minutes, were subjected to a power surge." At which, fearing blasphemy, Madame clamped the inhalator over his mouth.

THIS IS THE SORT OF SPECULATION THAT, SIX MONTHS AGO, would have set Penelope's imagination off and running. Now she examines it with dutiful dispassion; she no longer hopes for or expects relief. Nevertheless she forces herself to alertness and caresses her own right temporal lobe and contemplates streams of consciousness – waves, not particles – rising and falling through the empty reaches of space and the interstices of matter. She tries to imagine a little organ inside her skull, like eyes, or ears, attuned to convert the waves into the light of awareness — with varying degrees of acuity, she supposes, depending on the age and condition and evolution of the receiving set.

According to M. Truffault's hypothesis the loss of one receiver wouldn't have much effect, the universal waves would just wash over the darkened cranium and move on. An individual death shouldn't count for more than a hill of beans — but grief escapes Penelope's careful denial and wells up in her as she whispers, "But it does, it does."

Once again Penelope forces herself to concentrate. What if the brain itself, besides being a receiver, is also a *generator* of consciousness? Producing its own little waves in harmony with the ocean washing over it, broadcasting its insights into the universal stream, adding to the cosmic supply? Maybe *that* is the Meaning of Life, why we are all — insects, animals, humans — here on this earth, in this cosmos, evolving. She clings to the thought and wonders if more examination might uncover a modicum of comfort.

IT IS PERHAPS FORTUNATE THAT CLAIRE DID NOT SEND the subsequent issues of the *Globe* in which the resident philosopher was denounced by atheists and theists alike, the former charging that the fantastical thesis smacked of God, the latter charging that it reduced God to nothing more than a radio transmitter.

Later, when Claire went home to Roujan to have her baby, she brought with her a copy of the prestigious British medical journal, *The Lancet*. In an article entitled, "The Apparent Emergence of Simultaneous Cortico-cerebral Hyperfunction During a Five-

Minute Period," the author claimed to have uncovered statistical correlations proving that what had begun at precisely four o'clock in Bath and Bristol had not commenced until 4:01 in Birmingham, and 4:03 in London – in short, the five minutes had been constant everywhere, independent of time zones. In the same article a leading physician (who preferred to remain anonymous), speculated that blood samples taken in those minutes might reveal a rise in an as-yet-unidentified brain chemical (the consciousness factor?) that had perhaps been triggered by an environmental blip, possibly a delayed effect of atmospheric nuclear bomb tests. "Papa denounced these theories to the wilting postman," Claire wrote. "He was quite fierce in pointing to new evidence, only then being uncovered, that half a million people (some of whom went on to die), spoke of reassuring Near Death Experiences during those five minutes. Papa found himself greatly bolstered by these testimonials, particularly of those who, he said, didn't choose to die: they said they were emboldened, and were now serene in the certainty that they would eventually pass fearlessly into a greater light. The postman is still alive, and he told me last time I was home that he wasn't altogether sure in what way this reinforced Papa's favoured wave theory but he agreed that it was significant."

Penelope has trouble concentrating on the letter and thinks she'll take it to Brenda and perhaps reread it aloud. Brenda likes her to do that; it saves her small reserve of precious energy.

A STABBING PAIN UNDER HER RIB CAGE CATCHES BRENDA unawares and makes her groan. Diane, in the other bed, turns, her brow wrinkled with appropriate sympathy, but welcoming nonetheless any diversion that will distract her from her own breathless fatigue. "What's the matter?"

Brenda waves a dismissive hand and reaches for the button that will send relief dripping into her veins, but remembers in time and only pretends, for Diane's sake, to push it.

The phone rings. "Hello, Mother," Brenda says, and, keeping her voice hearty, goes on to say that she feels particularly well this morning.

Penelope is not deceived although she doesn't let on. "Can you believe it would turn this cold?" she says. "I'm glad it was nice while Gordon was here. Anyway, I'll be a bit late, I have to go to the dentist, his hygienist is threatening me."

"No problem, I'm not going anywhere..."

Glancing swiftly at Diane (it's safe, Diane is reading), Brenda buries the portable phone under the muffling covers and disconnects it, then continues the conversation as though her mother is still on the line.

"...except maybe home with you when you finish at the dentist's. The doctor said it would be okay for a few hours." Pause. "I'll meet you in the hall."

She sets the phone back on its cradle – but now the pain is attacking, seemingly fiercer for its brief respite. She turns her head to the window so Diane won't see.

Snow, the snow of her dreams, a pure line of dazzling white, a skirt slipped on over hairy trees, coating the North Shore mountains. A mist of artificial snow from the snow-making machine on Grouse Mountain veiling the white slash of the ski run. To the west a storm swirling around one of the twin peaks of the Lions.

"Listen to this," Diane says, holding up a worn paperback, *Life After Life*, tattered and shabby from constant perusal. Brenda steels herself. "Just as I burst out of the end of the tunnel I floated up, up into this crystal clear light, as white as the purest white, as white as snow...."

Brenda has tried, occasionally, to deflect Diane's fervour, but she might as well save her breath. Brenda thinks about that, about saving your breath, as if you can take breath on a day when you have breath to burn, when you are, say, sixteen years old and you and Gordon are skiing through powder and laughing at the sheer cold, exhilarating feel of breath, and stockpile it for when you might need it.

Diane's voice is quavering, trembling with her need to capture the radiance of a light said to be not like any kind of light you can describe, persisting with an energy born of evangelical dedication. Things seem truer, Brenda thinks, if others believe.

But she has things to do. She begins to push herself out of bed, struggling to put on her housecoat. Involuntarily she groans again, and when Diane pauses she says in a rush, "Damn! I always stub my toe on this stupid bed," and then, "I'm going home for a few hours."

Diane sighs and drops the book onto a pile that starts with Kubler-Ross's *On Death and Dying.* The book slides down, past *Enlightened Euthanasia, Assisted Suicide, Dying With Dignity,* and lands with a thud on *Living Wills.* Diane is not going to go either gently or unprepared into that good night, and she makes it clear that Brenda too, should be ready to meet the light that must, that surely must, be waiting at the end of the darkness.

Sometimes it does help. Once when Diane read aloud from the near-death-experiences book, Brenda felt a possibility, an identification, as though there had been a time when she had known about the tunnel and the waiting rapture and had flown toward the great whiteness and felt the sureness and the transcendence of peace. And she had liked the cold, clear sound of it – maybe that inspired the dreams.

Breakfast comes. Brenda forces food down, faking enthusiasm, remarking that she is actually hungry.

Afterwards she throws up, being careful to turn the cold tap on full so Diane won't hear. Then she creeps back into bed and turns again to the window. She thinks she can see black specks coming down the run on Grouse Mountain, although sometimes, during pain, her eyes fool her.

Rolling carefully onto one side she is able to open the metal cabinet without disturbing Diane. She finds the binoculars Gordon brought. Yes, little black stick figures are swaying against the white, back and forth, back and forth, a graceful, distant ballet.

When the doctor comes she is sprightly. He is surprised, but after some badgering agrees that she can have a day's pass. "Do you think it's wise?"

"Oh yes, it's good for...." she's about to say Jason, then remembers he won't be there, that she won't be seeing him again. "Mother," she amends. "She needs all the help she can get." She says this without thinking, and the doctor, unable to hide from himself the knowledge that she knows how helpless he is, warns her that she is very fragile, that she must take it very easy.

"My ball and chain," she reminds him, and he unhooks the intravenous.

Diane is, blessedly, asleep. Brenda eases herself out of bed. A wave of dizziness, followed by nausea, makes her lean against the bed frame and hang onto the cold metal until it passes. She creeps over to the cupboard and takes out her clothes, then carries them back to the bed. After a while she is able to pull on her underpants and untie the hospital gown. She decides not to bother with the bra, with its fake, unsuccessful, sewn-in breast. She pulls up the pants of her blue sweatsuit, and, in a final spurt of energy, drags the top over her head.

Trembling, she lies back. A nurse starts into the room and Brenda props herself up, then relaxes when the nurse changes her mind. Diane stirs. Brenda wriggles under the covers and dials the number of the cab company. She sets the phone down just as Diane wakens.

Brenda smiles at her, then reaches into the drawer and gets out the woolen toque she wears to cover her bare skull. "Bye-bye for now," she says brightly. "Mother's waiting at the door." She surprises a look of such naked envy on Diane's face that she feels something very like shame.

She walks out into the hall, resisting the temptation to hold onto the door frame, but in the safety of the hall she sits down, hard, on a nearby chair. For the first time she wonders if she will be able to go through with it. She reminds herself of the moment after waking before the pain clicks in. That is the place to park her thoughts.

Getting down the elevator and into and out of the taxi is a

blur, but once she is inside Penelope's empty house she begins to feel better. She goes into the kitchen and gulps down some sugar cubes, then goes upstairs and swallows several aspirins and lies on top of the bed in the room that will still be hers when she is no longer around to claim it.

It takes her an hour to get into her old, unfashionable crimson warm-up pants and heavy sweater, and by then her hands are shaking almost uncontrollably. Her mother will be leaving the dentist's soon, she may phone ahead to the hospital.... The mountains, the beauty, the hard edge of snow. She holds the bannister tightly while going down the basement steps.

FROM THE DENTIST'S OFFICE PENELOPE HAS A VIEW OF Mt. Baker. Sometimes Brenda and Gordon would go to Baker to ski when they were young. It stands by itself. No other mountains crowd or overshadow its lovely cone; it rises like an icon, pristine and snow-covered, from the misty border of the far-off horizon.

There must have been people who worshipped at its feet, who felt exultation when their interior darkness was overcome by the shape of the upthrusting, numinous mountain. Penelope thinks about worship and what an odd impulse it is. The west coast Haida projected the dark and unknowable onto their carvings — the occasional blackened and brooding raven in rotting cedar can still startle the hiker who stumbles on it in tangled underbrush. The awe they must have felt, the terror!

Brenda was lying. She never normally hangs up in mid-conversation.

Penelope leaves the hygienist and her guilt-inducing bleat about flossing and heads for the hospital.

Brenda's bed is neatly made, the hospital coverlet unruffled and turned back in a line of geometric precision. Diane is sleeping.

Penelope tiptoes over to Brenda's bed and strokes the coverlet, as though a trace of Brenda might linger still on the sterile smoothness. Diane wakens and mumbles, "Hi," and Penelope, dissembling, says that Brenda forgot her toothbrush. She goes into the shared bathroom and pretends to retrieve it. "Go back to sleep," she says to Diane, and gives a cheerful wave as she leaves. She sits in her car and puts her head down and prays (to whom? the Raven? Sigmund? Jung? Camilla? the disappeared Watcher? She couldn't have said) that Whoever or Whatever is running things will accept her as a substitute for Brenda. What good is she to herself or anyone else? Her search for the meaning of life would be meaningless without Brenda. Randomness seems to be coming up strong in the outside lane.

Brenda has made her decision, Penelope knows this. What she doesn't know is whether Brenda is opting for life or for death.

BRENDA'S BOOTS ARE WEDGED IN BEHIND A PAIR OF SKIS in the basement, and when she tries to pull them out gravity catches the skis and they crash to the floor. A spasm rattles her bowels and she doubles up. She barely makes it to the basement toilet, then has to lie down on the cool cement until the sweating and shaking stop.

Half an hour to get the boots on. Upstairs, the phone rings.

Mother might be leaving the dentist by now, may even have arrived at the hospital. Frantic, she lifts the heavy skis and carries them up, one step at a time. The mountains of her dream, the time lag for pain — she repeats it like a mantra. She grabs her jacket and phones for a taxi, remembering to tell them to send one that can carry skis.

When the taxi comes the driver fastens the skis on the roof, then opens the door for her.

She edges in carefully. Pain is stalking her. She thinks grimly of the new anti-stalking laws and toys with enforcement against pain, then fights down a sudden spasm that makes her twist and gasp aloud.

"You feeling all right?" the driver asks. She sees now that he can see her in the rear-view mirror, and she smiles enigmatically.

"Foot cramp. Tight boots," she says.

The driver laughs and switches the radio to a phone-in show with its opinionated callers, and she slides sideways so he can no longer see her. She fishes her goggles from the pocket of her jacket and puts them on, then leans her head back and thinks through the pain, to white peaks, to Everest.

Luckily there isn't much of a lineup for the gondola. She holds tightly to the railing, daring herself to look down at the ravines and deadly valleys. How they used to frighten her! Now she feels the same kind of interested, involved detachment she'd felt in the IMAX theatre, when the spacecraft Discovery tipped the room towards our fragile blue planet. Pain, a jealous torturer. Able to banish the minor anxieties.

When she steps off the lift into the cold mountain air she has to fight for breath. At the hospital they give her oxygen; here it is being taken away.

At the top of the run she rests on her ski poles while pain leaks out of her spine and down a nerve in her leg.

Around her, giant trees pose with their foot-thick burdens of snow. Now and then the snow slips off with a hollow pumph, occasionally onto the head of a skier. Below, in the distance, is Vancouver, a picture-postcard of a neat, orderly, pain-free city. The puffy balloon of BC Place, an easy landmark, and nearby the shiny golf ball of the Science Centre that houses IMAX. She locates Lions Gate Hospital outlined against the blue of Burrard Inlet, and she thinks she can identify the room where Diane is reading about the tunnel that leads to the light.

Beyond lies the ocean with its cargo of tugs and freighters and Love Boats. If you were floating over it, out of your body, you could turn to the west and find Japan, and the Great Wall of China, and finally the cool, clean peaks of the Himalayas.

Carefully, she positions her boot on one ski, is forced to bend to adjust it, and then, straightening, waits until the faintness passes. The second boot snaps into place easily. She sees with relief that the other skiers who rode up with her have whirled away. She had been afraid they would notice the shaking, but they were young, occupied with being young, with tightening the wonderful instruments of bodies that so far knew nothing of treachery.

Tentatively, she skies over to the edge of the run, and when she looks down, a needed rush of adrenalin steadies her.

Slowly, carefully, she slaloms a short way between moguls. She is holding the pain at bay; she thinks it doesn't have as much power up here. Perhaps it is warm-blooded. Perhaps it shrinks in the cold.

But the reprieve is temporary, she knows that – there isn't much she doesn't know about its treacherous ways. Her knees are shaking again, and she almost falls when a skier swooshes by, too close, throwing snow into her face, obscuring her sight. Trembling, she takes off her goggles and drops them in the snow. She doesn't bother to retrieve them.

Anxiously she looks about and sees, well over on the right, a tiny break in the trees and a flash of orange. Foot by laborious foot she makes her way to the clearing and the orange sign. EXTREMELY HAZARDOUS CONDITIONS EXIST OUTSIDE THIS BOUNDARY. PLEASE STAY ON THE TRAILS it says.

She rests against a great hemlock, aware that its bending boughs could dump their load on her, but forced now to trust something, a tree, until she can get her strength back.

The next batch of skiers go by in a small herd, and as she waits for them to pass the weakness returns and pain needles jab her flesh. Something like despair threatens; then, miraculously, there is nobody, and she steps carefully over the thin rope by the orange barrier and into an untrammelled world of soundless Christmas-card trees. Only a few steps to take her beyond visibility.

A clear spot of virgin snow lies on a gentle slope, no markings on it except for four little repeating paw-dents, two together and two following. Like a little family, a Mommy and Daddy and two little ones. She wonders if crippled rabbits leave three marks.

One all alone. Two following.

Then she is skiing through powder. Usually powder snow isn't fast snow; the skier sinks, depending on weight and speed, until a trail is broken. But Brenda is now so light she barely dents the white. She skims along in a rush of flying snow and happiness and laughter as the old expertise creeps back into her wasted muscles. She feels a forgotten sense of power as she leans into the curves, raising one ski slightly, putting pressure on the other, bending to accelerate through a tunnel of great trees whose heavy boughs meet above her and dull the glare from the snow, a Gothic arch of breathtaking beauty. The pain doesn't have a chance. She scarcely pauses when she breaks through into the light where the edge of the world looms.

Then up, up above the world, soaring through the wondrous blue, balancing, knowing with certainty that her skis will cut perfectly into the nearly-vertical slope, almost falling but managing in a wild rush of exhilaration to right herself and turn to slow her descent.

In front of her, a pure white peak. Everest.

Poised momentarily on the knife-edge she pushes with all her strength, throwing the powder into the blue in perfectly executed turns, using her ski poles to lift her just at the edge of extinction, flying as her body twists and settles and soars again, not once, not twice, but three times.

After that, the moment in her dream when she decides not to touch down. A thrill of spontaneous fear, tapping some final, hidden, emergency cache and shooting warm spurts of energy into her veins. She feels herself rise and soar above the whiteness, into the blue, into a moment like that in the giant, soundless 767 when all sensation has been temporarily suspended.

At the pinnacle she thinks she can see into the room at Lions Gate Hospital where she dreamed of soaring into the blue, and as she begins to fall a lightning flash of uncertainty darts through her brain. Something that is not exactly fear but more like sorrow, as though it is deeply, wrenchingly pitiable to be leaving the beauty of the snow-covered planet; and then she feels herself falling, falling through the frail air, hitting the slope, tumbling and whirling in alternate tunnels of light and dark for what seems an eternity.

She feels warmth seeping onto her face. When, finally, she makes the effort to open her eyes all she can see is a white milky light that envelopes her. She isn't sure whether it is snow, or that other, purer light. All she knows is that there is no pain anywhere, that pain seems to have been suspended for some time now, and because of that she is pretty sure she is no longer alive.

She pushes Jason, Penelope, and Gordon to one side, and thinks instead of Diane. She wishes she could tell her, could burst into the pale blue room where Diane is on the trail of the divine alchemy that will convert slippery death into life, and explain to her what has suddenly become clear, that it doesn't really matter very much. In fact, she would say, it doesn't really matter at all. It doesn't matter one way or the other.

EPILOGUE

O N THE DAY THAT BRENDA MADE HER SPECTACULAR
attempt to fly straight into heaven, Caleb Smith,
whose livelihood had disappeared with the sockeye
salmon, wondered if he could turn a hobby into badly-needed
cash before he lost his fishing boat.

It was still dark when he drove north past Penelope's house
and up St. Mary's to the BC Hydro access road. There he parked
his car, strapped on his snowshoes, shouldered his fancy new
Canon and the compact video camera he'd bought the last year
of the sockeye (which had netted him sixty thousand), and began
the slow climb up Fromme Mountain. He knew the area well
from summer hikes; all you had to do was to make sure that
Mosquito Creek stayed on the left and you wouldn't get lost, but
he stuck his cell-phone in his pocket just in case.

St. George's Trail crossed the Baden-Powell Trail, where David
Waters made his bid for escape. At first it was quite steep, then
it opened suddenly onto the Old Grouse Mountain Highway
and a gentler slope.

It was late morning by the time Caleb got to the little bridge that crossed the creek at Mosquito Falls, although he didn't cross the bridge. That trail would have taken him close to Blueberry Chair on the Grouse Mountain Ski Development. Instead he continued on above the falls, knowing that in summer a small trail eventually came out on another stretch of the Old Grouse Mountain Highway. It bent left and upwards bordering Grouse Mountain but didn't cross the creek again.

Here the ravine was deeper and the slopes treacherous. Caleb kept well back.

A species of rare chipmunk, possibly in danger of extinction, was said to burrow into the snow around there in winter. Its near extinction had come about because of tree squirrels that were not native and had no predators except for the occasional coyote. The tree squirrels made their way several years earlier across Burrard Inlet, hitchhiking, it was assumed, on a delivery truck.

Caleb saw a set of tiny prints and followed them until they disappeared near the base of a tree fairly close to the ravine — which at this point was more like a dizzying gorge. He parked himself and settled in for a long, chilly, silent wait.

He was uncorking his Thermos of coffee when his eye was caught by the flash of something crimson high up across the ravine that separates Fromme Mountain from Grouse Mountain. Grabbing his video camera he set it for distance and caught Brenda on her first, faraway rise, followed by her perfect landing on the nearly-vertical slope. This brought her closer to him so that he was able to record the full, breathtaking execution of her second leap into the air and her second touchdown.

Now, through the telescopic lens, she was so near that even

her absorbed, triumphant expression was clearly visible. The gorge stretched below her, almost vertical, only a few stunted pines clinging to the sheer rock face, and below that the boulder-strewn creek. Involuntarily he shouted, "No!" as she lifted off, the word hanging like a frozen balloon in air too fragile to support its weight.

At the height of the final lift, the same moment when Brenda thought she could see into Lions Gate Hospital, the camera caught a momentary expression of something akin to terror, as though, too late, she was changing her mind. The expression was so fleeting that, if it hadn't been for the magic of instant replays and stills, it would have gone unnoticed. Then there was something else, some beatitude of expression that made her seem to shine, although it may have been a trick of the sun slanting at its wintery angle and highlighting trees and peaks and every ripple in the snow in a dazzling glare.

Just before her final descent Brenda's head could be seen glowing in a halo-like radiance, like that of a carved medieval angel centred in stylized wooden rays. This was the picture that landed on the cover of *People* magazine.

Every TV in the land slowed the replay for the final tumble, so that Penelope suffered again and again through the sight of Brenda catapulting down and down through deep snow, and landing, finally, wedged against a small tree on the edge of the deadly gorge.

The helicopter rescue was photographed from beginning to end, a swinging Brenda flying through the sky on a stretcher and swallowed by the maw of the hovering aircraft.

PENELOPE WAITED AT THE HOSPITAL. BRENDA WAS suffering mild hypothermia and a broken shoulder, but, miraculously, that seemed to be about it. Of course, as the searchers pointed out, the snow was deep and the tumble hadn't been excessively far, but Camilla, viewing in Etobicoke along with millions of others from Rio to London and from Moscow to Nairobi, connected the blazing radiance around her head with the miracle of salvation.

THE NEXT DAY A CROWD OF REPORTERS AND CAMERAMEN ambushed her room. She was featured on CBC's *The National*, on CNN, ABC, and even PBS, and still is: the public can't get enough of Brenda's irreverent responses. In short, Brenda is having more, much more, than her allotted fifteen minutes of fame.

Penelope's neighbour, Mrs. Moore, loves TV-Brenda almost as much as she once disliked real Brenda, and, after learning that Oprah Winfrey has asked for and been granted an interview whenever Brenda is up to it, has decided – after Penelope con-sents to get Brenda's autograph for her – to give Penelope another chance before having her apprehended; after all, as she explains to Mr. Moore, eccentricity is permissible, indeed expected, in the best families. And she tells off that pushy Mildred. She herself is much too busy for petty interference in others' lives and she advises Mildred, too, to get a life.

THE ONE REQUEST BRENDA HAS DISMISSED OUT OF hand is from the Association for Assisted Suicide. They were quick to approach her to see if she would become a spokes-woman, and they offered help if she decided to make a better job of it next time.

Brenda more or less threw them out of her room. She is in love with sparkling life now, likes the excitement of being a celebrity, finds that she handles the media like a pro, has in fact been offered several excellent positions should she rejoin the living.

She intends to do just that. When the doctors set her shoulder they find that the tumour there is diminishing. They are astonished at the speed of her recovery. There are those among them who can scarcely believe that the radiation and chemotherapy have been so successful, and there are even those who cite some new studies about the benefits of freezing tumours and opine that it may have been exposure to cold that has caused this "spontaneous remission."

Camilla knows it was the healings. She says she felt a connectedness that Brenda had been blocking, an Inner Knowing that only needed accessing. Jason is sure it was an angel (among whom he numbers Camilla) and Gordon believes — but Gordon no longer knows what he believes. He who was once sure of everything, especially the rationality of science and the human brain, now recognizes that rationality may be nothing but a straight road in a curved universe. As for Penelope, she has kicked randomness out of her belief system altogether.

The effect on Caleb Smith who actually witnessed the event has been to make him realize that life is too short to sit around trying to recover what has been lost, and so he has taken the windfall from the sale of his video, sold his fish boat, and is going to do contract work for *National Geographic* at what he loves best — recording the numbered days of endangered species. He and Brenda plan to keep in touch; they both recognize divine intervention when they meet it.

PENELOPE IS FAST APPROACHING HER SEVENTY-FIRST birthday which, this year, will coincide with the monthly potluck dinner at her house. She has invited James from the Science for Seniors course and hinted to Mildred that there is someone coming she wants her to meet. Mildred will, she knows, be Really Mildred for the occasion, and Really Mildred is a warm and lovable person. By the time James meets No-name Mildred it will be too late, and anyway, James has his own *doppelgängers*. She thinks Mildred and James will hit it off and will live not happily, but not unhappily, ever after, and that when unhappiness now and then sneaks through the threshold of consciousness they will, as Tolstoy believed, relish their own unique brand.

IBM INSISTS ON CONNECTING BRENDA'S HOSPITAL ROOM to the Internet and e-mail, and to her surprise one of the first persons to log on is Claire Truffault-Clarke in Brazil.

"I saw it on TV! I am so proud to know you!" she writes, and Brenda is able to reach her at claire@brazil.forest.com.

"What happened to M. Truffault?" Brenda types. "My mother wants to know."

The reply comes the next day. "He died a year after our little Roger was born. Mother said he didn't seem to mind the death experience nearly as much as he had expected to."

"No new insights?" Brenda shoots back. "Nothing special after all his research?" and she is more than a little bemused when Claire replies, "Mother claims that he raised himself on one elbow and blessed his grandson, and then gazed heavenward and smiled."

In fact, Mme. Truffault swears that in the next instant, with her own two eyes, she saw the soul of her sainted husband being gathered to God by the Blessed Virgin, although Claire is reluctant to mention this. In light of Mme. Truffault's track record, neither Claire nor Tom has been inclined to dispute her testimony, although they can't quite quash a few doubts. The child, who is also called Roger and is now himself a doctor, was too young at the time to have an opinion.

Brenda is about to ask for a printer to type Claire's story out for Penelope when she remembers something she has wondered about. "Why did you choose Brazil?"

"We moved here so Tom could practise medicine and I could succour the poor children of Rio, and, in our spare time, work together to save the rain forest."

"Have you succeeded?"

"We've done some things. Helped to make the developed world aware of the forest. Saved a child or two."

"And your mother? What happened to her?"

"Mother? Don't you know? She's still alive and living in Roujan. Soon we leave for France to celebrate her hundredth birthday. She claims she has been ready to die ever since her vision, but I don't think she is in any big hurry."

"Good for her," Brenda types, and means it.

PENELOPE IS EXPERIENCING SUCH A LIGHTNESS THESE DAYS that on her walk she actually finds herself skipping. It's a year, she thinks, since she started her research, and for awhile it seemed that the Meaning of Life was being sucked into the Slough of Despond; that without Brenda life would have had no meaning.

Then Brenda must be the meaning of life, and Penelope snorts and starts to laugh aloud just as Anne Lewis and her husband drive by.

"Isn't that the old girl who used to walk past the other house every single day? Kinda nuts, isn't she?"

"No," Anne says. "She isn't. Eccentric maybe, but not nuts. Quite sharp, actually."

"Boy, some people's lives! I guess she hasn't got anything better to do, don't you wonder how people like that pass the time when nothing ever happens?" The Lewis's are fitting a visit to the school into their already burdened schedule (Anne is working now) because Kate has just made the Honour Roll after a near failure last year.

They wave, but Penelope doesn't see them. She crosses the road and starts up the hill.

Time, she thinks. Chaos. She laughs to think how Chaos theory had started by reassuring her, how by banishing randomness she thought she'd banished insecurity. Chaos theory had comforted her over the death of the fireman, but she hadn't been so crazy about it when it was Brenda's life on the line, had she?

"There are more things in heaven and earth, Horatio, than are dreamt of in your philosophy," she says loudly, and a woman snipping the dead blossoms off a hydrangea peers along the street to see who on earth would be named Horatio in this day and age.

Penelope thinks she's found traces of Hamlet's undreamt things. Outside the squarely delineated parameters of pure science, in the tiny cracks where weird blossoms flourish, where auras leak through, and brief ecstacies, and spontaneous remissions; it is in these holy places that she has come closest to something fundamental. In the thrusts and parries of unquantifiable energies that refuse to behave on cue, and so can't be gathered in under science's respectable cloak.

She imagines a giant thumb reaching down from heaven into the brew and stirring, mixing up cause and effect, sending the elements whirling into contention. Whose thumb? That's a whole new ballgame; she'll work on that next year.

At the top of the hill Penelope sits on her "resting bench." and through the thinning mist she sees a woman in the distance climbing the hill, a brisk, youthful woman holding her unlined face to the emerging sun. She could be Penelope herself, a younger, sturdier Penelope, when her hair was dark and her step light.

She is still too far away for Penelope to make out her features, but as she approaches Penelope thinks, I wouldn't care if she turned out to be my *doppelgänger*. She wouldn't scare me one bit. I'd just hold out my hand and shake hers. Penelope stands up and closes her eyes and sticks out her hand, even though the woman is still a block away.

Penelope knows exactly what she will look like. Tall, with dark hair that swings around her shoulders in what was once called a pageboy bob, brown eyes that have not yet learned the art of concealment, clear skin, and wearing a slightly flared wool skirt and red blazer. The young woman has worked hard at looking like everyone else but believes she has fallen short of the mark, far short of it. She has no conception of her own power, of her strength, her vibrancy, her vitality, nor of the sensuality which, like a silent explosion, bespeaks the magical fit of spirit and flesh. "How are you?" Penelope will say. "Yes, isn't it a coincidence? No, I'm sorry, there's no room at the inn, as they say. Yes, perhaps we will meet again. Goodbye!"

When she opens her eyes and checks the street the woman has disappeared.